All the
Broken Pieces

All the
Broken Pieces

Cindi Madsen

For Michael, who always believed this would happen. I love you!

Entangled Publishing, LLC
2614 South Timberline Road
Suite 109
Fort Collins, CO 80525
Visit our website at www.entangledpublishing.com.

Edited by Stacy Abrams and Alycia Tornetta
Cover design by Heather Howland and Grant Gaither
Interior design by Sabrina Plomitallo-González, Neuwirth & Associates.

Print ISBN: 978-1-62061-129-6
Ebook ISBN: 978-1-62061-130-2

Manufactured in the United States of America

First Edition December 2012

1

White ceiling, a fuzzy face hovering over hers.
Gloved fingers against her skin. A steady chirping noise
mixed in with words she couldn't quite catch hold of.

Opening her eyes took so much effort. And they kept
closing before she got a good look. One prick, another.
Tugging at her skin. A blurry arm moved up and down in
time with the pinpricks.

I think I'm going to puke.

Strange, dreamlike voices floated over her. "I think she's
waking up."

"She's not ready yet."

Cold liquid shot into her arm at her elbow and wound up
to her shoulder, through her chest, until it spread into her
entire body. Then blackness sucked her back under.

Her leg twitched. Then an arm. She wasn't telling them to
move; they kept doing it on their own. Her eyes flickered
open and she caught a flash of a white ceiling. The chirping
noise sounded out, steady and loud.

With a gasp, she shot up.

Hands eased her back down into the soft pillows. "Take it
easy," a blurry form said.

She blinked a couple times and her vision cleared.

A woman stood over her, a warm smile on her face. Her dark hair fell from behind her ear as she moved closer. "How are you feeling?"

Confusion filled her. She felt lost, scared. She wanted . . . she wasn't sure what. "I'm . . ." Her throat burned as she tried to form a sentence. "I don't . . ." The words didn't sound right. They were thick and slurred. Frustration added to the confusion as she tried again. "What's . . . going . . . am I?"

The woman reached down and cupped her cheek. "Shh. You were in an accident. But everything will be fine."

She searched her memory. There was nothing. Nothing but flashes of being in this room. "I feel . . . strange."

"But you're talking. That's an excellent sign." The woman sat on the edge of the bed. "Do you remember anything? The accident? Your name?"

Pain shot across her head as she searched through the fuzziness. Tears pricked her eyes. "I don't remember . . . anything."

"Olivia, honey, it's me. Your name is Olivia, and I'm . . . " Her smile widened and unshed tears glistened in her eyes. "I'm your mother. Victoria Stein."

Olivia tried to put the images together, tried to make sense of it all. But it didn't fit. Or she couldn't remember if it did. A tear escaped and ran down her cheek.

The woman—*Mom*—leaned down and hugged her. "It's okay. You were in a bad car accident and had to have several surgeries, but you're going to be just fine. Because I'm going to take such good care of you."

Mom squeezed Olivia's hand. "Let me go get Henry— your father. He'll be so glad to see that you're finally awake."

When Dad stepped into the room, he didn't look familiar, either. Olivia saw the concern in his eyes, but there was something else. He seemed reluctant.

Mom pointed at the chirping monitor. "Look at her heart rate. She can understand me, and she can talk."

Why is she saying it like that? Like it's a big surprise. Olivia licked her lips and forced the question from her dry throat. "Why wouldn't I be able to talk?"

Mom sat on the foot of the bed. "Because, dear, your injuries were so severe. The brain trauma, and your heart . . ." She shook her head, then placed her hands over her own heart, looking like she might start crying. "You're our little miracle."

Olivia reached up, feeling the tender spots on her head. Her fingers brushed across a row of—were those little ridges made of metal?

"Careful. The staples are almost ready to come out, but it's still going to be sore for a while."

Staples?! Her stomach rolled. *I have* staples *in my head?* She lowered her now-shaking hand. "Can I get a mirror?"

Mom looked at Dad, then back at her. "I don't think that's a good idea. Not until you've healed a little more."

Olivia gave two slow nods. If only everything weren't so strange. If she could just remember something. Anything.

"You're healing very well," Dad said. "And your heartbeat is strong. That's good."

Mom smiled at her. "That's because you're amazing."

Dad grabbed Mom's hand. "Darling, I need to talk to you about something. In the other room."

Mom patted Olivia's leg. "You just relax. I'll be back in a few minutes."

The two of them left the room, but when Mom swung the

door closed, it didn't latch. Olivia could hear their voices in the hall.

"I still think we should . . ." She couldn't make out the rest of Dad's muffled words. " . . . know if I can do this."

" . . . late for that," Mom said. "We'd lose everything, including . . ." Her voice faded as they got farther away. " . . . have to move."

She could tell the conversation was tense, but the words were impossible to decipher now. Holding a hand in front of her face, she turned it back and forth. A plastic tube ran from her arm to a machine next to her bed.

Weird. Everything was weird. She pulled a strand of her hair forward. Dark brown—like Mom's. But it didn't help her remember how she looked or who exactly she was. She kicked off her covers and stared at her legs. Running her gaze up and down, she assessed the damage: a few bruises and cuts. Her chest felt tight. She peeked into her nightgown and stared in horror at the long red stripe running down her chest.

Gross.

You're alive. You shouldn't be thinking about looks.

She dropped the nightgown, then put a palm over her heart. *Ouch.*

Lowering her hand, she scanned the room. *I wonder how my face looks. From the way Dad stared at me, plus the fact that Mom won't let me see a mirror, it must be bad.*

Brains are more important than looks.

That's what ugly people say.

Olivia put her hands on her head and squeezed. "Stop it," she whispered to her arguing thoughts, hysteria bubbling up and squeezing the air from her lungs. What was happening to her? Why didn't she recognize her parents or know where she was? *Who* she was? Tears ran warm trails down her cheeks. "Just make it all stop."

Mom swung open the door and walked into the room. "What was that, dear?"

Olivia swiped the tears off her face. "Nothing. Is everything okay?"

Mom nodded. "Of course. I'm going to take some time off from work to help you heal. As soon as we get you recovered enough, we're moving. After everything that's happened, I think we could use a fresh start."

Olivia was still too hazy to think about a fresh start. All she knew was that something seemed wrong. Make that *everything* seemed wrong. So she clung to the hope that she would recover quickly. And that when she did, all the wrongness would go away.

2

Olivia twisted a strand of her hair around her finger as she stared out her bedroom window. Women strode past wearing workout gear and swinging their arms; people walked their dogs; kids rode bikes up and down the street. The outside world was busy. But as usual, she was in her room, on the inside looking out.

A knock sounded on the door, followed by Mom walking in. "The clothes we ordered came today."

Olivia glanced at the cardboard box Mom set on the floor, then returned her attention to the window. A young brunette girl pulled a wagon filled with dolls and stuffed animals down the sidewalk, her mouth moving, even though no one else was near her. Olivia leaned closer to the window, unable to take her eyes off the girl.

I feel like I know her. Or not her, but . . . someone.

The image of a white cartoon kitten, red bow over one ear, popped into her head. A heaviness entered her chest, and she had the strangest urge to run outside and throw her arms around the little brunette.

The girl looked up to the window. Normally, Olivia stepped back before anyone saw her; this time, she wasn't fast enough. The girl didn't shrink away, though. Giant grin on her face, she lifted a hand and waved.

It took a few seconds for Olivia to wave back.

"Who are you waving at?" Mom asked.

"Just a little girl."

"Well, don't you want to try these on?"

She had been eager to get clothes that fit better—the first ones Mom ordered had been too big. But now that they were finally here, she wasn't in the mood. It wasn't like new clothes could fix what was wrong with her. "Why'd we have to move before I got a chance to talk to my old friends?"

Mom's head jerked up. "I thought you didn't remember your friends."

Hard as she tried, nothing from her old life—no memories of Rochester, Minnesota, besides the days in her room there—came back to her. She ran a finger down the window, leaving a smudge in its wake. "I don't, but maybe if I just saw them, I'd—"

"You kept to yourself. You were homeschooled. I've told you all this before."

Any time Olivia brought up the past, Mom got so weird. "Fresh start" was like her favorite phrase.

Olivia sighed, then crossed her room and lifted one of the shirts from the box. She slid it out of the plastic bag and stepped into her adjoining bathroom. Even though Mom had seen the scars before, she felt raw and too open when they were exposed.

She peeled off her baggy shirt and dropped her gaze to the line running down the middle of her chest. Over the past month and a half, the scar had faded from bright red to dark pink. But it still looked gross. The one on her neck wasn't much better, though at least she could hide it by wearing her hair down.

She squared off in front of the mirror and stared at the girl looking back at her. She kept waiting for the day when she'd see her reflection and remember who she was. The fact that it never looked right, never seemed familiar, always left her unsettled.

I guess I should just be happy my face healed. I looked like some kind of monster for weeks. Both of the voices in her head had been pretty horrified when she'd first seen her puffy, bruised face in the mirror. Even the one that claimed looks weren't important.

At first the voices had completely freaked her out—she knew it wasn't normal to have constantly arguing thoughts running through her mind. But she was such a mess when she woke up from the coma, and Mom and Dad had already been so stressed over her recovery, that she kept deciding to wait to tell them. Then week after week passed and she didn't know how to bring it up. How to tell them that in addition to being scarred and having no memories, something else was seriously wrong with her.

It's just a side effect from my injuries. They'll go away. They have to.

She pulled the stiff black T-shirt over her head, glad to see it not only fit but also covered her scar.

You should've gone with pink. All the muscles in her body tensed. She waited for the retort, knowing it would come.

I hate pink. It's like happiness threw up on me.

Olivia let out a long breath, trying to release tension, and then focused on what *she* thought of the shirt. With the intense desert heat, she'd love to wear nothing but tank tops. They didn't cover enough, though.

When they'd moved a couple weeks ago, they'd made the trip at night. Each time she'd woken up, they'd been in a new city, a new state. Until they'd ended up here, in Cottonwood, Arizona.

They pick hot, dry, middle-of-nowhere of all places. There's nothing but dirt and cactuses. Not that it matters. It's not like I ever go anywhere anyway.

"So?" Mom asked. "How does it look?"

Olivia pushed open the door. "Well, it fits."

"You want to try on the rest?"

Trying on another shirt meant facing the stranger in the mirror and the scar on her chest again. "Maybe later."

"Come downstairs, then, and I'll get you a snack so you can take your pills before we move on to your lessons."

When Mom had started reviewing school subjects with her, information popped into her head, slowly at first, then faster and faster. Math was her favorite—it was always the same. And at least something looked familiar, even if it was only proofs. "I'll be right down."

Olivia walked back to her window and pulled the curtains wide. All day she'd been trying to work up the courage to talk to Mom and Dad. Hiding in her bedroom wasn't getting her anywhere, and it was starting to feel suffocating—more like a cage than a haven. At first she'd remained isolated because of how hideous she knew she looked. But now, even after her face healed and her ugly scars could be hidden with her hair and clothing, the thought of being around people she didn't know terrified her.

I've gotta get out there sometime. Sooner rather than later if I'm going to follow through with my plan.

Yesterday she'd gone online to look up more about the town they'd just moved to and found out the new school year started in two weeks. Two weeks to get herself socially ready for public school.

Just thinking about it sent her pulse racing.

You're never going to change the world from your room.

Forget changing the world. How about a little social inter- action besides Mom and Dad?

Olivia pressed her fingers to her temples. Maybe getting out with other people would help make the voices go away, too. Or at least drown them out for a while.

She thought about the little girl who'd waved at her. All the people who passed her window, experiencing the outside world, smiling and talking to their friends. She wanted that. She also hoped that by being around people her age, she'd get a better grasp of who she was and then stop feeling so lost.

And smart women are powerful.

So are popular women.

"Argh! No more. Just shut up—both of you!" Trying not to think that yelling at her thoughts made her a total freak, she lifted her chin and took a deep breath. "I can do this," she said, then headed downstairs.

With every step she took, her chest got tighter. By the time she made it to the kitchen, she could hardly breathe.

Dad looked up as she came in. "There's my girl. How're you doing today?"

"I'm okay. How was your first day as the newest doctor at the Cottonwood Cardiac Care Center?" She knew he'd been nervous about it last night, even though Mom had assured him the center would be thrilled to have one of the Mayo Clinic's top cardiac surgeons working for them.

"I hate first days. I don't know anyone; don't know where anything goes. It's good to be home."

The courage she'd built up started to fade. Dad didn't make the outside world sound all that great. In fact, he made it sound intimidating.

Mom pointed to the crackers, cheese, and carrot sticks

she'd put out on a platter. "Have something to eat, and here..." She dumped a handful of pills onto the counter, filled a glass of water, and passed it over.

Olivia took the pills and washed them down with the water. She glanced at the table, where Mom had already set up for today's lesson. Just a couple of books and a lonely notepad. Hours of no sound but her pencil scratching against the paper, Mom's pacing, the clock ticking.

If I ever want to have friends, I'm going to have to face my fear.

Her pulse pounded through her head, and her throat went dry. "I've made a decision. I've decided that I want to enroll in school."

Mom's mouth dropped.

Dad grinned.

Reaching across the counter and putting a hand on her shoulder, Mom said, "Honey, I don't think that's a good idea."

"She wants to," Dad said. "If she wants to go, we should—"

"But there are germs out there that she's extra vulnerable to because of her condition and the meds she's on. Public school's not a good idea right now."

Disappointment filled her, bursting the image she'd dreamed up of laughing and talking with friends.

Of being normal.

"I'm not going to drop it this time." Dad set his jaw. "You've got to let her live, Victoria."

Mom's nostrils flared, and Olivia braced for the harsh words that were about to be thrown at Dad.

"I'm her mother, and I'll decide what's best for—"

"If you don't sign her up," Dad said, his voice calm but firm, "I will."

3

The morning before school, anxiety crept in along with excitement. She'd had two weeks of practice social runs: nightly walks; a grocery store trip that ended in only a minor hyperventilating spell; dinner at a restaurant; a drive to Jerome for window-shopping. Each trip started with the panicky, I-can't-do-this feeling. In time, it got easier.

Even after the practice runs, though, she still felt shaky at knowing how to act and what to say. And here she was, minutes away from going into an unfamiliar building filled with people. People her age who weren't missing all their memories.

What if I don't fit in? That would be all kinds of tragical.

I hope *I don't fit in. Most people are simple-minded followers.*

Her stomach clenched. *Oh, joy. I'm already going crazy and I haven't even gotten to school yet.*

She shook her head, trying to clear it of her worries. The voices, fitting in, not fitting in—right now she needed to push it all aside and focus on surviving the day. She'd never make it if she started doubting herself now.

Mom knocked on the open door and stepped into the room, wearing an expression suited for a funeral procession. "You know I'm happy to teach you at home. I just don't see why—"

"You're a great teacher, Mom, you really are. But this is about me getting back to a normal life, making friends, having that fresh start you're always talking about."

Germs, inadequate teachers, bullies, contact sports, and a slew of other things had been listed as reasons she shouldn't go. "I just worry about you, especially with your immune system so vulnerable right now." Mom sat on the foot of the bed. She picked up a notebook and flipped through its blank pages. "Since you insist on going, though, I think it's best you don't mention your memory problem. Or even your accident."

Olivia took the notebook from Mom and slid it into her backpack. "Why?"

"Kids can be so cruel. Even after graduating top of my class in med school, becoming a neurosurgeon for the Mayo Clinic, and running my own Huntington's trial, I can still remember the hurtful comments they made over the years." Mom grabbed Olivia's hand. "I don't want you to get made fun of. And if you don't like public school, let me know, and I'll go back to teaching you at home."

She nodded, thinking over Mom's suggestion. "So how do I explain that I don't know certain things? Like anything involving my past?"

"Give vague answers. And if you get cornered, call me, okay?" Tears formed in Mom's eyes. She stood and threw her arms around her. "I'm not ready to let you go. I've hardly had any time with you."

"You've had sixteen years with me."

Mom's suffocating grip tightened. "It doesn't seem like that long. You know I love you, right?"

Olivia patted Mom's back. "I know, Mom. I love you, too. But I'll be fine." She was telling herself as much as she was Mom. "I'm prepared for this."

"I worry you haven't had sufficient time to recover from your accident."

Mom seemed like she knew everything. But in this instance, Olivia desperately hoped she was wrong.

The drive to school seemed slow and fast all at the same time.

A flag hung on a pole at the entrance, and red railing lined the steps to the red doors. Even the letters painted on the building were red. The color was everywhere, and for some reason it made her entire body grow cold and clammy.

Students ascended the stairs, a steady stream entering the building.

That's a lot of people to deal with, she thought, her panic going into hyperdrive.

Hopefully there are some cute guys in there somewhere.

Who cares about guys? What if I can't keep up in classes?

A cute guy will make that more bearable.

Dad patted her knee. "You're going to do great."

Olivia turned toward him. "Maybe Mom was right. Maybe I should wait until next semester. We'll do more test runs and—"

"You're registered, you've got everything you need, and you're a strong, smart girl. I have complete faith in you. Now, do you want me to walk you in, or will that be too embarrassing?"

Don't do it. It's social suicide.

But I don't want to go alone.

Dad reached for his door handle.

"I got it. I'm going." She took in a deep breath and blew it back out. "Mom will be here to pick me up after school?"

"In just a few short hours."

She didn't think they'd be short, but at least it was something. Eyes fixed on the red double doors, she exited the car, slung her backpack over her shoulder, and headed for her first day of high school. For her first day of school ever. Her stomach clenched and her nerves were bouncing all over the place. Still, somewhere in that mess of emotions was a spark of excitement.

As people walked by, she recoiled, flinching whenever anyone got close.

Finally, she reached the doors and stepped inside. Fluorescent squares of light illuminated the hall, and red lockers lined the right side. The buzz of simultaneous conversations filled the air. This wasn't like the practice runs. It was louder and more cramped and ...

As her breath quickened, she started to get light-headed. Everything blurred together. Too much stuff everywhere. Way too many people. Sweat broke out across her forehead, and she tried to remember why she'd thought this was a good idea.

Okay. Deep breath. I can do this.

She forced her feet to start moving again. To her left stood a group of girls with flawless skin and hair, laughing and talking. *I'm guessing that's the popular crowd.*

Two other girls glared at the clique. "Bunch of followers," the one dressed in head-to-toe black said. It looked like she'd used an entire tube of eyeliner that morning.

"Look at Sabrina's skirt," the other added. "It barely covers her butt."

"She's undoing all the progress feminists have made."

The girl in the center of the popular group—Sabrina, apparently—turned back and glowered at the two girls. *Pretty* would be an understatement. She had shiny chestnut hair, tan skin, and large blue eyes.

"Why don't you losers take a picture? It'll last longer," Sabrina said, leaning closer to the girl in black. "Jealous much?"

"I'd be jealous if my goal in life was to be a vapid trophy wife someday."

Watching them exchange verbal jabs was all too familiar. *That's like what goes on in my head on a daily basis.* Between the perky voice, the anti-conformist voice, and her own thoughts, it sometimes felt like being three people. *Don't think about that right now. Focus on acting normal. Blending in.*

As if to spite her, the higher-pitched voice in her head whispered, *Making friends.*

The other quickly came back with, *Becoming independent.*

Olivia closed her eyes and took a couple deep breaths. When she opened them, both Sabrina and the two other girls were looking at her. Not wanting to get dragged into the mess, she hurried past them.

Studying the numbers on the lockers, she walked along the hall until she got to 207.

"You must be new," someone to her left said.

Olivia glanced around, checking to see if the person was talking to her. A blond girl was looking directly at her, eyebrows raised. "Um, yeah," she said. "I moved here over the summer."

"I'm Keira."

"Olivia."

"So do you always go by Olivia, or do you sometimes go by Liv? I've been obsessed with the name Liv forever. That's what I named my Barbie, my cat. I even asked my parents if I could change my name to it. I just love Liv. But if you don't like it, then I won't call you it. I'm just saying I know that's what I'd go by if my name were Olivia."

She stared for a moment, overwhelmed by how many words the girl had just thrown at her so quickly and trying to figure out how to respond. Finally, she simply shrugged. "Whatever's fine. You can call me Liv if you want to."

"Cool. Well, I'm going to go catch up with some of my friends. We've been talking about our first day of junior year for-like-ever, and I'm dying to see what's new. If you need any help, though, just let me know." She grinned, showing off her blindingly white teeth, then bounded down the hall.

See, it's not so bad. That Keira girl was nice. And I kind of like Liv, actually. Fresh start and all, maybe I'll try it out. It sounds...almost right.

A tall, lanky guy walked up to a petite girl a couple lockers down, wrapping his arms around her and leaning in for a kiss. Olivia's insides twisted, a combination of longing and embarrassment over watching the intimate gesture. There was something else, too—a pang in her chest that felt almost like . . . missing someone.

She jerked her attention to her backpack and focused on transferring her supplies from her backpack to her locker.

That smell. Musty, metal.

She knew she'd never been to public school, but the smell was so familiar. She stuck her head inside the locker and inhaled.

A sharp pain shot through her head, forcing her to raise her hands and squeeze her temples. The smell triggered . . . something . . . but she couldn't catch hold of what. That prickling sense of wrongness swept across her skin, giving her goose bumps. It was almost becoming as familiar as the voices.

"What's up, man?" a male voice said. A body bounced against the locker next to her, and she jumped. The guy laughed, shouldered his bag, and punched the arm of the guy who'd pushed him.

Relax. It's just typical high school boys being stupid, she thought, rolling her eyes. *Nothing to get scared over.*

Then she tensed, because how would she know what typical high school boys were like? She shook her head, her pulse still skipping a little from the near heart attack. Trying not to think about all the people or how many of them might bounce off lockers when she least expected it, she took her class schedule out of her back pocket and unfolded it. *First class: English Composition with Mrs. Tully, Room 121.*

Mentally checking off all she'd need, she grabbed her binder, slid a pen and pencil into the front pocket, and tucked it under her arm. She made her way down the hall, toward the stairs. Lots of people looked her way; she stared straight ahead, avoiding eye contact as much as possible. It was easier if she didn't have to figure out if she should smile or how she should respond if they said anything to her.

Near the bottom of the staircase, her arm spasmed and her binder slipped from her grasp. It hit the landing and popped open, sending papers everywhere. For a moment, all she could do was stare. The first few days she'd been awake, her arm had spasmed a lot—like it had a life of its own. It hadn't acted up in a while, but apparently it thought today would be the day to remind her how messed-up she still was.

Great. My first day of school and I get to start it like a total spaz.

Ew. You've got a great vocabulary somewhere. Why'd you choose the word spaz?

People tromped across the sheets of paper, scattering

them even farther. Olivia sighed, walked down the last two steps, then knelt and started picking them up.

Other hands joined hers. She looked up from her messy stack of papers, but all she could see was shaggy brown hair until he sat back and shook the strands out of his face. Square black frames covered his brown eyes. They were totally geek chic.

Geek chic? Sometimes these totally bizarre words or phrases just popped into her head.

He held out the pile he'd gathered. "Here you go."

Her heart picked up speed as she stared into his eyes. She couldn't remember how many cute guys she'd encountered before, but the one looking back at her was the cutest she remembered seeing, and she was sure that would be true with or without her missing memories.

He waved the papers. "Do you want them or not?"

She shook herself from her he's-so-cute trance and took the papers from him. "Thanks. Everything just kinda spilled. I don't know if I would've been able to get it all without your help."

"Yeah, well, the people here aren't the most helpful bunch." His gaze ran over her, and it seemed more critical than approving. "I'm sure you'll be fine, though."

Tilting her head, she studied him. "What do you mean by that?"

"Yep, you'll fit in just fine." He stood, readjusted his bag, and headed upstairs without even a nod good-bye.

∻

I made it to lunch. I guess that's something.

Olivia had tried to lie low, but small town and all, everyone else already seemed to know one another, making it harder to sneak by unnoticed. And even harder to know where to sit. She stood near the end of the lunch line, holding her tray, unsure which direction to go.

"Popular table's over there," a voice said.

Glasses Guy jerked his head toward a table to the right. A handful of girls—the one made up of Sabrina and her friends, along with Keira—was there. So were several guys who looked like they'd be grouped into the jock category.

She looked back at him. "Where do you sit?"

"Not there." He walked past her, sat at a table in the corner, and put in earphones.

I wonder what his deal is.

"Liv! Over here! I'll introduce you to everyone." Keira waved her over.

After considering her options and realizing she didn't really have any, she slowly made her way to what Glasses Guy had called the "popular table."

"Everybody, this is Liv. She just moved here from . . ." Keira looked at her. "I'm sorry, but if you told me, I don't remember."

"Minnesota."

"Minnesota. Anyway, her locker's next to mine."

Heat crawled up Olivia's neck and into her cheeks, and she pulled her hair forward to make sure her scar was hidden. *Okay. You can all stop staring now.*

"That's Sabrina." Keira pointed to her, then to the girls next to her. "And that's Candace and Taylor."

Wow. All these girls are so pretty.

And probably totally conceited. I bet they care more about looks than about what's going on in the world.

Let's just get through today. I'm sure the world will still need saving tomorrow.

"These are the guys. Clay, Austin, Jarvis."

The guys aren't bad, either.

Bunch of pretty-boy jocks. They're probably as conceited as the girls.

Olivia worked hard to smile, hoping it masked the thoughts buzzing through her head.

She mimicked Keira's casual pose, while trying not to stare so no one would know she was taking her cues from someone else. Being at school was more work than she'd thought it would be.

Sabrina started complaining about her classes, and everyone chimed in. Olivia was just happy the attention wasn't on her anymore. She poked at her food, choosing to eat the fruit cocktail and salad. The mystery meat didn't look appealing, so she left it untouched.

Once in a while, someone would look her way. It made her pulse quicken and her palms sweat, but she managed a couple of nods and one-word answers. Toward the end of lunch, a movement in the corner caught her eye.

Glasses Guy walked across the cafeteria and dumped his tray.

I wonder why he sits alone.

And why he was so cryptic when he was talking to me earlier.

Still, she couldn't seem to tear her eyes off him. Because whatever his deal was, there was definitely something intriguing about that boy.

4

Olivia shared her last two classes—chemistry and algebra II—with Keira. It was nice to spend the end of the day with someone who was not only super friendly, but also knew where she was going. When the final bell rang, Keira waited for her so they could walk to their lockers together.

The people filling the hall seemed eager to get home, which meant bodies cramming together and her personal space bubble shrinking to nonexistent. Any time someone brushed up against her, her breath hitched and her body went on high alert.

Keira hugged her books to her chest and moved closer. "So, first days are always hard, but hopefully yours wasn't too bad."

Olivia dodged a guy in her path, bumping against Keira's shoulder. "No, not too bad. I'm a little concerned about algebra, though. It was just so . . ." *Boring. And way below my level.*

Don't say that, or she'll think you're a nerd.

There's nothing wrong with being a strong, smart woman.

"I know," Keira said. "Mr. Walker is a super hard teacher. I didn't know what he was talking about, either."

"You mean that wasn't a review?"

"It was a foreign language, that's what it was." Keira opened her locker and shoved her books inside.

Disappointment filled her. Yeah, it was nerdy to be upset that math class was too simple, but it was her thing. Math spoke to her. In a sea of confusion, it was crystal clear.

Keira grabbed her bag and slammed her locker closed. "I'll see you tomorrow, Liv. I'm super glad I met you."

"Me, too." Olivia waved, then turned her attention to the combination lock on her locker. The first time she messed up halfway through. She went through the steps again, nice and slowly, inwardly grumbling that she had to stare at the bright red color that much longer.

Seriously. It's everywhere. She wasn't sure why, but it made her feel sick to her stomach. She grabbed the books she needed to take home, stuffed them in her bag, and closed the door.

The halls were already empty, with only a couple of other students milling around. Earlier, all the people had made her nervous; now, the lack of people made her feel just as uncomfortable. She rushed down the hall, pushed out the front doors, and looked for her ride. Spotting Mom's silver Lexus a few spaces back, she walked to it and climbed in.

Concern filled Mom's features. "How was your day? If you're done with public school, I completely understand. We'll tell Henry—"

"It was good." Saying it aloud, she realized that as stressful as parts of the day were, the majority of it had gone well. "I met a few people, and classes are good—although algebra is a little too easy. But maybe it'll get harder. I hope, anyway."

Mom kept opening her mouth, presumably to say something, but no words came out.

"I think I can do it. I mean, I can." Yes, she still flinched when people walked by or got too close, but she'd done it. Survived her first day of school. "I kind of . . . like it?"

"You like it?"

She nodded.

"What about sick kids? Were people coughing near you? Breathing on you?"

Olivia noticed all the cars lining up behind them. "We're blocking everyone. We should probably go."

With a huff, Mom pulled away from the curb and turned up the classical music she loved so much. Olivia wished that for once it could be something else. Anything else.

I wonder what kind of music Glasses Guy was listening to at lunch.

Everything the guy said seemed like a puzzle. But he *had* helped her with her papers. She thought about the way he shook his hair off his face, and how her heart beat like crazy when she'd looked into his eyes.

"Are you sure you're feeling okay?" Mom braked at the intersection and reached over to feel her forehead. "You're a little warm."

Olivia pulled away. "I'm fine." In less than a minute, Mom was already starting with the hovering. If her options were the challenge of school or Mom breathing down her neck all the time, she'd figure out the school thing, no matter what it took.

And if that also meant she'd get another chance to talk to Glasses Guy, even better.

5

Lunches were always filled with plenty of conversation. By other people. As Olivia ate, she tuned in and out of whatever topic everyone else was discussing, her gaze often drifting to Glasses Guy. All three days they'd been in school, he'd sat in the same place in the cafeteria, headphones on. He wasn't in any of her classes, and she hadn't talked to him since he'd pointed out the "popular table."

It seems like he prefers to be alone.

I'm shaky in social situations, and even I'd still rather not sit by myself all the time.

"So Liv, what are your big plans for the weekend?" Keira asked.

She pulled her attention away from Glasses Guy. "Um, I'll probably just stay at home with my parents."

"Ugh. Forced family bonding time's the worst. My parents insisted on it forever, but they finally realized it caused more problems than it was worth."

Clay Armstrong scooted down the bench until he was seated across from her. He was the jock with the whole tall, dark, and handsome thing going on. His eyebrows arched over eyes so blue she wondered if they weren't enhanced by colored contacts. "You guys talking about the weekend?"

Keira jerked a thumb at her. "Lame plans with the parents. Total waste of a weekend."

"We don't really have plans. I just assumed . . ." Olivia wasn't sure how to finish, since now Clay and Keira were both looking at her. "What are you guys doing?"

"There's a spot outside of town called The Gulch where we hang out on the weekends," Keira said.

Clay leaned in, propping his elbows on the table. "You should come. If you need a ride, I'd be happy to pick you up."

Going to school was one thing—she was just getting the hang of it. But no matter how lame her classmates thought it was, she was looking forward to a quiet weekend at home. She needed a break from worrying about what to say and how to act every second of the day.

Clay smiled at her. "So, whaddya say?"

"Maybe some other time." Her answer didn't get the attention off her like she'd hoped it would. Her heart picked up speed, and suddenly, she needed to get away from Clay's and Keira's questioning looks. She stood and grabbed her tray. "I'll see you guys later."

She threw away her uneaten food and rushed toward the exit. As she stepped into the hall, she glanced over her shoulder to see if anyone was still staring.

"Ugh!" she heard as she plowed into something solid.

She stumbled forward, barely managing to keep her feet under her. When she straightened, she saw it wasn't just something; it was someone.

"I'm so sorry," Olivia said to the scrawny kid she'd knocked down.

He sat on the floor, a stunned look on his face. Then he picked up his book and scrambled to his feet. Without a word, he ducked his head and hurried in the opposite direction.

Glasses Guy stood across the hall, a crooked grin on his face. "You're kind of clumsy, huh?"

Heat flooded her cheeks. *Why, of all people, did* he *have to witness that?*

He shook his head. "Poor freshman didn't even see it coming."

"I didn't mean to knock him down, and I already feel bad enough without you adding to it." To her dismay, her voice broke.

"I wasn't trying to make you feel bad," he said, stepping closer. "Watching you mow down that kid was actually the highlight of my day."

She frowned at him. "Somehow that doesn't make me feel any better."

"I guess you'll have to get all your new friends to cheer you up. I figured it wouldn't take you long to settle into that group."

I've noticed you don't have any friends didn't seem like a good thing to say, so she searched for something else. "They've been nice to me."

"Of course they have." He studied her for a moment, opened his mouth like he was going to say something, then shook his head and turned to walk away.

It would have been so much easier if she could feel indifferent toward him. But of all the people at Cottonwood High, he was the one she couldn't stop thinking about. "Wait."

Her pulse quickened when he looked back at her, and she almost lost her nerve. She swallowed and forced the words out. "I never got your name."

"Spencer."

She paused for a moment, not sure whether to go with Olivia or Liv. Everyone else called her by the nickname, and this seemed like a good moment to embrace being someone new. "I'm Liv," she said, liking the way it sounded.

"So I've heard." With that, he continued down the hall.

After their still-boring algebra class, Liv walked out of the classroom with Keira. As they neared their lockers, she spotted Spencer charging down the hall, a serious look on his face. Not only did he not hang around anyone, people seemed to go out of their way to avoid him.

He disappeared into the crowd and she turned to Keira. "Do you know a guy named Spencer?"

Keira glanced around, then draped an arm over her shoulders and leaned in. "Don't ever mention him in front of Sabrina, okay?"

"I wasn't going to . . . I don't even know him. I just . . . He helped me pick up some papers."

Keira's eyes widened. "And he talked to you?"

"Not really. In fact, he's kind of rude. But nice at the same time. It's hard to explain."

"He doesn't usually talk to anyone anymore."

"Why not?"

Keira shrugged. "You'd have to ask him, but since he doesn't really talk, it's kind of a parabola."

Liv lowered her eyebrows. "Parabola?" *He's complicated, but I doubt the quadratic formula is involved.*

"You know, like a catch-22."

"Oh. You mean a paradox."

"That's it. I knew it didn't sound right."

"Sorry," Liv said. "I didn't mean to correct you. My mom does it to me and it's so annoying."

Keira spun the combo to her locker without even looking.

"It's cool. Guess I should work on my vocab more. My brother always points out how ditzy I am."

"You've got that whole nice, sunny personality going for you. That trumps everything else."

Keira smiled. "Thanks, Liv. You're quiet, but I'll get you out of that shell yet. You really should come with us to The Gulch sometime. I think Clay likes you."

"I'm sure he was just being nice."

"You may be book smart, but me"—Keira leaned against her locker—"I know guys. And he's interested. So, what do you think?"

Liv had been so preoccupied with Spencer, she hadn't given much thought to Clay. Warmth tingled through her chest as she pictured his cute, smiling face. *He's totally hot.*

Irritation replaced the warm fuzzies, giving her emotional whiplash. *No way I'm going for a brainless jock.*

"I don't really know," she said. "There are too many thoughts swirling around to separate one from the other."

Keira gave her a funny look. "Did you have a boyfriend back at *your* old school?"

Since she'd never gone to school, at least she knew the answer, even if she couldn't remember. "Nope."

"Don't worry. I'll help ease you into it."

Hot air blasted Liv in the face the second she stepped outside. She made her way down the steps, happy to have survived another day, but then her feet slowed as she spotted Spencer. His headphones were in, his eyes focused on the parking lot. He walked up to an old, faded blue car, tossed his backpack inside, and got in.

A loud grinding noise came from the car. Scowling,

Spencer smacked the steering wheel. A few seconds later, the grinding noise filled the air again. The door flung open, and he walked to the front of his car and popped the hood.

Maybe I should go see if he needs help.

Yeah, except for the fact that you don't know anything about cars and the guy is impossible to talk to, that's a great idea.

At least staring at him from here, she could enjoy his cute profile without having to try to figure out his cryptic stares and comments.

But then she remembered how he'd helped her with her papers, and she figured she should at least go over and see if she could do anything. Maybe even offer him a ride when Mom got there. It would be the polite thing to do, right?

Even though she'd decided to go, her feet remained in place.

Come on, you're past being scared of talking to people.

She took a deep breath and strode over, her heart picking up speed with each step. Spencer was bent over his car, the muscles in his arms flexing as he messed around with the engine.

Between the heat and being so close to him, she felt a little dizzy. "Hey, do you need some help?" she asked his back.

No response. His headphones were still in.

She hesitantly reached out and tapped him on the shoulder.

He jerked up and banged his head on the hood. "Damn it!" Rubbing the spot he'd hit, he twisted to face her. "What?"

She flinched, surprised by his sharp tone. "I-I just thought you might need a ride. I'm sure my mom will give you one if you want."

He looked at her for a moment, that frustrating, hard-to-read expression on his face. "I'm fine." Without another word, he leaned over the hood again.

Resisting the urge to tell him he didn't have to be a jerk

about it, she clenched her teeth and headed back to the sidewalk to wait for Mom. She glared at Spencer's back, telling herself she didn't care that he didn't want to talk to her, then wondering why she wanted to talk to him.

He glanced up and caught her staring at him. Cheeks burning, she turned away. *From now on, I'm just going to ignore him.*

Maybe I'll even focus on Clay.

Clay's totally the guy to go for. Cute, athletic, popular—the whole package. Liv could practically feel the inner perky voice bouncing on the balls of her feet and clapping.

Sure. If by "whole package" you mean dumb enough to think he'll play professional sports instead of needing a real job someday.

"Geez. Not that I'm sure either way, but I think that's a little harsh." At least verbally responding seemed to shut up both the voices. Of course, that made her realize she was standing on the sidewalk talking to herself. *Awesome.*

Mom's car pulled up to the curb. Liv climbed in, the classical music making her inwardly groan. She leaned back in her seat as Mom drove toward home, thinking about Spencer, and Clay, and talking to Keira about boys earlier. "Did I ever have a boyfriend?"

Mom whipped her head toward her. "Of course not! You're too young for a boyfriend. I didn't have one until I was nineteen years old, and all he did was distract me from my studies."

"Nineteen? That's so old."

"Who's the boy?"

Spencer's face was the one that came to mind. Liv looked out the window at the houses flashing past. "There is no boy. A girl asked me if I'd had a boyfriend before. I told her no, but it made me curious." She glanced at Mom, thinking of another thing that she'd been curious about. "By the way, did you ever get the family pictures out of storage? I'd still like to see if they bring back anything."

A stern look crossed Mom's face. "Those memories are gone, Olivia. You're never going to get them back, and you need to move forward. Pictures won't help. Nothing will. You're just lucky to be alive. Isn't that enough for you?"

Mom had never snapped at her before, not like that. "I don't understand," Liv said. "It was just a simple question."

"Well, I think that's enough questions for one day."

The rest of the car ride passed in silence. As soon as they got home, she went straight to her room, frustration and anger burning through her. She no longer wanted to stay home this weekend. She wanted to get out of her house where she wouldn't have to deal with Mom—to go to that party everyone had been talking about. She didn't know anyone's phone numbers, though, so she couldn't call and ask Keira or Clay to come get her. Besides, what would she do when she got to the party?

Meet boys, have fun, get a social life.

Parties are lame. After they graduate, all the popular kids will still be stuck in this small town. It won't matter who you knew or what parties you went to.

A crushing sense of hopelessness filled her. Going to school was supposed to make everything better, but it wasn't working. Her life was still a confusing mess and the voices hadn't gone away. If anything, they were getting worse.

Liv sat at a dinner table. To her left, a young brunette girl

pushed her peas to the far corner of her plate. And she just knew her name was Elizabeth.

Elizabeth locked eyes with her and mouthed, "Okay, distract them."

Liv looked across the table at the dark-haired man, then studied the woman with pale skin and brown hair to his right. She felt the urge to hug her. Tell her she loved her. But she didn't even know who she was.

A kick under the table brought her attention back to Elizabeth. Elizabeth raised her eyebrows, staring at her like she should know what to do next and hurry up about it. With an eye roll and a loud sigh, Elizabeth said, "Don't you have something to say to Mom and Dad?"

The man and woman looked at Elizabeth, then at Liv.

"I'm thinking of piercing my nose." It came out of nowhere. She didn't know why she'd chosen it, but it definitely got their attention.

"You most certainly will not, young lady," the woman said. "I don't care what the other kids at school are doing, either, so don't even bother with that speech."

"Just think of how uncomfortable that would be anytime you got a cold and had to wipe your nose," the man said. "Not to mention how prospective employers would look at you. And before you tell me how unfair that is, I'm not saying it is or isn't fair, but it's how the world works. People judge others when they see piercings or tattoos."

Liv looked to Elizabeth, who grinned and gave her a thumbs-up signal. The pile of peas that had been on her plate was gone.

"Just seeing if you were paying attention," she said. "You know I'd never pierce my nose. Belly button, maybe . . ."

Both adults stared at her.

"Come on. When did they outlaw funny in this house?"

The woman shot her a reprimanding look. "Since you came home with a hot-pink stripe in your hair."

"It washed out," she automatically said. She pulled her hair forward to see. There was only brown, no hint of pink.

The woman shook her head, the start of a smile on her lips. "You girls are going to give me gray hair."

"You already have gray hair," the man said. "You just keep your hairdresser busy covering it up."

The woman's mouth dropped open as she looked at him. "Says the man who has a few grays himself."

He ran his fingers through his hair. "I'm proud of mine."

She smiled at him, then looked across the table at Elizabeth, doing a double take at the empty plate. "Did you eat your peas?"

Wrinkling her nose, Elizabeth said, "They were so disgusting."

When the woman turned away, Elizabeth shot Liv another grin. "I owe you," she mouthed.

A loud knock sounded through the room, but no one else seemed to notice, even when it got louder and steadier.

"Olivia?"

"Olivia, open up this door right now!"

The family around the dinner table dissolved as she opened her eyes.

What a weird dream.

Thinking about the thumbs-up from Elizabeth made her smile.

Liv jumped when the knocking came again. "Just a minute," she said, sitting up and blinking away the last haze of sleep. She didn't even remember lying down.

She crossed the room, unlocked the door, and opened it.

"You're locking the door now?" Mom asked, fists on hips, eyebrows knit together.

"I guess today's all about locking things up." She was a little surprised at herself—she didn't normally talk like that to her parents.

Mom shook her head. "I knew it—those kids at school are a bad influence. You used to be so sweet. And now . . ." She sucked in her breath. "You lock me out."

Liv tried to keep her voice calm. "It's not school, Mom. It's . . . You're kind of suffocating me. I was actually looking forward to spending some time relaxing at home this weekend with you and Dad, but it's not going to be relaxing if you're hovering over me, freaking out every time I try to talk to you."

"I don't mean to suffocate you," Mom said, the offense in her features clear. "I just worry, especially with everything you've already been through in the past few months. But I'll try . . . to give you your space. If that's what you want."

The tension in the room cleared, and her mind drifted back to her dream. Every time she pictured Elizabeth, the way she moved, the way she talked, she got the strangest sense of déjà vu. "The conversation in the car . . ." Mom seemed to be struggling for words. "I didn't mean to sound so harsh. I just want you to focus on your life ahead of you, not the fact that you don't remember your life before."

Liv leaned against her dresser. "Does that mean I can't ever bring it up?"

"Of course not." There was an edge to Mom's voice that said if she did bring it up, though, everything would be tense again.

Sighing, Liv looked down and focused on her shoes. Today she'd gone with her Converse sneakers. The who-cares-what-everyone-else-thinks voice approved; the girly, cares-about-being-popular side balked at the blackness. "Before the accident was I more the perky, happy type or the girl-power type?"

"You've always been my beautiful, intelligent girl."

Such a Mom response. Not really answering the question, but nice. "Who was a loner."

"What can I say? Like mother, like daughter." Mom folded her arms and rested her hip against the doorframe. "I've never been very good with people. I studied neurosurgery because I found it fascinating, then I used that knowledge to try to better others' lives. That was my way of connecting with people."

Mom gazed across the room for a moment, seemingly lost in the past, then straightened. "Anyway, I was hoping you'd come help me with dinner."

"Sure," Liv said. As she and Mom walked down the stairs, though, she couldn't get Elizabeth off her mind. "Hey, Mom, was I friends with any little brunette girls? Like nine or ten years old?"

Mom's steps slowed. She gripped the banister. "Friends," she said, drawing out the word. "Not that I can think of. Why?"

"I had the strangest dream. It seemed so real, like a memory. A faded, fuzzy memory. Only, people I didn't know were there."

Liv expected Mom to turn around to face her, but she continued down the stairs, all business again. "Your mind probably came up with those images while you were in a coma. It's your brain's way of keeping itself going."

Again Liv saw Elizabeth smiling at her, thumb in the air. The thought of her not being real made her heart knot. "So, they're just imaginary?"

"That's what dreams are, sweetheart. Sure, sometimes there are figments of reality mixed in, but it's usually all skewed. That's what makes them seem so real." Mom hit the bottom step and continued to the kitchen.

Feeling silly for getting so worked up over a dream, she tried to snuff out her emotions. As she walked into the kitchen, she pulled a strand of hair up front, like she'd done in her dream. *Pink might look kind of cute.*

It did look cute, but it got old fast.

That can't be right. No way Mom would ever let me do anything so crazy.

Yet, something tickled her memory. Elizabeth looking at her, eyes wide, saying, *You're going to be in* so *much trouble.*

Liv covered a yawn as she came down the stairs.
She'd slept in, so she shouldn't still be so tired. As she neared
the kitchen, she heard Mom's voice. "It sounds great, darling.
Someday I'd love to do it, but I've got to pick up Olivia from
school. Plus there's still the chance she'll change her mind
and want to take up lessons at home again. I want to be here
for her if she needs me."

Through the open entryway, she saw Dad seated on one
side of the table. "But Olivia's adjusting to school so well.
And—"

"No one else has the skills to care for her like I do.
Sometimes I'm still afraid that everything she's been through
. . . like one day we'll wake up and everything will be undone.
You're careful when you talk about Minnesota, right?"

Liv froze, a strange feeling pricking her skin. *What does
Mom mean by* undone? *And why does Dad need to be
careful talking about Minnesota?* Mom and Dad had told
her how she'd wrecked her car into a tree and almost died,
but they never went into much depth about that night and
would change the subject whenever she tried to talk about it.
Actually, they hardly talked at all about their lives from the
time before she came out of her coma.

Dad sighed. "Of course I'm careful. You remind me every

day all that's at risk. It's another reason you need something else to think about. I know you, Victoria. You're happiest when you're busy, and I think it would be good for you to get out of the house and meet some people. It's only a few hours, then you'd be home shortly after Livie was done with school."

Liv wasn't sure what they were talking about, but she didn't want to be the reason Mom couldn't do something. Plus, she didn't know how much longer she could deal with listening to them talk about her like she might break any minute.

She stepped into the kitchen. "What's going on?"

Mom was seated opposite Dad, a steaming mug in front of her.

Dad leaned back in his chair. "You know how your mom's always trying new cooking techniques and recipes?"

Liv nodded. "Yeah."

"I'm trying to talk her into taking a cooking class, but it's a little bit later in the day. It ends about thirty minutes after school, so she's worried about how you'll get home."

"You should take the class. I can ride the bus home."

Disgust overtook Mom's features. "You're not riding the bus. There are far too many germs, and no seat belts, and just—no."

Liv reached into the stainless steel fridge, took out the milk, and poured herself a glass. Walking home would take forever, and with the heat she'd dehydrate in minutes. But there had to be a way to work it out. "There's some benches in front of the school, so I could sit there and do my home-work while I wait for you to pick me up."

"There *are* benches outside the school. *Is* implies singular."

It took her a moment to realize Mom had been correcting her grammar. "*Anyway*, I think you should take the cooking class. It'll be fun." *And give you something to focus on besides me and how fragile I supposedly am.*

Dad slid the brochure across the table to Mom. "Several people will still be around for sports practice and that kind of thing, so Livie won't be all alone."

"It *would* be nice to have something to keep me occupied now that you two are out of the house all day." Mom looked at her. "But I don't want you to catch heatstroke."

Liv drained her glass of milk. "I'll take a water bottle, so I'll be fine. Just do it." When Mom didn't say anything, she pushed harder. "Remember the suffocating thing? Neither of us should miss out on new experiences."

"Well, I could always use more recipes to add to our dinner menu. And some adult conversation would be nice."

Behind Mom's back, Dad grinned at Liv and gave her a thumbs-up.

She smiled. Then she wondered if he'd done that before. *Maybe that's why the gesture was in my dream.*

"What?" Mom asked, looking from her to Dad.

"Nothing," he said. "I can't wait to see what you come up with next. You've always been good with experiments."

A weirdness blanketed the room as Mom and Dad exchanged nervous glances.

Liv placed her empty glass in the dishwasher. "What? Am I missing something?"

"You're perfect just the way you are," Mom said.

Mom's strange reply and the way she and Dad were looking at her made her feel self-conscious. And a little freaked out.

Mom shot out of her chair. "I've got to go change over the laundry."

Dad stared after Mom, then slowly looked up. "We're so proud of all the progress you've made. You know that, right?"

She nodded, still trying to catch up on what had just happened.

Dad came over and squeezed her shoulder. He tried to smile, but too much sorrow hung on his features to pull it off. "Thank you for being such an easy kid to love. You have no idea how much that saves me."

The hair on the back of her neck rose. "Saves you?"

"After everything that happened with the wreck . . ." His voice cracked. "We feel lucky you pulled through. That you're here with us. You're a good kid, that's all I'm saying." He squeezed her shoulder again, then walked out of the kitchen.

The something's-not-right sensation crawling across her skin was nothing new.

The flicker of mistrust for her parents was.

Her arm chose that moment to spasm. It smacked into the top rack of the dishwasher, sending shooting pain through her wrist and up her forearm and reminding her of the fact that she was far from perfect.

And now she was beginning to think that her parents might not be as perfect as she thought, either.

❧

"Olivia? Do you have a minute?" Mom stood in the open doorway.

At first she was going to say no. All day she'd steered clear of her parents, so she wouldn't have to face this sudden uncertainty she felt toward them. They'd helped her recover from her accident. They were all she had, really, and she needed everything to be okay between them. Then she saw the square black book Mom held in her arms.

"I found something you might want to look at." Handling

the book as if she thought it might break, Mom placed it on Liv's bed and flipped open to the first page.

Liv leaned in for a closer look. Mom and Dad stood under a floral-adorned archway. A frosty veil covered Mom's dark hair. Her white gown with lace overlay had a long train; she held a bouquet of calla lilies. Dad wore a tux with a black vest and a bow tie. Mom leaned in to him, a hand on his chest, smiling at the camera.

"Whoa," Liv said. "Dad used to have long hair."

Mom smiled at the picture. "He's always been so handsome. And tall—just like you."

From her earliest, fuzziest memories of waking up, she remembered Mom sitting by her bed and talking to her for hours. Mom had mentioned working with Dad in the hospital. "You said you guys first met at work, right?"

Mom nodded. "When he transferred to the hospital, all the women talked about how handsome the new cardiac surgical resident was. I was far too focused on work to think about men—handsome or not. But one day he grabbed my elbow and told me I needed to come to lunch with him. Turns out he thought I was too thin and that I needed to slow down and take better care of myself. I was furious at first—no one had ever talked to me like that."

A faraway look entered her eyes and she smiled. "Every day after that, he'd sit with me for lunch, we'd talk, and before I knew it was happening—before I could stop myself—I'd fallen in love with him."

Mom's face lit up as she relayed the rest of the story: squeezing dates into their busy schedules; Dad taking her to a fancy restaurant, dropping down on one knee and asking her to marry him.

The story ended with an account of their small wedding.

"All the other women at the hospital were so jealous—none of them could believe he'd fallen for me. In fact, they used to say I had brains but no heart. But meeting your father, well, loving him taught me there was more to life. I guess you could say he fixed my heart, no surgery required."

In a lot of ways, Dad and Mom seemed so opposite. But they somehow fit together. What those women had said about Mom sent heat through her veins. Sure, sometimes Mom came across as harsh, and she was definitely overprotective, but her intentions were in the right place.

Liv leaned her head on Mom's shoulder. "Those women were wrong. I get a daily reminder of how big your heart is when you're making sure I'm taking my pills, using my hand sanitizer, and eating healthy."

Mom kissed her forehead. "Thank you for that."

They continued looking through the photo album, and here and there, Mom would make comments about the pictures.

One photo near the end of the album showed Mom, side profile, stomach protruding, Dad's hand on her belly. The picture had been torn apart and taped back together.

"Why's this picture like that?" Liv asked.

Tears filled Mom's eyes. "The doctor told me . . ." Mom threw her arms around her. "I have you. They said I couldn't have a baby, but I have you."

When Mom sat back a minute later, her lashes were wet and clumped together; her nose and eyes were red. "Back in those days we had to go somewhere to get our photos developed, but now everything's digital." She closed the book. "All of our digital pictures were saved on our old computer. We should've backed them up, but we didn't, and when the computer died . . . All the pictures of you growing up are gone. I'm so sorry."

It all made sense now. This was why Mom had gotten so upset when she asked to see pictures. She patted Mom's hand. "It's okay. Like you're always saying, the past is the past. From now on, I'm just going to focus on the future."

But as the words came out of her mouth, cold filled her entire body, like something didn't want her to let go of the past. She got a flash of her younger self. A camera was aimed at her and she was smiling, telling whoever was taking the picture to hurry it up already. Then a twinge of pain shot through her heart, more like a memory of the ache she'd felt that day while her picture was being taken. As if in a dream, she watched herself crumple to the tile floor of an unfamiliar kitchen, felt everything inside of her aching, unable to catch her breath, the thought that this time she wasn't going to make it to the hospital echoing through her mind.

7

Liv sat in the empty classroom, math book open on the desk in front of her, tapping her pencil to her lip as she worked on the problems. Going home meant dealing with Mom's foul mood and a long list of chores, so the only way she could get her homework done was to stay after school.

As she moved to write her answer, the silver charm bracelet on her wrist caught the light. She lifted her arm and studied the large heart. J + L was engraved on the front.

Her nails were fake and French-tipped and her arms were toned and tan. She wore a lacy top that showed cleavage—she actually had quite a bit of it somehow—and tight jeans with rhinestones on the pocket. She shifted forward and her bangs fell into her face. Bangs that were pale blond.

Looking around, she noticed that the chairs attached to the desks were blue instead of maroon-colored, which wasn't right. Plus they looked beat up and old, their surfaces riddled with pockmarks and ink.

Liv experienced that same feeling she got when she immersed herself in the tub, everything muted yet warm. Her cell phone rang, pulling her out of her daze. She took it from her pocket and stared at the pink floral covering. The name Courtney flashed across the display. She tossed her pencil on her book and answered.

"Where are you?" Courtney asked. "The girls and I are heading to the mall. We might even catch a movie later."

Under no circumstances would she tell her friend she was hiding out at school, studying math. "I can't tonight. I've got to . . . pick up an extra shift."

"You're always at that damn restaurant. Can't you take a night off?"

"You know how it is," Liv said, even though Courtney didn't. Not really. Liv was careful not to let any of her friends see what her real life was like.

"Fine. See you tomorrow at school. You won't be too busy for me then, will you?"

"I'll try to fit you in. If you're lucky." She'd found that making a joke was the best way to keep people from taking too close a look or asking any more questions.

Courtney laughed. "You better."

Liv hung up and got back to work on her assignment. She might not be the best at many subjects, but math was her thing, and she was determined to get amazing grades this year. It was her only shot at college, and college was her ticket away from Mom and out of Rochester.

Besides, she actually liked math. Always had. It wasn't anything that her friends would beam with pride over—in fact, they'd mock her endlessly. But she loved that moment when she saw how to solve the problem she'd thought might be unsolvable only seconds ago.

"What are you still doing in here?" a deep voice asked, making her jump.

Mr. Schaeffer stood in the open doorway. He'd decided she was a problem student, and nothing could change his mind. Liv didn't like him, either. She didn't trust older men in general. Too many bad run-ins, thanks to Mom.

It didn't help that Mr. Schaeffer had also given her a couple of referrals for things she couldn't help. Like being late because her car wouldn't start and Mom was too hungover to drive. Or the time she'd sworn in class—okay, that one was probably a little her fault.

She swallowed, trying to hide the fact that her heart was beating too fast and her hands were shaking. "Mrs. Taylor knows I'm here. She'll be right back."

Mrs. Taylor did let her study in her classroom and was usually there to help out if she needed it. She was the one teacher Liv liked—that was another secret she hid from her friends. But Mrs. Taylor'd had to leave early that day.

Mr. Schaeffer narrowed his eyes, staring at her for an agonizing eternity, then finally left. As soon as he was gone, she stood and gathered her books. Time was up anyway; Mom would be calling soon, asking where she was. Later, when Mom was asleep or busy and Liv was so tired the numbers would swim together, she'd have to finish her homework.

All the extra hours of studying would be worth it someday. Because someday, she would do something amazing with her life. She was going to be somebody.

She just needed to survive the next few years first.

✦

Monday morning, frantic energy coursing through her veins, Liv entered the school. Today was going to be different.

All morning she'd thought about her odd dream, where she wasn't really herself but everything still felt hauntingly familiar. Even though it hadn't really been her in the dream, it gave her this boost of confidence, as though the skills to fit in—even if it was a fake, hidden part of herself—were buried in her brain somewhere, if she could just dig deep enough.

She spotted Sabrina, Candace, and Taylor. Usually she kept to the fringe of the group. Even then, she'd only go over if Keira was there. Not today, though. The need to be accepted was in overdrive, telling her to go up and be bold.

All you have to do is find the right thing to say to Sabrina and you're in. Everyone else will follow. Don't think about it as sucking up; think about it as making your life easier.

Liv waited for the argument from the other voice in her head—which probably didn't bode well for her mental state—but it never came. It was so nice to not deal with the bickering thoughts, she decided to listen to the one.

Maybe I can ditch a voice if I embrace one and push the other away, she thought as she strode toward the group. Sabrina was going on and on about some college guy she'd met at a party. She had on a flowy floral shirt, chunky silver jewelry, and tight-fitting distressed jeans. Her hair was sleek and shiny, her makeup impeccable. Looks obviously meant a lot to her.

"I love your necklace," Liv said, and for some reason it came out a little ditzy-sounding. "In fact, your whole outfit is awesome."

Sabrina looked at her and smiled.

Could it really be that easy? A compliment and I'm in, just like that?

Everyone in the group was looking at her now. Out of habit, she pulled her hair forward.

"I noticed you wear a lot of graphic tees," Sabrina said. "Is that what everyone wore at your old school?"

Liv put a protective hand on her chest, over her other hidden scar. "I guess so."

Lips pursed, Sabrina looked her up and down. "I mean, it's cute and all. You just might want to change it up once in a while."

"Thanks," Liv said, then immediately wondered why she was thanking Sabrina for basically saying her fashion sense sucked. She wanted to back away but didn't want it to look like she was offended or hurt, even though she was both.

I warned you they were like this. All they care about is looks and tearing other people down.

Oh, sure. *Now* the other voice chimed in. *Where were you a few minutes ago?*

She wasn't sure if she was more angry or relieved there was no answer.

Out of nowhere, Keira showed up. She stepped in front of Liv, facing Sabrina. "So, what was Grant's deal the other night? He was acting like a total idiot."

Sabrina added her opinion, a few more chimed in, and thanks to Keira's diversion, the spotlight was off Liv.

"Missed you at the party," a voice said near her ear. "It's too bad you couldn't come." Turning toward the sound, she saw Clay. "By the way," he said, "I think you look nice no matter what you wear."

Her cheeks burned from the compliment, combined with the fact that he'd witnessed her humiliation. "Thanks."

"See you at lunch?"

"Yeah, sure." Liv watched him walk away.

Keira nudged her. "I told you he likes you."

"He was just being nice."

"Because he likes you."

"Why would he like me?"

"Um, hello, because you're super pretty, and you've got this whole mysterious vibe, kind of like Angelina Jolie, like you might have a vial of blood around your neck or something."

A shudder ran through her at the mention of blood, though she tried to forget about it and focus on the rest of what Keira had said. "Angelina Jolie?" The name sounded so familiar. "Who is she again?"

"Hello! The movie star?" Keira stared, eyebrows scrunched together. "I can never tell if you're joking." She linked her arm in Liv's and they started toward their lockers. Keira glanced over her shoulder, then leaned in and whispered, "Sabrina's just jealous of all the attention you're getting, since you're the new pretty girl in town. She'll thaw out in time. She just needs to get to know you."

"I'm sure that's it," Liv said, even though she was thinking she wanted to keep her distance from Sabrina. Even the fringe of the group wasn't as safe as she'd hoped it would be.

Powering through her lack of sleep hadn't been too hard that morning, but the longer the day went on, the more she felt it. Even though she'd sworn to focus on the future, her mind wouldn't shut down as she'd lain in bed last night, trying to fall asleep. It kept trying to find information—namely, information about Elizabeth—that just wasn't there.

Then she'd had the weird . . . memory? . . . of collapsing in the kitchen, and the dream about the girl doing her math homework.

Since Liv didn't have to work hard to keep up in algebra, she folded her arms across her desk and put her head down. If she wasn't going to learn anything, she might as well take a short nap.

"Liv?" Mr. Walker's voice echoed through the room. "Care to answer?"

When she'd laid her head on her desk, she didn't realize it would attract attention. The math she knew, but now everyone was staring, and that made speaking difficult.

"Well, first off, I wouldn't use that method." She cleared her throat and tried to sound confident. "Polynomial division takes way too long. But if you're looking for the answer, it's two Y squared, plus three Y, plus one."

"What method would you use?"

"Synthetic division."

"That's higher-level math." Mr. Walker stepped up to her desk and tapped the top with two fingers. "Why don't you see me after class. Now, let's look at the next problem . . ."

Panic welled up in her. She'd never had to stay after class, but she knew it wasn't a good thing. *Why didn't I just keep my mouth shut?*

Rapid pulse pounding through her head, Liv approached Mr. Walker. "I'm sorry. I'll never try to sleep again, and I'll use whatever method you want, even if my mind automatically wants to use the other." She glanced at the doorway, not liking the fact that she and Mr. Walker were now the only two people in the room. He seemed nice enough, but once again her dream came to her, the same panicky feeling the blond girl felt when she'd been cornered in the classroom now tightening her own chest.

"Relax, Liv." Mr. Walker was known for being one of the scariest teachers in school—that's what Keira had said, anyway. But he was smiling and his voice was calm. "I think you're bored with the math we're doing."

"It's just *so* basic."

Mr. Walker handed a piece of paper to her.

Liv ran her eyes down the page. *Now this is more like it. Real math that takes a few minutes to analyze and tear apart.*

Could you at least try *to hide the fact that you're such a nerd?*

No way! I'm smart and that's okay. Not all guys go for shallow idiots.

Yeah, nerdy guys.

Mr. Walker's eyebrows rose as he looked at her. "So, how do those problems look to you?"

Liv shrugged. "Like fun?"

One placement test later, she was set to switch math classes. Starting tomorrow, she'd be in honors pre-calc.

Nerdy or not, she couldn't wait.

8

One of Liv's limited non-T-shirt tops was a short-sleeved purple button-down. That morning she'd gone back and forth, debating whether she should wear something new or go for another T-shirt just to spite Sabrina. In the end, she decided if wearing a different style would keep her from snarky remarks, she'd conform. Just a little bit.

As she started up the stairs of the high school, she saw the two Goth girls who'd clashed with Sabrina huddled together in heavy discussion.

They eyed her with the same disdain they did Sabrina. "Just what we needed at this school," the one with short hair said. "Another follower."

Surely they're not talking about me.

"Better run off to your queen," the other girl said. "I'd hate for you to have to come up with your own ideas."

"Me?" Liv asked, pointing to herself. "I like you guys. I'm all about girl power and being whoever you are and that kind of thing."

The short-haired girl ran her eyes up and down her and gave a pointed look to her shirt. "Could've fooled me."

Liv knew she shouldn't care what two girls she didn't even know thought about her. And it actually wasn't even so much what they said but the fact that deep down, she knew she'd dressed up more for Sabrina than for herself.

Don't worry about them. They look like death warmed over.

No, they look like they don't want to be like everyone else.

Conforming to a different style is still conforming. Right now it's about surviving high school. I can take a stand after I graduate.

If I still remember what I wanted to stand for after not using my brain for so long.

Liv squeezed her head, wishing she could push out the voices. Maybe it was time to see a psychiatrist? Only then Mom might pull her out of school, and she'd never have any hope of being normal. Or of being a strong person who made a difference.

"Ugh. Here comes the rest of the group." The girl's disgust was exaggerated and impossible to miss.

"Just ignore them," her friend said, pulling her toward the entrance. "No sense in trying to talk to people who only care about being popular."

Sabrina, Candace, and Taylor all slowed as they approached. Sabrina glanced at the Goth girls' backs, then to Liv. "Are you friends with those guys?"

Here was her chance to say something—to show Sabrina she didn't care what she thought. But instead she said, "I don't really know them, but I don't think they like me."

"I don't think they like anyone with an actual pulse." Sabrina's gaze flicked to Liv's shirt. "Nice outfit, by the way. Glad to see you stepped out of your box." Her inflection suggested it wasn't a compliment. Sabrina shot her a tight smile, then stepped past, the two other girls in tow.

Suddenly she felt lost and alone, like she wanted to sit on the steps and cry. She hated that Sabrina obviously didn't like her and hated even more that she cared.

I don't want to be this girl anymore. I want to be me.
I just have to figure out who the hell that is first.

Keira's face dropped. "You're not going to be in algebra anymore? That totally sucks!"

Liv finished chewing her bite of roll and swallowed. "We'll still have chemistry together."

Sabrina leaned in to their conversation. "You know Keira's *my* lab partner for chem, right?"

I'm so fed up with her and her bossy, better-than-everyone-else attitude. If it wasn't for Keira, I wouldn't still be sitting at this table.

"We can all get together and study, though," Keira said, a big smile on her face. "Trust me, you want me as a study buddy, because I bring the best snacks."

Sabrina looked at Keira, her eyes lingering on Keira's stomach. "Maybe you should lay off the snacks."

Smile fading, Keira glanced down, then set her fork on the table.

Without the slightest hint of remorse, Sabrina continued. "So Liv, if you want any more fashion advice, I'd be happy to help you out."

Yeah, 'cause I'm just dying to look like Barbie. Seriously, she called, and she wants her outfits back. Liv wished she had the guts to say it out loud. Even more, she wanted to tell Sabrina to leave Keira alone. Instead, she gritted her teeth and focused on her peas.

"What are we talking about over here?" Clay asked, scooting next to Liv.

"Boring stuff," Liv said.

"If you're involved, I doubt it's boring."

Sabrina rolled her eyes. "I think I'm about to lose my lunch." She picked up her tray and walked away.

A crease formed between Clay's eyebrows. "What's her problem?"

Keira glanced around, then leaned in. "All I know is that Spencer's in her class before lunch, and she's always grouchy afterward."

"She still hung up on Hale?"

"Hale?" Liv asked.

"Spencer Hale. Sabrina's been even bitchier since he dumped her."

For once, the topic they were discussing over lunch actually interested her. "How long ago was that?"

"Beginning of the summer," Keira said. "He dumped her about the same time he stopped talking to everyone else."

Liv looked to the spot where Spencer always sat. As usual, his headphones were in, and no one else was near him. And as usual, her stomach flipped as she looked at him.

"It's a shame. He used to be cool." Clay nudged her. "Enough about him. We've only got a few minutes to kill before class. Entertain me."

"Me?" Liv shook her head. "I'm more of a listener."

"Well, how do you feel about knock-knock jokes?"

Liv shrugged. "I'm not sure."

"Knock, knock." He stared at her, eyebrows raised, for several seconds. "You say who's there."

"But I don't know. You're the one telling the joke."

Keira laughed, and she wondered what she was missing. "Are you being funny," Keira said once she got her laughter under control, "or do you seriously not know what a knock-knock joke is?"

"I guess I've never heard one before."

"Where'd you grow up?" Clay asked with a laugh. "The North Pole?"

Liv looked from his amused face to Keira's. *No, but if everyone keeps looking at me like I'm crazy, I might just have to move there.*

Liv hoped her new, higher-level math class would be the pickup she needed after this wretched day. She knew what a joke was, but the whole knock-knock thing? Not in her memory at all. It was like when she couldn't think of the word *napkin* last night and Mom and Dad stared at her with concern in their eyes. Another reason she didn't want to tell them forgetting a word was the least of her problems.

Keira had giggled as she explained the whole knock-knock setup. Then, after all that, the punch line ended up being: *No, dogs bark, owls who.* It wasn't even funny, so they shouldn't bother calling it a joke.

I'm sick of feeling stupid.

Liv glanced at the numbers next to the doors. *Room 112. This is it.*

She hovered outside the door. Each new class had been hard enough—deciding where to sit, making introductions, getting used to the teacher's method of teaching. And now, since it was four days into the semester, she also had to worry about taking someone else's seat.

Footsteps approached and she automatically turned.

Spencer's eyebrows drew together. "You're still lost?" He sighed. "What's the name of the class you're supposed to be in and I'll tell you where to go."

I'll tell you where to go.

Sometimes she hated the random thoughts that popped

into her head. But that one, she liked. If only she had the guts to say it aloud.

He sighed again, like he was completely put out by her being there. "Come on, the bell's going to ring and we'll both be late."

Liv tilted her head toward the classroom. "I go to this class."

"I think you're confused." He spoke slowly, enunciating the words like he thought she was stupid. "This is honors pre-calc."

"And you're in it?" she asked, her anger growing. She'd had enough of this guy and his attitude.

"Yeah."

"So you've got to be smart to be in it?"

Spencer shrugged. "I guess some people would say that. You've got to have a good grasp of math, anyway."

Liv glared into that cute, smug face of his, and for the first time felt more irritation than attraction. "So you're implying that I'm not smart enough to be in here?"

"No. I just know you weren't in here before, and that you were lost a few days ago."

"Right. On my *first* day. You think that after three days I'm still confused?" She crossed her arms. "The insults just keep on coming."

Frustration filled his features, and she thought it was about time she'd gotten one on him. "I wasn't trying to insult you. Man, you're sensitive."

"Maybe that's because you treat me like I'm an idiot."

"It's not . . . I wasn't saying . . . Look, I think that we—"

"You need some help with those sentences? Believe it or not, I'm pretty good at English, too." Okay, that was a stretch. Mom always corrected her grammar. Still, it had the desired effect. The stunned look on his face was priceless.

The seats in the classroom were almost full now. Liv walked in and took one, deciding she didn't care if it was someone else's. She was claiming it.

When Spencer walked in, he didn't so much as glance her way.

Liv sat down on the bench outside the school to wait for Mom. *The Great Gatsby* was assigned reading, so she decided to start on it.

Cars came and went until the place was mostly deserted.

"What are you doing?"

Liv looked up and saw Spencer. The same irritation she'd felt toward him earlier that day rose to the surface again. "Why? Are you surprised I can read?"

"Never mind," he muttered, heading toward the bike rack. He unlocked a silver bike, throwing it around like it had done something to offend him, and rolled it past her.

She tried to keep her eyes on her book, but watching him walk away was a hard habit to break.

He hesitated, glanced over his shoulder, then propped the bike against the end of the bench and sat next to her. "I'm sorry, okay. I guess I judged you a little bit because of the way you look."

Liv crossed her arms and glared at him. "And how do I look?"

"Like a snobby, pretty girl who'd fit in with the popular crowd."

That hadn't been what she'd expected him to say. She looked away, somehow feeling embarrassed, insulted, and flattered, all at the same time. "Oh."

"You waiting for a ride?"

She licked her suddenly dry lips. "Yeah. I'm, um, not sure how long I'll have to sit here. My mom's got a cooking class, and she's going to pick me up when it's over."

He nodded. Tapped his fingers on the bench. Seemed to struggle with what to say to that. Liv wished he'd figure something out, because she didn't want him to go, yet didn't trust her limited conversation skills to say something herself.

"There's this place near the football field that's got some good places to jump. Since I had to bring the bike today, I figured I might as well do some riding." He twisted toward her. "You want to come down and ride with me while you wait? It's better than pretending you're really into reading . . ." He flipped her book up to look at the cover. "Yeah, it'll definitely be more fun than reading that."

"I don't know if I *can* ride a bike." Liv lowered her gaze to her lap, feeling stupid again.

Spencer threw his hands in the air. "Okay, I get it, I was wrong about you. You're smart; you know how to do things."

"No, I mean I really don't know. It's . . . hard to explain."

"Now who's calling who stupid?" He grinned at her. She hadn't seen him smile like that before. It definitely looked good on him. And it made her chest feel all tingly.

"What I'm trying to say is, I never learned." That seemed better than admitting she might've learned but didn't remember.

"How can you have not learned to ride a bike? It's a rite of passage for a kid. It's up there with Happy Meals from McDonald's, going to the park—all that stuff." He raised an eyebrow. "You've done *that* stuff, right?"

Liv shrugged. She could say yes, but she was sick of trying to keep track of all the lies and constantly holding back. She wasn't exactly ready to reveal the truth, though, either.

"Come on, then," Spencer said.

"Come on, then, what?"

He stood and grabbed his bike. "Let's see if you can ride."

"No, thanks."

"Why not?"

"Because I don't want to fall on my face, and my mom will be here any minute, and if she sees me riding a bike, she'll freak out."

He studied her for a moment, then nodded. "Yeah. It's all starting to make sense now."

She lowered her eyebrows. "What's that supposed to mean?"

"You're one of those."

"One of whats? Why do you say everything in code?"

"It's probably for the best anyway." Gripping the handles, he straddled the bike. "I guess I'll see you in class."

Liv watched him ride the bike away. It looked simple, and she regretted not giving it a shot. His voice ran over and over through her head. *You're one of those.*

Liv stormed up to her bedroom and flung open the door.

Elizabeth was sitting on Liv's bed, fingernail polish and makeup everywhere. When she looked up and saw Liv, her eyes widened.

"I thought I told you to stay out of my stuff," Liv said.

"It was just a little bit. Aren't you supposed to be staying at Jackie's house tonight?"

"We had a fight. Just like you and I are going to have a fight if you don't clean this up and stay out of my stuff."

Elizabeth put the bottles of nail polish in a big plastic box. Her eyes had gray shadow from her lashes all the way to her eyebrows.

Gritting her teeth, Liv flopped onto her bed and gathered her makeup. Her metallic gray eye shadow was a crumbled mess. "You ruined my favorite one! I swear, you mess up everything."

Elizabeth's lower lip stuck out. Tears formed in her eyes. "I didn't mean to. Don't be mad."

Now she felt bad. She wasn't angry with Elizabeth—well, she was a little angry. Mostly, she'd just had a bad day and the fight with Jackie had been a big one. She reached out and squeezed Elizabeth's knee. "I'm sorry, okay. You don't mess up everything."

"I'm sorry you got into a fight with Jackie. She is kind of a witch with a B, though."

Liv smiled. "True. Just don't let Mom hear you say that."
She grabbed a tissue and wiped some of the eye shadow from Elizabeth's lids. "Less is more, kid."

"Hello, have you seen your eyeliner these days?"

Liv turned toward the mirror. Her eyeliner was heavy. Way too much black—she was even wearing a black tank top, as well as a dark leather studded cuff. All her other features were the same, but there wasn't a big scar on her chest. For the first time in a long time, she almost recognized herself.

Eyes glued to her reflection, she moved for a closer look. There in the corner of the mirror was a picture of the woman and man from the dinner table. She and Elizabeth were in it, too.

Liv reached for the picture, knocked over a box, and it rattled as it fell to the floor. She picked it up, studying it. It was a pillbox, little compartments for every day. Three of them still contained pills. She set it aside and bent down to study the picture. But then the world spun, and she was no longer in the room but lying down, a blindingly bright light directly overhead. A person with a surgical mask appeared over her, and the light gleamed off something large and silver in the person's hand ...

Liv shot up in bed, her pulse racing. Something had freaked her out in her dream, but she couldn't remember exactly what, only the echo of the fear deep in her chest. The scar over her heart burned. She rubbed it, taking a few deep breaths to calm down.

Closing her eyes, she tried to catch hold of the images. The last thing she could remember was ...

Elizabeth. Her chest ached in a completely different way now, not from the scar but from the heart beating under it.

She untangled her legs from the covers and kicked them off, as the start of a headache worked its way across her skull.

Holding a hand to her head, hoping the pressure might help, she padded into her bathroom and took a couple Tylenol. When she closed the medicine cabinet, she stared at her reflection. Briefly wondered about using lots of black eyeliner.

Sabrina would for sure call me on it.

It didn't look that good anyway.

But Elizabeth . . . Wearing all that eye shadow, looking and talking like a little adult. The familiarity and warmth that she always felt when she thought about Elizabeth filled her. She wanted to hug her tight and protect her from the world, even when she was kind of being a pain.

A lump formed in her throat. "Why does she feel so real to me?"

Breakfast eaten, teeth brushed, and bag ready to go, Liv hurried downstairs.

Today she'd decided to go back to wearing a T-shirt, even choosing a black one. Screw Sabrina and her fashion advice.

Mom slung her purse over her shoulder. "Ready?"

"As I'll ever be."

They were almost to the school before she got up the courage to ask about Elizabeth again. Mom might not be aware of her being friends with any younger girls, but maybe the name would trigger something. "Did I know someone named Elizabeth?"

For a moment, Mom didn't move, just remained perfectly frozen, as if she didn't hear. Then she turned down Mozart's

"Queen of the Night," and even if she didn't have a good answer, it at least gave her a break from the opera music. "Why? Do you think you remember something?"

Explaining the whole dream thing and how real it seemed would be difficult, especially if Mom was going to brush it off again. "The name popped into my head, and it seems familiar."

Gaze fixed on the road, Mom said, "I had a friend named Elizabeth. She used to come over for dinner, that kind of thing."

Liv's heart dropped. "Oh."

"Something wrong, sweetheart?"

"Nope. That explains it."

But it didn't explain it at all.

There were things about the past that just didn't add up, and Liv was sure there was something Mom was keeping from her. The more she thought about it, the more the missing pictures bothered her, too. How could they lose sixteen years' worth of family photos? This was the same woman who labeled every container in the kitchen and color-coded her closet.

Mom pulled up to the school and put the car in park. She dug into her purse and took out a cell phone. "I programmed home, my cell, and your dad's numbers into this phone. Even when I'm in my cooking class, I'll have mine on vibrate, so call if you need me."

Liv took it. "Cool."

"Don't get into trouble with it. It's for emergencies, not so you can collect boys' numbers." Mom locked eyes with her. "Understand?"

Liv nodded.

"I'll see you not too long after school. Have a good day."

"I'll do my best." Liv climbed out of the car and charged up the steps to the school, one thing on her mind: she was going to find Spencer and ask what exactly he'd meant when he told her she was "one of those."

After all she'd been through, it irked her that he thought he could just look at her and know who she was. *She* didn't even know who she was.

A hand clamped on her arm, and she whipped around to see who'd grabbed her.

Keira's eyes were wide, her cheeks flushed. "You'll never guess what happened on my way to school."

She seemed to be waiting for some kind of response, so Liv said, "You're right. I probably won't."

"This idiot ran a red light and almost plowed into my mom's car. We swerved and went up on the curb and the truck barely missed us. My heart is racing. Feel it." Keira lifted Liv's hand and placed it over her heart. "Can you feel it?"

The lack of personal space? She liked Keira, but she felt odd standing in the hall, her hand over Keira's heart. She pulled back. "Really fast."

"I know, right? Time totally slowed down, and I swear my life flashed before my eyes. I thought, 'Oh my gosh, I'm too young to die.'"

Keira took a deep breath. "Anyway, it was so freaky. It's pretty much the most scared I've ever been, and at first I told my mom I was too traumatized to come to school, but I swear, she doesn't even care about my emotional well-being. She just told me to stop being so dramatic and get to class. But if I close my eyes, I see it over and over again."

Maybe it's a good thing I don't remember the accident. Just knowing it happened is enough to freak me out. "I'm glad you're okay."

"Yeah, and I'm so glad my face didn't get banged up. I mean, my nose is the kind people get surgery to look like." Keira patted her nose, then dropped her hand. "That was pretty vain-sounding. I just like my nose, and having a big scar would totally be awful."

Pain radiated from Liv's chest—from the scar she never wanted anyone to see. Wrapping her arms around herself, she walked down the hall with Keira, abandoning her mission to confront Spencer.

"Hey, Liv," a voice said from behind her as she exited the cafeteria. "Wait up."

Clay stepped next to her. "You didn't say much at lunch."

"Well, that's how we do things at the North Pole."

His face dropped. "I was afraid we made you feel bad yesterday."

"Not bad. More like . . . stupid."

"That wasn't what I was going for at all." He put his hand on her shoulder. "Let me make it up to you. How about I walk you to class?"

Liv nodded. "Okay. I've got pre-calc with Mr. Barker."

They started down the hall. Unable to think of anything to say, she stared straight ahead, hugging her books to her chest. When they reached the classroom, she turned to Clay. "Um, thanks for walking with me."

Clay grinned. "Sure thing. I'd say have fun, but since you're going to math class, I don't think that's possible."

"Oh, I like math."

Of all the things to say, that's what you go for?

Don't say I didn't warn you if he grunts and makes caveman noises now.

"Pretty *and* smart. Sounds like a dangerous combo." Clay grinned again, then turned around. And almost bumped into Spencer. "Oh hell, it's Hale."

The disdain was evident as Spencer glared at Clay. "Clever. Now move out of my way."

They regarded each other for a moment, both staying rooted to their places.

Clay shook his head. "Not worth it." He stepped around Spencer and continued walking down the hall.

Spencer's gaze moved to her. "Nice choice of friends."

Liv raised an eyebrow. "Are you talking about you or him?"

"I'm not your friend." Spencer walked past her, into the classroom.

It took her a minute to pick her jaw off the floor and recompose herself. When she walked into the classroom, she avoided looking at Spencer. She was done wondering what his deal was. She already knew. He was a jerk. A jerk she planned to avoid as much as possible.

Classical music played through the kitchen, culturing the food from boring beef stew to a French stew Mom called *pot au feu*—which she explained meant pot on fire.

"What's next?" Liv asked.

Mom wiped her hands on the dish towel hanging from the oven door. "Get the celery, carrots, and onions."

Liv grabbed the veggies out of the crisper, rinsed them, and laid them on the cutting board. There was an art to the way Mom chopped vegetables. She was fast with a knife, yet her speed didn't mess up her precision.

"Oh, before I forget, I need some information so I can write my paper for my English comp class."

"Like what?" Mom asked, her knife gliding through the carrots.

"Basic stuff. Like traditions, what happened on the day I was born . . ."

Knife still in motion, Mom whipped her head up.

"Mom, be"—the knife went down again—"careful," Liv finished. But it was too late.

Mom dropped the knife and brought her hand over the sink. "Oh, drat!"

"I'll get you a Band-Aid." Liv ran to the bathroom and dug through the medicine cabinet. The bright red letters made the box easy to find. Frantic, she took out a Band-Aid and rushed back into the kitchen.

The paper towel Mom had over her finger had turned red.

"What's going on in here?" Dad asked as he came into the room.

"Oh, I just cut myself."

Shock crossed Dad's face. "You? Steady Hands Stein?"

"It's nothing big."

Dad stepped up to her. "Let me see." He removed the paper towel and studied the cut. A crimson stream ran down Mom's finger. "Good thing no one here's squeamish at the sight of blood."

The room tilted and Liv reached out to steady herself on the counter. *Blood. There's blood everywhere.*

"You okay, Livie?"

Faint and distant, mixed in with the sound of rain pounding metal, she heard a song. A song that she knew by heart. But she had no idea what it was. There were drums. Loud drums. A female voice belted out the lyrics with power and conviction. Something about swirling shades of blue, the sun kissing the earth, and hushing the urge to cry.

Blood poured down, soaking her shirt, leaving large drops on her jeans. Lifting her head was impossible. Everything hurt.

You're going to die.

10

"**Whoa**," **Liv said as Mom's fuzzy outline** sharpened. "What happened?"

"Dad carried you to the couch when you fainted. Do you remember? You saw the blood and—"

"Don't say blood." Liv put a hand up to her throbbing head. *I feel like I never quite get rid of this wretched headache.*

Mom frowned. "You're the daughter of two surgeons. You should be able to handle a little blood."

Liv groaned. "Mom, please."

Dad handed her a glass of water. She sat up and took a sip.

"How are you feeling now?" he asked.

"Better." Liv glanced at Mom's finger. A Band-Aid covered the tip of it. "Are you okay?"

"It's fine. Now you rest here, and I'll get you a snack to tide you over until dinner. And don't worry, none of the blood got on the food."

"Seriously, Mom, can you please stop talking about it?" Liv shuddered. It wasn't so much the blood as the feeling seeing it had given her.

Like the life was slowly draining from her.

Mom smiled, then leaned down and hugged her. "It's okay if you're squeamish, just don't faint like that again. You scared me."

"Believe me, I'll do my best."

Mom disappeared into the kitchen. Dad sat on the couch and picked the *National Geographic* off the coffee table. His expression changed as he scanned the pages, reading the different stories.

Sitting there, supposedly relaxing, wasn't really relaxing. It was boring. And it made her start thinking about everything that was wrong with her. "I feel like I'm falling apart."

Mom stepped into the doorway, vegetable plate in her hands. "You're not falling apart. In fact, you're very lucky to be as healthy as you are." She placed the plate on the coffee table and Liv saw the snack she'd brought. Carrot sticks and celery. The same thing she'd been chopping when she'd cut her finger. *Yeah. No thanks.*

"Your mother's right. The fainting was a reaction to seeing blood, not because anything's wrong with you." Dad lowered his magazine. "Although we are going to have to get you over that. You can be anything you want to be except afraid."

"I've got two doctors living under my same roof," Liv said. "If there's a situation involving the word that I'm not going to say, I think I'll be fine."

"Well, what about when you go to college?"

A crease formed between Mom's eyebrows. "I don't even want to think about that." She sat next to Liv and patted her leg. "We just got you, and I'm not letting you go."

Liv tensed as cold crept up her spine. "Just got me?"

"I mean, we just got you healed, and it seems like only yesterday ... Just no more talk of leaving. As far as I'm concerned, you're living with us forever."

Dad shrugged. "Fine by me."

Mom's and Dad's eyes landed on her.

"I'm not planning on going anywhere," she said. "I can't

even seem to make it through a day without some kind of tragedy."

Later that night as she was crawling into bed, Liv realized she'd never gotten the answers from Mom so she could start on her English composition paper. In fact, all night Mom and Dad had been exchanging odd glances. After Liv and Dad had taken a walk, something that was becoming a nightly ritual, Mom pulled Dad into the kitchen and told her to go start on her homework. When she said she needed information for her paper, Mom's tone sharpened, and she'd told her to do her *other* homework and worry about the paper later.

Clenching her jaw so she wouldn't scream—which was what she felt like doing—she flipped onto her other side. *What are they keeping from me? And* why *are they keeping it from me?*

She tried to connect the dots, but without her memories, too many of the dots were missing. It all came down to the wreck, though—that much she was sure of. *They act like the full truth would break me. Does that mean they know about the voices? Or maybe there's something else.* Liv's stomach knotted.

Something even worse.

11

The sun beat down, hotter than normal. Liv squeezed into the small square of shade covering the bench, but it didn't help much. The shade widened and she automatically looked up.

After her eyes adjusted, she realized the dark outline belonged to Spencer. Ever since he'd so nicely pointed out they weren't friends, she'd done her best to avoid him. When he'd come into math class earlier, she'd purposely kept her head down. Now that he was here, she clenched her jaw and stared down at the book in her hands.

"I take it from your ignoring me that I made you mad again," he said.

"I'm not mad. I just don't talk to mean, rude people."

"Fair enough." Spencer unlocked his bike from the rack and rolled it up to her. "Were you telling the truth about not knowing how to ride a bike or never going to McDonald's? Because I was thinking that would be almost impossible. Which made me think you were . . . I can't figure out if you were making a joke, or if you thought that I was stupid, or what."

"Think whatever you want." She kept her eyes down, but she could feel him standing there staring at her.

"I was rude yesterday, and I'm sorry. I didn't mean for

it to come out like that. I just think you've got bad taste in friends."

"At least I *have* friends. You hang out with yourself all day."

"It's just better that way. Then I don't have to deal with people I don't like."

Lifting a hand to shade her eyes, she shifted her gaze to his face. "So, you're basically saying that you're the best company you could have?"

"Not exactly." He put out the kickstand on his bike, propped it up, then sat next to her.

With Spencer so close, her heart started doing that fluttering thing again. His hair fell down over one side of his glasses, and she had the urge to reach up and swipe it back.

He shook it out of his face, saving her the trouble she never would've actually gone to. "So where'd you move from?"

"Rochester, Minnesota."

"Was there a lot to do? There had to be more going on there than here." He looked at her, eyebrows raised, obviously waiting for an answer.

She shrugged. "I don't know. I guess there was."

"What do you mean, you don't know? What did you do for fun?"

"Would you like a report on the city or something? I just don't know, okay?"

"You always get so damn defensive."

"Only around rude people." She crossed her arms and twisted toward him. "And hello, I get defensive? Look in the mirror."

"*You* look in the mirror."

"Whatever." Never before had she felt so angry. He drove her completely crazy. She wanted him to go away and stay at the same time, which made no sense.

"Come on," Spencer said. "Let's see what you got."

"You want to fight me now?"

"I'm talking about the bike. Nobody can't ride a bike. And if you really can't, it's about time you learned."

"Why? Why do you want me to get on your bike?"

"I'm kind of bored. I beat my *Mass Effect 3* video game already and I don't have anything better to do." Amusement flickered in the eyes that met hers. "You do know what video games are, right?"

"I know what they are."

"You ever play one?"

"Not that I know of."

"You make the most difficult-to-understand comments."

"Like you're any better." She didn't want to start talking about everything she didn't know, so she stood. "Fine, hand over the stupid bike."

Spencer stood and rolled the bike to her.

Mimicking the way she'd seen other people get on, she gripped the handlebars and kicked her leg over. As she straddled the bike, she realized this probably wasn't the best idea. Yesterday she'd fainted, and her arm still sporadically twitched. No way was she going to admit to Spencer that she was scared, though. Besides, it did have an almost familiar feel to it.

"Okay, most important thing . . ." Spencer tapped the metal bars on the handles. "These are the brakes. For now, you should use them both. The left's the front brake, and if you hit it hard enough, you'll end up launching yourself over the handlebars."

She squeezed the brakes, getting a feel for them. "Got it."

Liv looked up to find his eyes on her, and there was a softness she'd never seen in them before. Then his typical serious expression took over, and he stepped off to the side. "Now you just pedal and try to keep your balance."

It sounded easy when he put it like that. And it couldn't be *that* hard. She'd seen lots of people ride bikes around her neighborhood—most of them a lot younger than she was. She got the gist, so now she simply had to let the bike do what it was made for.

Her right foot found the pedal as if she'd done it dozens of times before.

I totally know how to do this.

Taking a deep breath, she put her weight onto one pedal and sat on the seat. Then she moved to push the other pedal down, but the bike started tipping. She seemed to be falling in slow motion, yet she couldn't do anything about it. "Whoa . . ."

She got her hand down seconds before hitting the sidewalk. The bike landed on top of her, the handlebar digging into her side. "Ouch."

Okay, so I totally don't *know how to do this.*

Spencer looked down at her, a baffled expression on his face. "Wow, you actually don't know how to ride a bike. I was sure you were lying."

Liv frowned at him.

"Are you okay?"

"I'm fine." Beyond embarrassed, she scooted from under the bike and stood. Her palm and the bottom of her elbow burned, and she turned her arm over to look at it. When the color red registered, she jerked her eyes away. "Oh, no. I think I'm bleeding." She held her arm up to Spencer. "I can't look at it. Am I bleeding?"

"Way to shatter that tough-girl facade."

"Just tell me if it's bleeding. I can't look at blood because it brings back bad memories."

"Of what?" Spencer asked.

"I don't know."

"You say that a lot."

"I can make up something if you're going to be obnoxious about it."

"I'm not the one freaking out over a little blood."

"So there *is* blood?" She hated how her voice came out all high-pitched, but she couldn't help it. Already, her head was spinning.

Spencer grabbed her hand and studied it. "Barely. It's scraped up, so there's a little blood, but it's not like it's pouring."

Her stomach churned. "Just stop talking about it before I pass out."

Spencer laughed.

"It's not funny."

"It's a little funny," he said, half-cocked grin on his face.

The smile cut through her panic, allowing her to focus on the fact that he was holding her hand. Her heart pounded out an erratic rhythm. Time froze.

A flash of silver sent it ticking again. Liv pulled her hand away as Mom's car turned onto the road in front of the school. "That's my mom. I can't let her know I rode your bike."

"You didn't ride it. You crashed it."

She shot him a dirty look.

"Why would she care about you riding a bike?"

"Because as you pointed out, I crashed it." Holding her arm down so she wouldn't see the blood and freak out again, she hurried back to the bench.

Spencer didn't immediately take off like she thought he would. He rolled the bike over to her. He watched her gather her belongings, crease between his brows, mouth set in a straight line.

"What are you always doing here, anyway?" Liv asked. "Are you in sports or something?"

"Or something."

Mom pulled up to the curb, so she didn't bother asking what his comment meant. She had a feeling he wouldn't tell her anyway. If only because he knew it would drive her crazy.

"I guess I'll see you later." She locked eyes with him. "Any idea which personality you'll be going with tomorrow? Should I expect total jerk or evasive irritator?"

A slow grin spread across his face. "You better be nice. I know your weakness now, and I won't hesitate to use it."

With him standing there grinning at her like that, she couldn't help but smile back. There was just something about him. When he actually let the nice guy shine through. "Goodbye, Spencer."

She stepped down the concrete steps and got into Mom's car.

"Who were you talking to?" Mom asked.

"His name's Spencer." Liv looked out the window and watched him ride his bike away. "He's . . ." *Annoying, frustrating, cute, occasionally nice . . .* "In my math class."

Taking that spill off Spencer's bike had removed a layer of skin from her palm, and her forearm was red and raw. She stood in front of the bathroom sink and ran cool water over it. That had helped earlier today, when she'd first cleaned it out. Looking at it now didn't bug her, and she felt silly for having made such a big deal about it.

Still, every time she thought about blood, her stomach clenched.

Think about something else.

Like how Spencer grabbed my hand. Or when he smiled and said he knew my weakness.

"I wonder if he meant bikes or blood."

He's so cute. And funny.

Plus, he's not like everyone else. He's got his own style.

And he's smart, too. See? Not all smart guys are nerds.

At least she wouldn't have any internal battles while around him. All three of her personalities seemed to like Spencer. *Too bad he'd never talk to me again if he found out I have three personalities.*

She groaned. She wanted to think about Spencer, not the fact that voices were constantly whispering to her, slowly driving her insane. *I shouldn't be thinking about him, anyway. Chances are, he'll be a huge jerk again by tomorrow.*

But I really hope he's not.

She brushed her teeth, then walked across her bedroom to her window. The sun was gone from the sky, off illuminating another world. Dark clouds reduced the moon to a smear of light. Earlier today, during her and Dad's walk, she thought it might rain. But it never rained here.

Good. I hate the rain. That night, the rain was horrible.

A strange feeling settled over her.

"What night?"

12

All day, Liv had been anticipating this moment.
Her feminist side told her to wait for him to come to her.
But the other part of her—the one that had picked out the
pink top—kept telling her to go for it. When she saw Spencer
sitting in his normal spot in the cafeteria, looking cute as
ever, she couldn't help but pick the side that wanted to go
talk to him.

Her throat went dry as she took a step toward his table.
Then she remembered him saying he liked sitting alone, and
her courage faltered.

He looked up. It was subtle, but there was definitely a
smile that hadn't been there seconds ago.

Balancing her tray in her steady hand, she lifted the other
to wave.

Fingers clamped around her arm and she was jerked in the
other direction so fast the mandarin oranges slid off her tray
and splatted on the floor.

"Sabrina has huge news," Keira said. "Hurry up."

Liv got her feet under her and followed Keira to the table.
She set down her plate and frowned at the empty section
in her tray. Those baby oranges were all that had looked
appetizing.

Every face turned to Sabrina as she sat down. She was

clearly basking in the attention, smiling like she'd just won a beauty pageant. "So, my daddy got us VIP tickets to the One Direction concert."

The girls shrieked and clapped. There were "OMGs," "No ways," and a couple of other high-pitched responses. They even started yelling out names and arguing over who was the hottest.

Sabrina held up her hands and the girls quieted down. "Daddy got four tickets so we can all go, and he said he'd drive us to Phoenix." She looked across the table at Liv. "I hope you don't feel bad. Candace, Taylor, Keira, and I have been planning this for a long time."

"I don't." Liv kept to herself the fact she didn't even know who One Direction was. "I hope you guys have a good time."

"But maybe you can talk to your parents and see if you can buy a ticket and come with us," Keira said, flashing her usual warm smile.

The look Sabrina shot Keira made it clear she didn't appreciate the suggestion.

Keira was quiet for a moment and then seemed to recover. "There's another party at The Gulch tonight. Are you going to come with us this time, Liv?"

"Um, I don't know . . ."

"We can give you a ride if you want. Right, Sabrina?"

Liv wanted to tell Keira not to bother. Obviously Sabrina didn't like her and she didn't want Keira getting in trouble with Sabrina over it.

Sabrina took a sip of her bottled water. "I suppose it wouldn't be too big of an inconvenience."

The smile was back on Keira's face as she leaned closer to Liv. "And it'll make Clay happy."

"I'll pick you up around six," Sabrina said. "Don't expect

me to wait on you. You're either ready when I get there, or
you find another ride."

*She's actually inviting me to go with them? Semi-inviting
me, anyway.* Even after Sabrina's snide comments, she still
had a desire to get on her good side. It didn't make sense, but
she wanted the girl's approval. And she really wanted to go
to the party.

"I just have to talk to my mom and dad first." *And Mom
will never let me go.*

Keira held out her hand. "Give me your cell and I'll
program my number into it."

Keira called her phone with Liv's, then handed it back,
pulled her phone out, and punched buttons. A beep sounded
from Liv's phone. She opened up the text Keira had sent her.

I'll let Clay know you'll be there. Don't worry, I'll
be subtle.

Liv smiled at Keira. She slipped her phone into her pocket,
then looked up to see Spencer watching her. When her gaze
met his, he quickly looked away.

Liv walked into Mr. Barker's classroom, sat in her normal
seat, and flipped her notebook to the section she reserved
for pre-calc.

Spencer sat at the desk in front of her and twisted to face
her. "So, would you like to hear about the time I split my
head open?"

"Hearing about it doesn't bother me. I just can't see the
blood."

A wicked grin spread across his face as he leaned closer.

"Oh, 'cause blood was pouring down from my eyebrow, into my eyes, and—"

"Okay, you got me," Liv said, giving him a light shove. "That's enough."

He grabbed her hand, turned it over, and studied the scrape on her arm. "Not too bad."

Her throat went dry and she had to work harder than usual to get words out of her mouth. "Now that it's not bleeding."

Spencer gently ran his thumb over the raised, red skin, then looked up at her, a spark of some indefinable emotion in his eyes.

For a moment he didn't say anything, then he set her hand on her desk and released it. "So it looked like some intense UN meeting was going down over lunch."

"First we talked about the crisis in the Middle East . . ." Thanks to Dad's *National Geographic*, she actually knew about that situation. "After we solved it, we moved on to discussing some One Direction concert. They were screeching and clapping like seals about it."

"Not a fan?"

Liv shrugged. "I don't know who they are."

"Their music's awful, but I thought every girl knew who they were. Next thing you'll be telling me you don't know who Justin Bieber is." He looked at her, like he was waiting for her to say, *Of course I do*. His jaw dropped. "You've never heard of . . .?" He shook his head. "How is that even possible?"

She opened her mouth, searching for a believable answer. She didn't want to lie, but the truth—what would Spencer do with that information?

Mr. Barker walked into the room. "Okay, everybody. Eyes up here. We've got lots to cover and not much time to cover it in."

Spencer spun around to face front. Even the back of his head looked cute, his shaggy hair curling up at the bottom. While he was obviously surprised she didn't know who One Direction or Justin Bieber were, it didn't feel like he was judging her. Talking to him felt natural—there was something about him that made it easy to let down her guard and be the person she really was underneath all her issues. For the first time in a long time, she felt like she might just belong somewhere after all.

"What's your next class?" Spencer asked as he and Liv exited the room.

"Chem with Mrs. Smith," she said.

"That's not far from where I'm going." He stuck by her side as they walked down the hall. For over a week, she'd imagined what it would be like to talk to him, and now she was almost scared to say anything, for fear she'd mess it up. "So, you never answered my question," he said.

"You never answer any of mine."

"Who's being evasive now?" He nudged her with his elbow. "Come on. Tell me why you've never learned to ride a bike, or how you don't know who one of the most popular singers in America is."

"It's a long, complicated story that I don't want to get into right now." She glanced at him. "Especially since I don't know if I can trust you. Or even how you'll act tomorrow."

"Okay, how many times do I have to apologize?"

"Once more wouldn't hurt."

Spencer caught her arm and said, "I'm sorry I was a jerk."

She'd thrown it out as a joke; she hadn't really expected him to apologize. She looked into his brown eyes, surprised by the sincerity in them. "A-apology accepted."

They started down the hall again, and she remembered what she'd been dying to ask for days. "Hey, what did you mean when you said, 'You're one of those'?"

"One of whats?"

"Exactly," Liv said.

A crease formed between Spencer's eyebrows. "When did I say that?"

"By the bench. After we talked the first time."

"Wow, I really made an impact on you."

Liv rolled her eyes. "Don't flatter yourself." She tucked her books under her left arm, since she still couldn't trust the right not to spasm. "It just bothered me. That you'd judge me without knowing anything about me."

"Well, if it makes you feel any better, I am starting to change my mind about you."

"Which means?"

"Wouldn't you like to know?"

Liv shook her head. "You really enjoy pushing my buttons, don't you?"

He broke into a wide smile. "You know, I kind of do."

The crowd filling the halls started to clear.

"I better get to class." He put his hand on her arm, just above the elbow, and gave it a light squeeze. "I'll see you later."

"Later." Grinning like an idiot, she turned to take the few remaining steps to class.

And saw Sabrina staring at her, arms folded, anger evident across her face.

"Oh. Hey, Sabrina."

Sabrina narrowed her eyes. "Why were you talking to Spencer? And why was he talking to *you*?"

"We're in the same math class."

Sabrina blocked the entrance. "So, you were talking about math?"

Liv looked past her, into the classroom. "It looks like class is about to start."

Stepping aside, Sabrina said, "About that ride to the party. I just realized I don't have any more room in my car."

"So, I've been thinking," Spencer said as he neared the bench where Liv was sitting, reading her book.

She glanced up at him. "Sounds dangerous."

That irresistible grin spread across his face. "I was thinking you need to get out more. Experience a few things."

"Says the guy who hangs out at school after hours and sits alone all the time."

He plopped down next to her. "I guess we should both get out more."

One thing had been on her mind since she'd been told she no longer had a ride. "What about the big party tonight?"

"I don't go to those things. They're stupid, and people just get stupider by the minute." A distant look entered his eyes, and for a moment, it was dead quiet. Then he seemed to snap back to the present. "Are you going? To the party?"

"I don't have a way to get there. And I doubt my parents will let me. But I do kind of want to go." She sighed. "Even if I could, though, the thought of coming up with things to say, or knowing what I'm supposed to do when I get there, totally intimidates me." She dropped her gaze to her lap and shook her head. "I don't know why I told you all that."

"Sounds like you're not ready for your first party. I'd recommend starting with something lighter. Like McDonald's."

"Oh, my mom would never go there. We eat meals with foreign names every night while listening to classical music."

One corner of his mouth turned up. "What I meant was, come with me to McDonald's. I'll ease you into the crazy life."

"Now? Isn't it too far to walk? Or ride to?" When she looked at the rack, she didn't see his bike. "Where *is* your bike?"

Spencer dug a set of keys out of his pocket and held them up. "I got my car back. New alternator, just waiting to be used."

The way he held up the keys, eyebrows raised, smile on his face, made it hard to say no. Unfortunately, it wasn't up to her. "Let me call and ask my mom." *Who's going to say no.*

Mom didn't have cooking class on Fridays, but she'd called to say she'd stuck some bread in the oven that wasn't quite done, and she'd be coming as soon as she pulled it out. Liv decided to try the home phone first, hoping Mom hadn't left yet.

With every ring, Liv's hope faded a little more. Spencer had actually asked her to go somewhere with him, and it devastated her to think of not being able to.

"I'm pulling the bread out now," Mom answered at the same time that Dad said, "Hello?"

"Henry? When did you get home?"

"I barely walked in the door," Dad said. "Thought you'd be off to get our daughter, so I answered the phone."

"I was just about to leave. Unless you want to go pick her up."

"Actually, I was wondering if I could hang out with a friend," Liv said. "We're going to grab something to eat, and I'll get a ride home so you don't have to worry about it."

"I'm sorry, but I'm afraid—"

"Victoria, we talked about this," Dad said. "We agreed to let her be a normal teenager. She can't do that if we never let her go anywhere. Now, Livie, who's driving?"

"His name is Spencer."

"A boy?" Mom asked, disapproval tingeing her voice. "What is this, a date?"

"It's just grabbing some food. There will be other people there, too." Liv was sure other people would be at the restaurant, so it wasn't a total lie.

"Is he a responsible driver?"

She looked at Spencer, who was spinning his keys around his finger. They flew off and landed in the nearby bushes. "Yeah. He's a really responsible driver. It's all anyone talks about."

"Olivia," Mom scolded.

"It's a joke, Mom."

"Safety on the road is no joke."

There was an awkward silence as that sunk in. They all knew what could happen if you lost control of a vehicle.

Mom heaved a sigh. "I suppose it's okay. Be careful, and not too late."

"Thanks. I'll be home in a while." Liv disconnected the call and turned to Spencer. The keys were back in his hand. "I told my parents you're a responsible driver. I hope I wasn't lying."

"I haven't had any complaints. Of course, I don't usually let anyone ride with me." He jerked his head toward the parking lot. "Let's go, then. And trust me, this is going to be so much better than that lame party at The Gulch."

13

Spencer unlocked the passenger door of the rusted, used-to-be-blue car, then leaned in and tossed the papers littering the front seat into the back. He straightened and gestured her inside. "You can throw your bag anywhere."

Liv got in and placed her backpack at her feet.

The other door opened with a creak. Spencer climbed in and turned the key. The engine chugged a few times before firing up.

"Are you sure the car's fixed?" Liv asked.

"Hey, don't diss Rusty. Not all of us can afford nice, fancy cars."

She pointed at herself. "Is that a jab at me? Because I don't have a car. I can't even drive."

"What exactly *can* you do?" Spencer asked, putting his car in gear and easing out of the lot.

"Right now, I'm just happy to be spending time away from the house. Not that my parents are hard to get along with. It's just . . . it's nice to do something different."

Spencer's eyes flicked from the road to her. "I know what you mean."

A couple minutes later, they were standing in the lobby of McDonald's, the scent of food filling the air. Liv studied the glowing red and yellow menu. "So, what do you suggest?"

"Normally, I'd say go Quarter Pounder or Big Mac, but since you didn't come here as a kid, you gotta have the whole experience and get a Happy Meal. But you should probably order a double cheeseburger on the side, too, or you'll still be hungry." Spencer stepped up to the counter. "Just leave it to me."

"For a boy or girl?" the cashier asked when Spencer ordered the Happy Meal.

"Girl."

"Wait," she said, her feminist side protesting. "What's the difference? Girls shouldn't get treated differently from boys."

The cashier sighed and scratched the back of his head. "Cars or ponies." He pointed at the poster behind him. It showed a variety of cars on one side, a collection of multicolored ponies on the other.

Spencer glanced over his shoulder at her. "Are you saying that even though you're a girl, you want the car?"

Liv saw the cute little ponies with their big eyes. "Actually," she said with a sigh, "I kind of want a pony."

Spencer shook his head, but he was smiling. He finished his order, refused when she offered to pay for hers, then handed her a cup for soda.

She looked over the options on the drink dispenser, wondering how much Mom had been exaggerating the effects of sugar and caffeine.

"You've had soda, right?" Spencer asked.

"I have to be careful what I eat."

"Long story?"

"Exactly."

Spencer got Coke, so she did, too. A couple minutes later, their food was up, and they went into the playland to eat.

Fries were awesome. Soda was awesome. Junk food—the

stuff Mom called empty calories—might've been empty, but it was deliciously empty.

"Okay, you were right," Liv said as she finished off her food. "This is good."

"I know my fast food."

"But I feel kind of gross now."

"That's normal. Running through the playland makes you forget about that, though." He tilted his head toward the maze of plastic tubes. "Ready?"

"I don't think we're supposed to go in there. It's for little kids."

Spencer grabbed her hand and pulled her to her feet. "We're on a mission to make up for what you've been missing out on. We're lucky, too. There aren't any little kids in there right now."

They kicked off their shoes and entered the small yellow circle.

Stuffy, ketchup-and-sweat-smelling air hit her. "It smells wretched in here."

"Who says wretched?"

"I do. And you'd be wretched if you made fun of it."

He glanced over his shoulder, a smile on his face. "Just follow me."

Liv crawled into the tubes after him. It was hot and she felt trapped, but she took a deep breath and powered through.

"This way," Spencer said, going into a blue tube.

The light glowed through the space, tinting everything the same color as the plastic. As they entered the red section, Spencer's clothes and skin took on a reddish hue. The hard plastic was unforgiving on her knees, and she still felt a little claustrophobic, but excitement shot through her stomach, taking over her other emotions. They reached a clear bubble overlooking the eating area.

"Oops. I didn't mean to bring us to the wave-at-your-mommy bubble. It's been a while since I've been in here."

"Where exactly are we going?" Her legs were burning from being crouched over.

"The slide, of course." On hands and knees, Spencer crawled past her, back the way they came.

"Of course. How silly of me to question our quest."

Spencer's laugh echoed through the red plastic tube. Hearing him laugh was worth the burning muscles, the stale ketchup smell, and the panicky feeling that she might be trapped in the playland forever.

They crawled across the mesh netting and reached a landing where she could almost stand.

"We made it to the slide." He waved his arm toward the circle. "Ladies first."

In order not to bang her head, she had to slip into the slide without sitting. A couple seconds later, the ride was over, but getting out was a struggle. She had to hook her feet over the bottom and pull herself through.

Spencer exited a moment later. "That seemed a lot bigger when I was a kid."

"Well, that makes sense. You were smaller, so it felt bigger." She raised an eyebrow. "I thought you were good at math."

"And I thought you were a nice, quiet girl."

As soon as they got back to the table, Liv took the sanitizer out of her bag and put it on her hands. Spencer was staring, so she held it up to him. "Want some?"

"That's such a mom move, disinfecting your hands."

"When we crawled past the ball pit I saw part of a hamburger in there." Thinking about the germ-filled breeding ground made her shudder. "I have to be careful about germs."

"Okay, time for your long story. It's basically impossible to avoid everything you have unless you've been locked in a basement all your life."

He'll think you're a total weirdo if you tell him.

And he'll think the same thing if you act all sketchy about it.

Liv took a deep breath, wondering if she was really about to do this. Mom had advised against it—had said to give vague answers—but the vague answers weren't getting her anywhere. He'd asked straight out, and she didn't see anything wrong with giving him a straight answer. About the wreck, anyway. No way she'd tell him she was currently arguing with herself.

"It's not that I've never done these things before. I just don't remember doing them." She glanced at the playland. "Although, knowing my parents, I probably never have eaten here."

Spencer rested his forearms on the table, bringing him closer. "You don't remember?"

"I was in a car wreck earlier this year. I had heart and brain surgery and was in a coma for a while. All my memories from before the wreck are gone."

Eyebrows raised, he stared at her. "You're not joking, are you? That would be a pretty messed-up joke."

She shook her head. "Not a joke. I need to keep my heart rate from going too high or too low, which is why I have to be careful about what I eat, and also why my parents gave me a thirty-minute lecture on how bad it would be for me to mix my meds with alcohol. The meds suppress my immune system, thus the need for hand sanitizer."

"Wow. That's . . ."

"Frustrating. Confusing. A thousand other things."

"I was going to say crazy." He lowered his eyebrows. "No memories of your past? At all?"

"Sometimes I know things even though I don't remember learning them. It's why I like math. It makes sense. It's all there. When I'm solving equations, I feel in control. But when people are talking about movie stars, or pop culture, or, say ..." She threw her hand in the air. "Riding bikes, for instance, it's just blank. It's really frustrating and it makes me feel stupid."

"Why didn't you just tell me that when I was giving you a hard time about it?"

"My mom's afraid of what people will say or how they'll act when they find out." She gazed into his big brown eyes, terrified he'd never look at her the same way again. "I probably shouldn't have told you."

A solemn expression overtook his features. "It's weird how one moment can change everything. Forever."

A group of kids ran into the room, their excited cries piercing the air. Their moms—she assumed they were their moms, anyway—came in behind them, trays filled with food. Yelling and laughing, the kids charged for the playland.

Spencer piled the trash from their meal onto the tray. The carefree, playful guy from earlier was gone. "Ready to go?"

Liv grabbed her pink pony off the table and nodded. Panic welled up as she followed him out. Sharing her secret had seemed like a good idea, but now she wanted to take it back.

I shouldn't have told him. Mom was right that people would be weird about it.

And of course she was right. Not remembering anything about your life is freaky. Add in the two clashing personalities, and ...

Her heart sank. *I don't stand a chance of ever having a close friend, someone I can actually share everything with.*

Without another word, they walked across the parking lot

and got into the car. Liv's phone beeped as Spencer merged with traffic. Thinking Mom was sending her a message, she dug it out of her pocket. The text was from Keira.

> What happened? Sabrina just said you didn't want to come to The Gulch.

She'd forgotten all about the party. Though it irritated her that Sabrina made it sound like she had decided to back out, when she'd been the one to un-invite her. Because of Spencer. Who was quiet and distant now.

Liv typed out a response.

> Sorry, couldn't make it. See you Monday.

She sent the text, then pocketed her phone.

"Where are we going?" she asked.

Spencer looked at her, seeming surprised to find her there. "I wasn't thinking. I just started driving home."

"I freaked you out, huh?"

"No."

"Liar. You were talking nonstop until I told you about my accident."

He took a deep breath, then blew it out. "It's not you, I swear. I started thinking about something else."

"What?"

"Nothing."

"So we're back to this." Liv crossed her arms, so frustrated she wasn't sure if she should scream or burst into tears. "Just take me home. You'll need to flip around and go back the other way."

Spencer turned onto a side street, made a U-turn, and

headed back down the main road. "Just tell me where to go."

"Down this street, left on Oasis."

Spencer turned up the music instead of attempting a conversation.

Earlier, things had been so light and fun; now tension filled the air, and Spencer didn't even seem to care. She'd expected him to say something. Anything.

The longer the silence stretched between them, the more her chest ached, and the more she wished she could rewind time and take back her confession.

He took the left, and they drove past the familiar houses. She pointed at the four-bedroom house that had recently become home. Lately, though, it didn't even feel like home, just another place she didn't quite belong. "It's the one on the end."

Liv bent over and picked her backpack off the floor. Frustrated or not—and she *was* extremely frustrated—she decided she should at least thank him for taking her out. Her mom had taught her manners.

"Thanks for dinner." She pulled the handle, opening the door.

"Wait," Spencer said.

Liv turned back, relieved he wanted to smooth things over.

"Don't forget your pony." He picked it up from the seat and held it out to her. The pink toy looked tiny in his hand.

As soon as she took it from him, his gaze returned to the windshield. The urge to slam the door was strong, but she managed to swing it closed with normal force. She tucked the pony into her pocket, walked up the sidewalk, and stepped inside her house. Through the frosted-glass window, she watched Spencer drive away, sure she'd screwed up everything that could have been.

14

The girl next to Liv passed her the brown sack. *"Hurry, the game's about to start."*

The girl—Courtney—was wearing a cheerleading uniform. The same uniform Liv also had on.

Green's so not my color.

The hem of her skirt was flipped up and she smoothed it back down with her free hand. She was wearing the silver charm bracelet with the engraved heart hanging from it. Her acrylic nails were painted in a pale pink, with a jeweled flower on the thumb.

"Either drink or pass it back," Courtney said. Her dark hair was gathered into a high ponytail; green and black ribbons cascaded down, mixing with the curls.

Looking into the brown sack, Liv saw the thick, clear bottle. "What is it?"

Courtney took the bag out of her hands. "That's it. You're cut off. You better remember the cheers when we get out there. I'm not going down because you can't remember something as simple as 'Go, fight, win.'"

Cheers? I don't know any cheers.

Another uniformed girl stuck her head around the corner. "Mrs. Willis is coming! Put it away and let's go!"

Courtney spun around and shoved the sack into a locker. "Let's go cheer on our team."

Liv reluctantly followed her. As she passed a big glass trophy case, she did a double take. Leaning in, she stared at her reflection. Thick blond hair was gathered into a high ponytail, colored ribbons wrapped around it. Her face was round, her lips done up in bubblegum pink.

That's not how I look.

And yet . . .

"Come on!" Courtney yelled.

Liv turned away from the trophy case and started down the hall. Walking in a straight line wasn't working, no matter how hard she tried. The walls kept coming closer.

Courtney clamped onto her arm. "You're such a light-weight. Pull it together. You know if we get caught again, your mom will ground you for life."

"I don't care what my mom says." The words came from her mouth, as if they were second nature. She sensed more coming, not even knowing what they'd be. "She can't tell me how to live my life when hers is such a mess."

"Save the speech for after the game when she says you can't go to the party with Jace." Courtney dragged Liv toward the open doors of the gym. "Just be cool."

"But . . ."

Courtney pulled her into the gym. People filled the bleachers, guys in uniform ran onto the shiny wood floor. Liv and Courtney lined up on the sidelines with the rest of the cheerleaders.

The girl front and center turned back and shot her a dirty look. "It's about time." She returned her attention to the floor and clapped her hands together. "Ready . . . ?"

All the other girls straightened, getting ready for . . . she had no idea. Panic clutched her chest. She didn't know what she was supposed to do next.

"Okay!"

Liv jerked up, the dream fading away as she looked around her room. Her heart hammered against her rib cage, and it took a couple deep breaths before she finally stopped gasping for air.

Like the dreams involving Elizabeth, this one was more vivid than usual. As sad as she felt when those dreams ended, she'd take them any time if drunken cheerleader was the other option.

It didn't even look like me.

But it felt so real.

She thought about the dream where she'd been studying math. The bracelet, nails, hair … It was the same girl, she was sure of it. *But what does it mean?*

Sunlight glowed around the blinds in the window, and she smelled the faint scent of bacon and something sweet. *Mom must be cooking breakfast.*

The pink pony on the side table caught her eye, and last night came rushing back to her. The playland. The awkward ride home. Spencer had said it wasn't her, and she wanted to believe that. It did seem like he was a million miles away there at the end.

Just forget about him. He's obviously got issues.

Says the girl with no memory and voices in her head.

As she got out of bed, she felt the familiar pounding of an oncoming headache.

Without the commotion of school, the voices had a lot of time to talk to her, pulling her thoughts all over the place. *I should get new clothes; I should burn the frilly clothes I have.*

I should figure out how I'm going to fix things with Sabrina; I wish Sabrina would choke on her own giant ego.

Back and forth, all day, until she was physically and mentally exhausted. Since Mom and Dad would either overreact or lie, that left her to figure it out on her own.

So when she was sure Mom and Dad were busy downstairs, she slipped into the office and closed the door. She stared at her distorted reflection in the computer screen for a moment, not sure she was ready for what it might tell her, while at the same time sure she couldn't put it off any longer.

Finally she clicked onto the Internet and pulled up Google. Her fingers trembled as she typed in: *hearing voices*

She glanced over her shoulder, double-checking that she'd closed the door.

Better lock it. Liv turned the lock as slowly and quietly as possible, then moved back to the computer. Her stomach was a knot of jangled nerves as she scanned the results.

The top items were on schizophrenia symptoms. *Great. Just great.* It was what she'd been afraid of, and a big part of why she'd put it off for so long. But as she scanned down, there were words under the titles that gave her hope.

> People who hear voices in their heads don't always need psychiatric help. Sometimes the voices within can guide you in everyday life.

Well, that doesn't sound so bad. Even though my voices are more about shouting and bickering than guiding. She clicked on that link. It talked about how the voices were usually a result of trauma. Obviously wrecking your car and nearly dying was traumatic, so big check on that one. It even said the greater the trauma, the more likely the voices will sound threatening.

After scanning through that article, she clicked back to her original search and moved to the second result on the page.

> Hearing voices is a common symptom of severe mental illness, although many people with no other symptoms also hear voices.

Liv glanced at the door again, listening for any sounds that might mean Mom or Dad were coming upstairs, then read through the article. One of the subheadings was Practical Advice for People Who Hear Voices.

Perfect, she thought. *That's exactly what I need right now.*

She frowned as she read the "practical advice." It suggested talking to other voice hearers. *Oh, sure, guess I'll go up to people and ask, do you hear voices? No? Never mind then, and of course I don't, either.*

One article on schizophrenia said there was often a connection between creativity and mental illness. She didn't feel very creative, though maybe she should see if she could pick up a paintbrush and create an amazing painting, or ... *What else do creative people do? If I don't know, does it mean I'm not one?*

Judging by the outfit you put on today, you're not creative at all.

I suppose you call sticking a flower in your hair on par with a Da Vinci painting?

More like Monet—he was much more into painting flowers. And you think you're *the smart one?*

"Could you two shush now?" Liv hissed. "I'm trying to convince myself I'm not crazy, and it'd be much easier if I wasn't arguing with myself."

She read through a few more articles, until she had more information than she knew what to do with swirling through her head. From what she could find, the possibilities were schizophrenia and bipolar disorder. Their symptoms included hallucinations, which she didn't have, unless she counted the dreams. But they were only extremely vivid dreams, right? Borderline hallucinations, at most.

Okay, so as long as the voices stay in my head and the dreams are only during the night, I can deal with this. I'm not the only one.

After staring at the screen for a moment, she moved the cursor to close the window, but then she had an idea. What would she find if she looked up her parents? She went back to the home page and clicked inside the search bar.

Each beat of her heart was faster and harder than the one before. The thought of doing the search made her stomach clench. Still, she hovered her fingers over the keyboard, wondering if she should start with Mom or Dad.

She jumped when her phone rang. She dug it out of her pocket, desperate to quiet it before Mom and Dad came upstairs and caught her.

"The party was so lame," Keira said when she answered. "All the same people were there, and I was totally bored. I wish you would've come."

She didn't know why Keira had decided to like her, but she was glad all the same. "It's not like my being there would've made it more exciting," she said as she cleared the Internet history and shut down the computer.

"Adding a new element always makes it more exciting. Clay was disappointed you didn't go, by the way."

Warmth tingled through her chest and she could feel the goofy smile on her lips. "He said that?"

"*Hello*, he didn't have to. I could just tell. So, what have you been doing today? My Saturday was *so* boring."

Liv walked to her room as she relayed the day's events to Keira—skipping her Google search—then sat on the bed and listened to Keira go on and on about Samuel, a guy in her literature class. They chatted for about an hour, until even Keira ran out of things to say.

After she hung up the phone, she got into her pajamas, planning on turning in early. She and Dad had teamed up to convince Mom to go hike one of the Mingus Mountain trails tomorrow morning. According to several of Dad's colleagues, there was a killer view once you got to the top.

Wondering what shoes would be the best for hiking, she opened her closet doors.

It's going to be nice to do something new. A rush of excitement ran through her and she clapped.

"Go. Fight. Win." As she said the words, her arm came up in a square in front of her, raised in a fist, then thrust in the air.

She repeated the cheer again. Then did it faster.

Goose bumps broke out across her skin, and the hairs on her neck stood on end. "Now that's just weird."

15

Sweat broke out across Liv's forehead.

"Are you sure you don't want to pull your hair back?" Mom asked.

At this point, looking good wasn't even an option. Her T-shirt had sweat marks around the collar and under the arms, and her hair had cemented itself to her neck. But people passed on a constant basis and she felt less exposed with her hair down. "I'm okay."

Mom thrust a bottle toward her. "Drink some water."

Liv took a swig. At the beginning of the hike, the water had been cool; now it was just as warm as the sticky air surrounding it.

"Better let Dad check your heart rate."

"I'm fine, really," Liv said. When Mom frowned, she lowered her voice and leaned toward her. "It'll be embarrassing. I swear, if I feel bad, I'll let you know."

A man came down the trail, a dog tugging him forward. He lifted his hand. "Dr. Stein! Nice to see you."

Dad introduced her and Mom to Dr. Harris, who worked at the clinic, too. The yellow Lab pulled against his leash, heading for Liv. She backpedaled a couple steps, but then an image of a dog bringing her a stick popped into her head. A calm feeling washed over her, and she felt a surge of affection for the Lab. Palm up, she extended her hand to the dog's nose.

He sniffed it. Then licked it with his warm tongue. His tail swished back and forth.

"This is Tag," Dr. Harris said. "It looks like he likes you."

Liv knelt in front of the dog and scratched his ears. "Hey, Tag."

As Mom, Dad, and Dr. Harris continued to talk—some kind of medical mumbo jumbo— Liv ran her fingers through Tag's coat. Something about the coarse hair against her palm tugged at her memory. Even his nasty breath only made him more endearing. If anyone had asked her earlier how she felt about dogs, she never would've said she liked them. But now she realized she did.

"Guess I better get going," Dr. Harris said. "I'll see you later, Henry." He nodded at Mom, then Liv. "Nice to finally meet you both."

Liv reluctantly stood. As she watched Tag walk away, a sense of longing washed through her. "Did I ever have a dog?"

Dad shot her a sidelong glance. "Have you met your mother?"

"I don't have anything against dogs," Mom scoffed. "I just don't want to be cleaning off dog hair and picking up after them with little Baggies."

Every time something felt familiar, it seemed to contradict her life, which made her feel even more lost. *When am I going to get over this awful sense of wrongness?*

And what am I going to do if it never goes away?

They continued up the trail, finally making it to the top. The air was a couple degrees cooler, and she took deep breaths, trying to ease the cramp in her side. Red-hued hills contrasted the deep blue sky, shrubbery dotted the land below, and a tree-lined river cut a trail through the valley. It looked like a picture straight out of Dad's magazines.

Okay, so it sucks that I messed up everything with Spencer and that I miss a dog I never had. But I made it up this hill, and I didn't flinch once when other people passed me on the trail.

Out of the corner of her eye, she caught movement. But she didn't get her hands up in time. The spinning yellow Frisbee binged her in the side of the head, then fell to the ground. Rubbing the spot where it had hit, she turned around.

"Sorry," a younger boy with a round, flushed face said, making his way over.

"It's okay." Liv bent down to get the Frisbee, right as he reached for it.

The kid looked up and his eyes widened. "Ew, that looks disgusting! What happened to you?"

Glancing down, Olivia saw the tip of her scar peeking out of the top of her shirt. Her hand shot up, flattening her neckline as she stood.

Pain radiated through her chest, not from the physical contact but from somewhere deep inside.

"Yo, Felix," a voice yelled, making Liv flinch. "Hurry up."

The kid grabbed the Frisbee and ran back toward his friend, leaving her standing there, fighting tears. *I should chase that chubby kid down and bing him over the head with the Frisbee.* The voice held venom, but underneath it, there was pain.

J-just ignore him. It doesn't matter what he thinks.

It felt like every ounce of her energy had been drained and in its place was now suffocating sadness, weighing her down. Often, with all the fighting going on in her head, she felt like three people constantly at war. Right now she was feeling the ache of all three of them. It was even worse than the bickering.

Mom came over and draped an arm around her shoulders. "I'm glad you and Dad talked me into this. The view's so pretty up here." Worry creased her brow. "Are you okay, sweetheart? Is it your heart? Did we push you too hard?"

It *was* her heart, but it had nothing to do with the hike. Liv lowered her hand, blinking to keep the tears from spilling out. She swallowed past the giant lump in her throat. "I'm done. I just want to go home."

And never leave again.

Monday morning came too fast. Liv had dragged herself out of bed at the last possible minute, thrown on a pair of jeans and a T-shirt she'd found on her floor, and hadn't even bothered with makeup. Since she'd fallen asleep with wet hair last night, her locks were half-wavy, half-smashed, and all-the-way frizzy. The girly voice was appalled.

Now, as she stood at the base of the steps to the school, her legs felt as heavy as her heart. *It was stupid to think I could ever be normal. My chance at normal ended the night I wrapped my car around that tree.*

Keira was the only potential for a close friend, and maybe Clay, but that was because they didn't know about her missing memories.

They hadn't seen her repulsive scar.

And she was going to make sure no one else ever saw it again.

Those words that had tortured her since yesterday's hike ran through her head again: *Ew, that looks disgusting! What happened to you?*

She was broken. Unfixable.

People rushed by, bumping into her like there wasn't a whole freaking stairway. *Back the hell off*, she wanted to yell. Instead, she gritted her teeth and trudged up the stairs. Her eyes burned from crying herself to sleep.

The second she walked into the building, there was Sabrina and the gang, all polished perfection. Unfortunately, Keira wasn't there, and she was the only person she thought she could stand this morning.

Sabrina's eyebrows shot up. "Whoa," she said, managing to pack a hundred insults into such a tiny word. "What look were you going for this morning?"

Taylor and Candace giggled.

Something inside Liv snapped. "I was going for, I don't give a shit what you think."

Eyes widened, mouths hung open. The words had burst out of her, and Liv liked how they sounded now that they were there, mixed in with the gossip.

The fear hit a few seconds later.

She's going to destroy you.

Doing her best to throw on an indifferent front, she turned to leave and almost ran into Keira.

Keira's smile disappeared as she looked from her to Sabrina, then back to her. "What'd I miss?"

"Ask Sabrina. I'm sure she'll fill you in." Liv walked away, too angry to care what else they said about her.

The momentary strength Liv had felt from standing up to Sabrina quickly faded, and she'd ended up sitting outside for lunch to avoid the drama with the popular group and the awkwardness with Spencer. Since it was in the high nineties, she'd basically sweated off her lunch as she ate it, and by the time she made it back to her locker, she felt depleted. It was only halfway through the day, and three and a half more hours seemed like a torturous eternity.

Then I'll tell Mom I want to go back to being homeschooled. I won't have to worry about where to sit or what anyone else thinks. She grabbed her math book and slammed her locker door. *Do I really want to go back to that life again? Sure, no one told me how disgusting my scar was*—her heart gave a painful squeeze—*but it was lonely.*

Look around. It's not like I'm swimming in friends here.

Because you're not even trying. Wasn't there a flyer for cheerleading tryouts on the wall?

I'd rather choke on my own vomit than only get noticed because my butt's hanging out of a short cheerleading skirt.

"Great," she mumbled. "Back to arguing with myself. Just what I need, more issues to deal with."

A girl sitting on the bench in the hall looked at her, face all scrunched up.

Discouraged and confused, and needing to get away from the girl who'd heard her talking to herself, she tucked her books under her arm and strode down the hall.

"Hey, Liv." Clay jogged up to her. "I missed you at lunch." He nudged her with his elbow. "I hope you're not trying to avoid me."

"Not you. Life in general."

"On your way to the math class that you like?"

"The very one." Liv slowed as they neared the classroom. "Don't you like any of your classes?"

He shrugged. "I guess history is less awful than the rest."

She leaned in and whispered, "Don't worry, your secret's safe with me."

The grin he gave her lit up his whole face, and it was impossible not to return it. "I thought you were going to be at the party Friday night. It would've been better if you were there."

Liv spotted Spencer coming down the hall. She didn't want to stare, but she couldn't help it. He always looked so grouchy. But the rare times she saw him smile, and the time she'd made him laugh in the playland — those moments stuck in her mind, making it hard to give up on him completely.

He glanced her way, his usual serious expression on his face.

Liv turned away, hoping he didn't notice she'd been staring at him. "Sorry," she said to Clay when she saw his expectant expression. "What were you saying?"

"Just that you should come to a party sometime. You might be surprised how much fun we can pull off using our limited resources."

"Maybe I'll catch the next one."

See, not everyone at school is hard to deal with. Clay went out of his way to find me, and I don't even have to decode what he's thinking.

I can do this. I can stick it out. There are a lot of other people here besides Sabrina and her group.

Maybe I'll even get involved in something. Not cheerleading, but some other extracurricular activity. Something not physical.

Or nerdy.

Okay, so joining a group might have to wait.

The people in the hall were clearing out. She jerked a thumb toward the classroom. "I better get to class. But I'll see you later."

Big smile on his face, Clay did this charming head-nod/eyebrow-raise combo move. "Count on it."

Feeling much lighter than she had earlier in the day, she slipped inside Mr. Barker's room. Spencer didn't look up when she came in. His eyes were glued to the notebook in front of him.

Fine, Spencer Multiple-Personality Hale. Be that way.

Liv sat at the desk in the far corner, the one she knew no one else sat near. As Mr. Barker started the lecture, she glared at the back of Spencer's head. The longer she stared, the angrier she felt. The least he could've done was say hi or wave. *That's it. This time, I really am done with him.*

The instant Liv walked into chemistry, Sabrina started with the dirty looks.

She's such a bitch. She talks crap about me, then acts like I'm *the one who attacked her.*

Liv glared right back, holding her head high, even though there was still a tiny part that wanted to win Sabrina over.

I don't need you. Clay likes me, and you and Spencer can just get over yourselves.

When she glanced at Keira, though, a pang went through her chest. Out of everyone here, Keira had been the nicest. She thought they were friends, and she didn't want to give her up. But apparently, Keira was going along with Sabrina, which meant *she* was willing to give *her* up.

What did you expect? They're all the same.

Telling herself she didn't care, and feeling a mix of relief and sorrow about letting it all go, she settled into the empty table behind Keira and Sabrina.

Mrs. Smith went on and on about how fun today's experiment would be, but Liv seriously doubted making elephant toothpaste was going to be the pick-me-up she needed. It wasn't even real toothpaste. Just breaking hydrogen peroxide into oxygen and water. Apparently it looked like toothpaste, but larger, and for some reason, that made Mrs. Smith really happy.

"Now put on your goggles," Mrs. Smith said, giant grin on her face, "and let the fun begin."

Of course I got the scratched goggles, Liv thought as she put them on. *If only they were scratched up enough to block my view of Sabrina's perfect shiny hair and frilly red top.*

Mrs. Smith frowned in her direction. "Liv, you don't have a partner?"

Several faces turned to stare at the odd girl out. None of them had put on their goggles yet, so she felt like even more of a loser.

"You can work with Sabrina and Keira, if you'd like."

If looks could kill, Sabrina's would've dropped her on the spot.

"It's fine. I don't mind working alone." *I've got a couple warring voices in my head to keep me company, anyway. I'm sure they'll be real helpful.*

Liv read the first step on her lab handout and got to work on the experiment. Once the potassium iodide was dissolved, she poured eighty milliliters of hydrogen peroxide into a graduated cylinder. Next, she added forty milliliters of Dawn detergent to the cylinder, then picked it up to swirl the ingredients together, like the directions told her to.

Her arm spasmed and the foamy mixture flew out of the cylinder.

Several foamy drops splattered onto the back of Sabrina's shirt.

Mrs. Smith had specifically warned them that the high-grade hydrogen peroxide would bleach clothing.

Mouth hanging open, she stared, not sure what to say or do.

Sabrina glanced back, eyebrows knit together. She scowled at Liv.

"What are you looking at?" Liv said, surprised at how bold and snarky she sounded.

Sabrina rolled her eyes, gave an exaggerated sigh, and faced front.

Liv's eyes remained fixed on Sabrina's back. White spots were already forming where the mixture had hit the red shirt. She kept expecting Sabrina to notice, but with all the ruffled layers, she must not have felt it.

I should tell her before it completely ruins her shirt.

No way. She deserves it. Plus you know she's going to freak if you tell her.

It *had* been an accident, none of the mixture had gotten on her skin, and it wasn't like Sabrina would tell her if the tables were turned. Besides, there was a tiny part of her that got a thrill at what she'd done to Sabrina. Okay, make that a big part. Her body felt lighter than it had all day, and her lips twisted into a smile that was all genuine satisfaction.

If she's going to hate on me anyway, I might as well give her a good reason.

After school, Liv sat on her usual bench to wait for Mom. The minutes were dragging, and after what seemed like a forever-long day filled with a whole lot of downs, she was eager to get home. The heat wasn't helping her mood, either. She took a swig from her water bottle, but the warm liquid didn't do much to cool her down. The *clang* of someone pushing open the door sounded, and she automatically glanced toward the entrance. *Spencer.*

Twisting away from him, she dropped her gaze to her book. *The Great Gatsby* was as annoying as her day. People playing games. A stupid girl and a stupid boy.

When a shadow crept across her page, blocking her light, she leaned closer to the book.

"You know he's a jerk."

Without looking up, she said, "I hate it when people refer to themselves in the third person."

"I'm a jerk, too."

"I know you are. That's what I just said."

"What happened with your friends?"

"See, when you say friends, I'm not really sure who you mean. You've made it clear you're not my friend."

"I mean the girls you've been hanging out with," he said. "You didn't sit by them at lunch."

"I'm sick of rude people, I'm sick of drama, and I'm starting to think I'm just going to go back to home school."

Spencer sat next to her. "Don't do that. You'll go crazy. Besides, it makes kids socially awkward."

"I'm not exactly excelling in that department anyway."

He was quiet for a moment, then he leaned close enough that the tips of his hair brushed her cheek. "You ever gonna look away from that book?"

"Not until you're gone." It took all her self-control to keep staring at the novel. "See, if I don't look at you and start thinking that we're friends, I won't be as disappointed when you go into jerk mode."

"I admitted I was a jerk."

"I know. And I agreed with you."

His hand grazed her leg as he reached for the book. He pulled on it, yanking it out of her hands.

Nose in the sky, she crossed her arms and twisted away.

"Why's your mom coming into the parking lot the wrong way?" Spencer asked.

Liv turned to see.

And saw nothing. She pushed Spencer. "Argh! What do you want?"

His glasses reflected her angry expression. It definitely wasn't her most flattering look. Not to mention her hair was still a frizzy mess. "You were the one who said you wanted to go home the other night," he said. "I just did what you asked."

She clenched her jaw. "Don't even pretend you were totally innocent. We had a good time, then you went all weird on me."

The corner of his mouth lifted. "So you had a good time?"

That maddening touch of arrogance irritated her even more. "Until I told you I have no memory of my past, which you obviously couldn't handle."

"I swear it wasn't that. I was thinking about something else. I had fun with you. More fun than I've had in a long time, actually. Then because of . . . some stuff, I decided it was best if I didn't get too close to you. But then today . . . let's just say I changed my mind."

Liv studied his sincere expression. Her frustration faded, but the confusion was still there. "I have no idea what to make of you and your multiple personalities. Or the fact that you can't ever just say anything in a normal way so that I can understand what it means."

Spencer locked eyes with her. "I had fun the other night, and I hope that you'll forgive me so we can hang out again sometime. Is that clear enough?"

Liv sat there, trying to decide how to respond. If he hadn't grinned, she might've been able to keep her steely resolve. But she was a sucker for that smile. "Clear as mud."

16

Tuesday, Liv stayed away from Sabrina and her group, avoiding everyone except Keira as much as possible. After she got her lunch, she eyed the so-called popular table, wishing she could sit by Keira without having to deal with Sabrina.

Spencer stepped next to her. "Still in a fight with the girls?"

Keeping a tight grip on her tray, she sighed. "I'm not sure. *Fight*'s not really the right word. More like fed up. Some of the girls are cool, but I'm not sure it's worth dealing with the snide remarks and backhanded compliments from the rest of them."

"There's lots of room at my table."

"Wouldn't that mess up your loner rep?"

Spencer gave her a half smile and shrugged. "I'm not too concerned."

They crossed the cafeteria to his usual table and sat facing each other. "Wow. You're not even going to put your headphones in?" Liv twisted her spaghetti around her fork. "Now I really feel special."

"The blood thing," Spencer said. "Is that because of your accident?"

Fork halfway to her mouth, she froze. Looking down at the red tomato sauce, her appetite disappeared. "Really? You're going to talk about blood while I'm trying to eat?"

"Sorry. I was just curious."

She shook the noodles off her fork. "Salad it is."

"Okay, no more blood. We'll talk about something else."

"How about we talk about you for a change?"

Spencer shook his head. "I'm not that interesting."

"Oh, come on. How about the basics? Like brothers and sisters?"

"One sister. I live with her and my mom. Dad's been out of the picture for a while." He took a drink of his water. "How about you?"

"It's just me and my mom and dad. They're both doctors. Or were. My mom's not working right now, and it gives her way too much time to worry about me."

Spencer's gaze drifted behind her. "If you weren't in a fight with the girls before, you might be now. We're getting some dirty looks."

Liv glanced over her shoulder. When she saw the girls staring—Sabrina had an especially angry expression—she smiled and waved, then faced Spencer again. "Better or worse now?"

"I'd say shocked." He tilted his head, a smile playing on the corners of his mouth. "Just when I think I've got you figured out, you surprise me."

"Well, I'm just surprised you didn't decide to revert back to your cold personality today. I'm not exactly sure what to make of you."

"Oh yeah? What's your opinion so far?"

Leaning forward, she raised an eyebrow. "Wouldn't you like to know."

Spencer grinned, and she hoped that meant he did.

They talked through the rest of lunch and left the cafeteria together. Spencer said he had to grab something out of his locker. Unsure whether that was an invitation to join him, she told him she'd see him in class. As she walked toward Mr. Barker's room, she was feeling pretty good about life in general.

Clay stepped up beside her. "So you and Hale? What's that all about?"

"It's not really about anything." Liv turned to face him. "We share a class, we see each other around. We're friends. Getting to be friends, anyway."

His eyebrows drew together, and it looked like he was waging some kind of internal struggle. "Just be careful. One day he's your friend, the next he's not." With that, he kept walking down the hall.

"So I had this idea." Spencer sat on the bench next to Liv. "We write out a list of things you need to experience, and then we do them, checking them off as we go. That way, you make up for all the things you missed out on. Or don't remember doing, anyway. And you might as well tell your parents that I'll bring you home after school. That way they won't have to worry about it."

"My mom's a professional worrier," Liv said. "She'll find a way."

He pulled out his notebook. "Okay, we can cross off McDonald's. I think bike riding should wait until your coordination gets better."

She glanced over his shoulder as he jotted down the list.

1. McDonald's
2. Catch a lizard

She read it twice to make sure she wasn't seeing things. "I don't want to catch a lizard."

"That's what you do when you're a little kid. It's fun, I swear."

"Yeah, but I'm a girl, which means I don't really want to catch scaly, crawly things."

"I taught my little sister. If she can do it, you can do it. Now, *shh*. I'm trying to think."

3. Sports: baseball, basketball, volleyball

He tapped the pen to his lip. "You know how to swim?"

"I don't think so." Swimming meant a bathing suit, which meant scars on display. "Better move that one to the end."

"Why?"

"Because I asked you to."

"These aren't in any particular order. We'll go through them however we feel like doing them. You've missed so many good movies. And music."

4. Movies: Lord of the Rings trilogy. Matrix trilogy. The three Spider-Man movies.

"That's a lot of trilogies."

"This is just a start. We'll add more movies as we think of them."

5. Music: 30 Seconds to Mars, Radiohead, 311, Green Day, Shinedown

"I like a mix of old and new rock and alternative. Once I get a feel for what you like, I'll be able to add more to that list, too. Oh, yeah, I still have to put swimming on here."

6. Swim
7. Bike
8. Drive

"Your handwriting is really sloppy," Liv said. "I can hardly read it."

Spencer glanced at her, then wrote another item on the list.

9. Teach Liv to give a compliment once in a while.

He used the pen to point at it. "Is that clear enough?"

"There's plenty I could put on a list for you."

"This is about you, though. Call your mom and tell her you've got to go lizard hunting right now."

"Now?"

"Look at this list. It's already pretty long. We should get started, and right now" — he tipped his head to the sky — "it's a perfect day for lizard hunting."

Stepping over the cactus, she scanned the ground. Instead of mentioning the lizard hunting, she'd simply asked to hang out with Spencer. Mom had surprised her by saying yes after only a brief hesitation.

Liv spotted one of the little creatures sunning itself on a rock. Most of them had run off before she'd even gotten close. She was kind of hoping this one would get up and run, too. "I don't think I can touch it."

Spencer put a finger to his lips. "Talk quietly or you'll scare him away. Now stop being a wuss and just do it."

No way could she back away from the challenge now. One inch at a time, she crouched near the lizard. She hovered her hand over it for a couple seconds, then snatched it around the stomach.

"Ew, ew, ew," she said as it wiggled in her hand. Its belly was soft, but the jagged scales on the lizard's back rubbed against the palm of her hand. Its clawed feet swung wildly through the air. "Now what?"

The lizard whipped around and bit the fleshy part between her thumb and index finger. "Ouch!" She shook her hand until the lizard released its grip and fell to the ground.

Mouth hanging open, she looked from her hand to Spencer. "I swear, if it starts bleeding, I'm not going to do any more of these stupid things with you."

Spencer stepped across a big rock, grabbed her hand, and looked it over. "I think you'll live."

She yanked her hand out of his grip and smacked his arm. "Why didn't you tell me they bite?"

"I thought you were smart. Everything with a mouth bites."

"I'm going to bite *you*."

He gave her a smile that sent her pulse racing. "I think I'd like to see that."

Heat crept into her cheeks, her heart went into overdrive, and as they stood there, looking at each other, she swore his gaze moved to her lips.

Then he looked over at his car. "So now that you've caught a lizard, we can—"

"Don't even think you're getting away that easily. We're not leaving until *you* catch one."

Eyes running over the ground, Spencer took a large step forward. "Watch and learn."

꒰ᵕ꒱

"I still can't believe that's what you did for fun as a kid," Liv said as Spencer turned onto Main Street.

"In case you didn't notice, there's not much to do here."

Show-off that he was, Spencer had caught four lizards before calling it a night. Red scratches showed on his hand where the creatures had clawed at him. Two of the brown scaly things had bitten him before he'd let them go.

Spencer turned up the volume on his car stereo. "How about this? It's a far cry from classical music."

The male singer scream-sang the lyrics over heavy drums. "Sounds like he smashed his finger or something. Why is he so angry?"

"Maybe a lizard bit him and he's making a huge deal about it."

Liv laughed. "Okay, let's listen to something else."

Spencer pushed the scan button on his radio.

"Yuck. What is that?" she asked when it landed on a station.

"That's country. And yes, it *is* horrible, so you get extra cool points for not liking it."

She threw her hands over her heart. "Just what I always wanted. Cool points."

Smiling, Spencer shook his head. They were back to this comfortable place she loved, laughing and joking, everything so easy and fun. It felt amazing to be the person she was deep down, when the past was in the past and her voices were stripped away.

He pushed the numbered buttons on his stereo, listening for a second or two, then pushing the next.

"Wait. Go back. That sounded good."

He dropped his hand, nose all wrinkled up. "You've got to be kidding me. Chick power music?"

"It makes me want to go protest all the wrongs in the world. And maybe do a little headbanging."

"Why is it okay when the chicks are screaming, but not the guy?"

Liv shrugged. "It sounds better."

The song ended and a commercial came on. Spencer started hunting again.

"That sounds good," Liv said.

"Katy Perry?" Spencer stopped at the light. "Don't tell me you like this synthesized pop crap. This isn't even music."

"I want to hate it, but it's kind of catchy. I hate it and like it at the same time."

"You're a little schizo."

"I know. I can't figure it out. I feel like . . ."

A huge grin spread across his face.

"What?" she asked.

"I was making a joke, and you start explaining how you're schizo. It's funny, that's all." The light turned green and Spencer accelerated through the intersection.

"It's just that sometimes I feel like I'm living a life that's not mine. I'm sure it's because of my missing memories, but it feels like everything's . . . off or something." Her insecurities flared, and she leaned back in her seat. "Okay, now that I hear it out loud, I realize how weird it sounds. Just pretend I didn't say it."

A crease formed between his eyebrows. "No, I think everyone feels that way at some point. Memories or not. In fact, it's probably nice to not remember all the crappy stuff you've done."

"But what about the good memories I've missed out on?"

The song ended, and for a moment, silence hung in the air.

"Well, that's why we have the list. Being out there tonight

brought back good memories of how easy things used to be when I was a kid." Spencer pulled up in front of her house and threw the car in park. "Tomorrow, I'll take it easy on you. We'll go with a movie."

Suddenly tomorrow seemed way too far away.

17

The promise of another adventure with Spencer was enough to help her get through her morning classes. The closer it got to lunch—to seeing him again—the happier she felt. By the time she walked into the cafeteria, she was dizzy with anticipation.

She got her food and headed toward Spencer's usual spot. Unlike last week, he didn't have his earphones in. His eyes met hers and he returned her smile.

Keira stepped in front of her. "You need to come with me."

"What's up?" Liv asked.

"Trust me, okay? I'm fighting for you, but I can only do so much. Just come sit by me today. Please."

Liv looked at Spencer, shrugged, and reluctantly followed Keira in the other direction.

"What's the deal?" Liv asked as she and Keira sat down.

"Some of the girls were talking, and they were saying you're not as nice as I think you are."

All the crap she'd put up with from Sabrina, and now the group was blaming *her*? The more she thought about it, the hotter the blood running through her veins got. "Sabrina's the one who was constantly taking shots at me. All I did was stick up for myself."

"They said she was just talking and you were rude about

it." Keira threw up a hand. "I believe you, I do, because I know how Sabrina can be. She's used to getting her way, and she can sometimes come across as mean, but once you get to know her better, you'll see she's got another side to her, too. I think you should try to make up with her."

Liv crossed her arms. "What if I don't care what she thinks?"

"It's not only about her, though. I've been friends with Sabrina, Candace, and Taylor forever. We've grown up together. We've had our differences, but when I needed them most they were there for me. Right off the bat I knew that you and I could be friends. But if you and Sabrina start fighting . . ." Keira shook her head. "I don't want to have to choose. I just wish everyone could get along and be happy."

Some of Liv's anger deflated. She could tell Keira truly believed it was possible for them to all get along, and she wished that was true, but she wasn't holding her breath. "You're a very sweet person, Keira. I hope you don't get walked on because of it."

"It's not so bad. Once in a while I have to give in on something I don't want to do, but I get invited everywhere, and it's nice having a big group of friends."

I remember when all I wanted was to fit in. I thought it would be easier, but it wasn't.

Wait. What?

Liv thought that if she just focused hard enough, she'd be able to grab the memory that was tickling her mind.

"So, like, what are you guys?" Sabrina asked, shattering her concentration.

Out of nowhere, Sabrina, Candace, and Taylor had appeared opposite her. All three of them stared at her, obviously waiting for an answer.

"Keira and I are friends, so we're sitting here having a conversation." Liv forced a smile onto her lips. "Care to join us?"

Sabrina narrowed her eyes. "You know that's not who I'm talking about. What's going on with you and Spencer?"

Why is everyone so obsessed with my relationship with Spencer? "We're friends."

"You know, he and I used to date."

"He never mentioned it." Okay, so she knew they'd dated, but only because Keira and Clay had told her. Determined not to let Sabrina get to her, she kept her voice calm, like they were discussing nothing more serious than the weather. "I assume there's a reason for the *used to* part."

Rage filled her eyes. "You just got here, so I'll let you off with a warning. Stay away from him. It's rule number one in girl code. You don't go for a friend's boyfriend, crush, or ex-boyfriend."

The calm started to crack as Liv glared back. "Funny, Sabrina. I didn't know you and I *were* friends."

"Keep acting the way you are, and we never will be. You won't have *any* friends." Sabrina glanced at Candace, then Taylor, and finally Keira. "I think Liv needs some time to think about this on her own."

Keira looked up at Sabrina. "But I haven't even eaten my—"

"You can eat it down there." Sabrina pointed to the other end of the table.

"Sorry," Keira whispered, then picked up her tray and joined the rest of the girls.

Liv watched them settle in. Keira had an apologetic look on her face; the other three girls were going overboard pretending she didn't exist.

The room blurred, a similar scene unfolding in her mind of three girls sitting across from her in a cafeteria. One looked like the punk version of Sabrina—pretty with shiny brown hair. Only this girl had a blue stripe up front and eyes ringed with lots of black eyeliner. She wore a leather band on her wrist and enough earrings to provide jewelry for an entire army, and she had her fingernails painted black. The two other girls flanked her, and she could tell they'd back the girl up, no matter what happened next.

The hazy form of the girl leaned forward, her image sharpening, eyes narrowed. "You want to go back to being a loner?"

Liv stared at the girl, a riotous mix of anger, frustration, and panic coursing through her. "So if I don't agree with you all the time, we can't be friends?"

"Friends back each other up. So either you're in or you're out." The girl stood, and so did the other two with her. "We'll give you some time alone to think about it."

The images faded, and the noise of people eating and talking, along with the smells of food and cleaner, came back into focus. Liv gripped the edge of the table so hard it dug into her palms, but she couldn't let go, because it felt like the room was spinning. Where the hell had that scene come from? Was it a hallucination?

No, because if it was . . . Cold spread through her entire body. If it was, that meant she was leaning less toward occasionally hearing voices and more toward serious mental illness.

She glanced at the end of the table, where Sabrina was still pointedly ignoring her. She wondered what would've happened if the scene in her mind had played out all the way. Would she have eventually given in to the girl so she didn't have to be a loner?

Had any of it actually happened?

Liv shook her head. It didn't matter. Because right now, in

this moment, she wasn't going to give in. She had someone else to talk to. *If Sabrina really wanted me to stay away from Spencer, she shouldn't have left me on my own.*

Fully planning on joining him, she gripped her tray. But when she looked over to the spot where he'd been earlier, he wasn't there anymore.

Spencer sat at the desk in front of Liv and spun around to face her. "Looked like some serious mutiny was going down at lunch today."

She propped her cheek on her fist. "I'm being punished. Apparently there's a girl code and I'm breaking it."

His mouth dropped open in mock horror. "You broke girl code? How dare you!"

"You'll never guess what it's about."

"Well, don't keep me in suspense," he said, smiling.

"You. Sabrina demanded I stay away from you."

His smile faded.

"Why is she still so hung up on you?" Liv asked.

"I don't know."

"Well, how long did you guys go out?"

His familiar mask descended again. "This is one of the many reasons I hate this tiny town. All the drama. And everyone thinks it's their business when it's not. It's over. She knows it, I know it, end of story."

Wow. He really doesn't want to talk about it. Maybe he's still hung up on her, too. That thought made her sick to her stomach.

He ran his fingers along the back of his chair, eyes focused on the movement. "So, are you going to have to stay away from me now?"

"That'll be pretty hard, since we've got a whole list of

things to complete and you promised to be my ride home."

"It's not that far of a walk, you know."

Liv opened her mouth, but the shock made it impossible to form a coherent sentence. "Oh, I ... uh ..."

He reached out and squeezed her knee. "Hey, I was kidding. You didn't think I'd actually make you walk home?"

"With you, I never know."

"Ouch." He put a hand over his heart. "I thought we were past that. I mean, we caught lizards together."

Liv smiled and made an extra large eye roll. "Talk about dramatic."

"Just wait. You're going to love our movie marathon. Even more than you love math."

Spencer glanced around. "Okay, we got the popcorn."

Liv held up the bowl. "Check."

"Movie's in the DVD player and the curtains are drawn for minimal glare."

"Wow, you're taking this really seriously."

"I'm setting the mood. You've got to get the whole movie experience."

A few minutes later, they were side-by-side—not too close, and definitely not as close as she would like to be, but close enough to share the popcorn—watching the first *Lord of the Rings* movie.

Halfway through, the front door swung open, flooding the room with light, and a little girl walked in. "Hey Spence, whatcha doing?"

Spencer picked up the remote and pressed pause. "Trying to watch a movie. I thought you were going to be over at Hailey's for a while."

"Got boring." The girl grabbed a handful of popcorn and shoved it in her mouth. A couple kernels didn't make it and fell to the floor.

"This is my little sister, Katie. Katie, this is my friend, Liv."

"I didn't think you had friends anymore."

Spencer gestured for Katie to move out of the way of the TV. "If you want to watch with us, you have to sit down and be quiet."

Katie sat on the floor in front of them and Spencer started up the movie again. Liv couldn't focus on it anymore, though. The same feeling she always got around girls Katie's age—girls with brown hair—filled her. This awful, aching sensation in her chest that made her want to cry.

When Katie swung her backpack off, Liv noticed the picture on it—a white cartoon cat with a red bow over the ear. The words Hello Kitty were in large letters across the top. Staring at it, she was sure she'd seen it before. It brought back . . . something. She thought of Elizabeth, makeup and nail polish strewn about the room.

"Is she always getting into your nail polish and makeup?" Liv asked.

Until Spencer looked at her like she was crazy, she didn't realize how stupid it sounded. "Yeah, it's a real problem," he said.

"Oh, I just heard that about little sisters. That they get into your stuff." Tears filled her eyes. She blinked, trying to keep them from breaking free.

Confusion flashed across Spencer's face. He leaned in and put his hand on her knee. "What's wrong?"

Liv shook her head. "Nothing. Everything. I don't really know." The answer was that she missed somebody. Somebody she didn't know. Which made no sense. Now that Spencer was staring at her, she had an even harder time controlling her emotions. "Can you just take me home?"

"Everything okay?" Dad asked as Liv walked into the living room.

I'm just a crazy person who sees people who aren't there in the cafeteria and had a meltdown for no reason in front of Spencer, but everything's just dandy. "Yeah. It's fine."

The ride home had been filled with awkwardness. She had no idea what to say or how to explain, so she hadn't bothered, and Spencer hadn't said anything, either. Just when she thought they were making progress.

The smell of food and violin music filled the air. "Sounds like Mom has already started cooking dinner."

Dad nodded. "She's got some new thing she's trying."

"I think I'll go help her." She needed something else to focus on.

"I'm sure she'll appreciate that."

Mom's back was to Liv. Her hands were kneading something in a large bowl—hamburger maybe. On the TV screen in front of her . . . it couldn't be what it looked like.

Humming to the music, Mom added more salt, then took out the ball of meat and pressed it into a loaf pan. All while watching what looked like a bloody human brain.

Red flashed across Liv's vision. She heard the ghost of a chirping noise and felt strange pricks across her scalp. A wave of dizziness crashed into her as she stumbled back and knocked into a chair.

Mom turned. "Hi, sweetheart. How was your day?"

Sure she was going to lose her lunch, she put a hand over her mouth.

Mom glanced from her to the TV. "Oh, it's some old surgeries. To keep up my surgical skills. I'll turn it off if it bugs you."

No wonder I'm so screwed up, she thought as she hightailed it out of there.

Taking deep breaths, she managed to make it back to the living room. The love seat was closest, so she took a couple shaky steps and flopped onto it.

Dad lowered his magazine. "You okay, Livie? You look a little pale."

"Mom's in there watching brain surgery while making dinner."

"I saw that she'd gotten out her old tapes."

"You don't think it's a little weird to be making food and staring at brains?"

One corner of Dad's mouth twisted up. "I suppose it does seem a little crazy to someone who isn't used to seeing it, but to your mom, it's where she excels. It's like math is to you; it's what makes sense to her." He paused for a moment. "I do worry about her. She loved her work."

"Then why'd she give it up?" Liv asked.

Dad looked at her for a moment, the wrinkles on his forehead deepening. "Well, after your wreck, she put all her efforts into getting you better. She needed a break from work anyway and had always wanted to be a stay-at-home mom. I'm sure someday she'll ... Besides, there's not exactly a lot of need for it in Cottonwood."

"Then why did we come here? Mom always says we needed a fresh start, but I'm still not sure why we moved at all."

"If you're not going to help your mom, why don't you go start your homework?"

"But—"

"Now." Dad's tone made it clear there wouldn't be any more questions. Normally, Mom was the one to get upset. Dad had never sounded so harsh.

Hurt and frustrated, she made her way up to her room. Spending time with Spencer, she'd let herself think her life could be normal. But now there it was again, all her instincts whispering that she was anything but. Ignoring the signs wasn't working anymore—if she was honest with herself, she'd known something bad had happened in Minnesota. More than the car wreck. Something so awful that Mom and Dad were keeping it a secret from her.

And since they obviously weren't going to confess, she would have to start digging for the truth herself.

18

"Hey, about yesterday and the makeup thing. I was just teasing you. I didn't mean to hurt your feelings."

Pulling her book out of her locker, Liv spun around and faced Spencer. "It wasn't what you said, I swear. Besides, isn't giving each other a hard time kind of our thing?"

His solemn expression softened, and a smile played on the corners of his mouth. "Yeah, I guess it is. I felt bad, though. I was sure you were going to tell me what a jerk I was."

"Not today, but don't worry, I'll call you on it if you start acting like one again."

This time, his smile broke free.

Together, they started down the hall. "What happened, then?" Spencer asked. "I take it you weren't crying because of the cinematic beauty of the movie."

She exhaled, trying to figure out what she could possibly say. "Here's the thing. Since I broke girl code and all, you're kind of my only friend—no pressure, by the way. I'm sure Keira will still be nice to me, but I don't want her to get in trouble, so . . ."

"So you're saying you don't want people to know we're friends. I'm making things worse?"

Liv shook her head. "Not at all. In fact, I want to show Sabrina that she can't push me around. She can't tell me who I can and can't be friends with."

Spencer lowered his eyebrows. "Then what are you saying?"

"I guess I'm asking if we can just forget yesterday's meltdown ever happened."

"Forgotten." He shook his hair out of his face, and the overhead lights reflected off his lenses. "But if you ever do want to talk about it, you can."

"And if you ever want to talk about anything, you can talk to me, too."

"I don't have anything to talk about."

Liv raised an eyebrow. "Sure you don't."

"So today after school," he said, ignoring her implication, "you want to finish the movie or do something else from the list? I added bowling and mini-golf last night. Those are definitely things you've got to experience."

The fact he'd added to the list after she'd acted all crazy made her want to hug him. But since she couldn't get up enough courage to actually do it, she smiled at him. "Bowling sounds fun."

"Bowling it is."

Sabrina and her group walked down the hall, headed toward her and Spencer. Pinpointing the exact moment Sabrina realized that she hadn't listened to her threats was easy: the smile turned into a sneer, and she shot her an icy glare.

"This should be interesting," Liv muttered.

Spencer draped his arm around her shoulders and leaned in. "What was that?"

Pulse racing, she stared into his eyes, trying to remember what she'd been talking about. Oh yeah, Sabrina. Getting mad. But with his arm around her, she really didn't care.

✧✦✧

Liv was having trouble focusing on her English comp paper. For one, she was thinking about how Spencer had put his arm around her, replaying it over and over. Then there was the fact that she didn't have anything to put down. With Mom and Dad both freaking out any time she brought up the past, she didn't have the information for the family paper she was supposed to write. Taylor and Candace were both in the class, too, and they took turns staring daggers at her.

Mrs. Tully gave a pointed look at Liv's blank computer screen. "You should get started, Olivia. This is going to be a big project."

Liv put her hands up on the keyboard. "Okay."

"Why don't you start with your family history."

Believe me, I'm as curious about that as you are. "I'm not sure about the details."

"Then write about a tradition your family has. Like what you do for birthdays or holidays."

Again, not something she knew. She supposed she could start with how every morning they sat around the table and she threw back a handful of pills. Then there were walks with Dad and making dinner with Mom—she doubted anyone else's mom cooked while watching brain surgery. Of course, she didn't exactly want to write about that. Especially since it might lead to her puking all over her keyboard.

Typing her name and a couple of generic facts was enough to get Mrs. Tully to move on. Liv stared at the blinking cursor.

Blink.

Blink.

Blink.

Like it was taunting her.

How can you not remember? The loud, demanding voice in her head made her jump. Her heart rate spiked and her palms felt slick against the keyboard. *You're not even trying.*

Yes I am. Liv glanced at Mrs. Tully, now seated behind her desk. *Starting now.*

She opened the Internet and typed in Dad's name. She got a bunch of links that weren't him—an artist, a real-estate guy. She tried again, typing in *MD* and then *PhD* after his name. Information came up on where he did his schooling, residency, and fellowship, along with several medical articles. One had a subheading that read:

Genomics and Genotype-Phenotype Relationships in Heritable Cardiovascular Diseases Predisposing to Sudden Death

The article itself was full of words like *DNA* and *ion channels*. Nothing helpful like, *Hey, this is why your dad acts weird every time you bring up the past.*

A chair scraped the floor and Liv looked up, feeling her heart thudding against her rib cage. Candace sneered at her, then leaned in to say something—most likely an insult about Liv—to Taylor.

Ignoring them, she typed in Mom's name. She got about the same results: her credentials and articles that might as well have been in Latin. Liv bit her thumbnail, trying to think of what else she might be able to look up. After a moment, she moved her fingers back over the keyboard and searched for the Mayo Clinic. Within a couple minutes, she'd found out that it was known for its innovative treatments, was huge in medical research, and was on a list of the "Best Companies to Work For."

So why would they give up such great jobs to come here?

Something didn't add up. And as a math person, that bothered her.

"I thought you and Spencer were just friends," Keira said as Liv shoved her books into her locker.

Liv closed the door and turned toward Keira. "We are."

"Everyone's talking about how cozy you two looked this morning."

"By everyone, I'm assuming you mean Sabrina."

Gripping her open locker door, Keira leaned in. "She's really upset. She thought that Spencer would come back around eventually. One day they were together, the next he just stopped talking to her. Talking to anyone, really. Then you move in, and just like that," she said, snapping her fingers, "he's talking to you."

"We didn't exactly have an easy start," Liv said.

"But he *is* talking to you."

Liv nodded.

Keira glanced around, then leaned even closer. "Sabrina and Spencer went out all last year. They were the couple everyone gossiped about. She was totally crushed when it ended."

"Something must've happened between them."

"Everything changed at the end-of-the-year party. Spencer got arrested. After that, he was a different person."

A sinking feeling went through Liv's stomach. "Arrested? Are you sure?"

"I'd already left, so I didn't see it, but that's what I've heard. Since he cut himself off from everyone, no one really knows what happened. Plus the story always changes based on who tells it." Keira's eyes widened. "Oh, crap. Here comes Sabrina. You know I'm not mad, but if she sees me with you . . ."

"It's okay. I don't want to make things hard for you."

Keira shot her an apologetic smile, then stepped past her. Liv's mind spun over Keira's revelation. *Spencer was arrested?*

Bad boys are *kind of hot.*

Yeah, until they take out their rage on you. Then it doesn't matter how hot they are.

"Hey." Fingers grazed her back and she jumped. Turning, she saw Spencer. "Sorry. I didn't mean to scare you."

Liv put a hand over her fast-beating heart. "Hey."

"Ready for lunch?"

She nodded. Then she walked down the hall with Spencer, wondering if everyone in the world had something to hide.

As Liv sat on the bench after school, waiting for Spencer, she replayed Keira's unexpected news about his arrest; how Clay had told her to be careful.

Maybe I should rethink spending so much time with him.

It was true she didn't know him that well, but she couldn't believe he was dangerous. Occasionally cold or distant, sure, but dangerous? Wouldn't she be able to sense something like that?

Spencer exited the school and made his way over to her. He flashed her a smile that shot straight through her heart. "Ready to go?"

So maybe she didn't know everything about him. But this was a guy who'd written a list to make up for the experiences she couldn't remember. Her gut told her he was a good person.

Sometimes you just had to trust your instincts. She tossed her book in her bag. "Ready."

Music rang out and Spencer reached into his pocket.

"That's my phone. One second." He answered it. "Yeah." Pause. "Okay, hang tight. I'll be right there."

He hung up and sighed. "My sister and her friend got in a fight, so she doesn't want to go over to her house to wait for me or my mom to get home. It looks like our options are finishing the movie at my house, I can take you home now, or I guess we could still go bowling, but we'd have to bring Katie, which we probably don't want to do because she gets really chatty."

"I don't mind chatty," Liv said.

"You sure?"

She nodded. Her main concern was that she'd look at Katie and start crying again. But she liked the idea of spending time with her.

When they got to Spencer's house, Katie was sitting on the front step, cheeks propped against her fists, elbows on her knees.

"She looks so sad," Liv said.

"She'll get over it. She and Hailey fight all the time." Spencer unrolled his window. "You want to go bowling?"

Katie's brows drew together. "With you?"

"And Liv."

"But you never take me anywhere anymore."

"I do, too."

"You do not."

"Do you want to come or not?" Spencer asked.

A smile broke through the sadness, and Katie shot up and bounded toward the car.

Liv studied the multicolored balls lining the racks at the bowling alley. She pointed to a blue swirled one. "This is pretty."

Spencer shook his head, but he was smiling. "Typical girl. Choosing a ball because it's pretty."

She grabbed the ball and almost dropped it on her toe. *Whoa. It's heavier than I thought it would be.* She lugged it over to the lane they'd been assigned, then sat down to put on the ugly black-and-maroon shoes she'd rented. Katie and Spencer showed up with their shiny bowling balls shortly after.

Katie plopped in the seat next to her. "Hailey said that I'm a baby because I wanted to play Barbies. How old were you when you stopped playing with dolls?"

Liv glanced at Katie, then at Spencer, hoping he'd give her a good answer. He just shrugged. "I think you can play with them however long you want," she said. "I hate to break it to you, but girls are just kind of mean sometimes."

"Why?"

"I'm not sure. I guess we all feel a little insecure from time to time, and it's easier to pick on someone else than focus on ourselves. Just look at Spencer. Instead of thinking about how bad I'm going to be at bowling, I'm going to tell him that he better watch out, because he's going down."

Katie laughed. "You must be really good, then, because Spencer's way good. Dad used to take us every Friday night." She looked at Spencer. "Remember that?"

Spencer nodded. "Yeah. And as for Liv, she can't even handle a little lizard bite, so I don't think beating her will be that hard."

"Oh, it's on." Liv stood and grabbed her ball. Looked down the lane at the bowling pins, then over her shoulder at Spencer. "Um, I just roll it, right?"

"I keep forgetting that you don't know what you're doing." He walked up to her. "You have to hold it like . . ." His gaze dropped to the ball in her hands. "First off, I think we should get a ball with holes you can actually put your fingers in. This one is way too big." He took it from her and set it down, then ran to the rack. He grabbed another ball and brought it over to her.

She frowned. "It's black and ugly."

"Just put your fingers in it and let's get started." Spencer showed her how to hold the ball, then, using his ball, demonstrated the basic moves.

Liv swung her arm back like Spencer had. Started forward. And dropped the ball.

It barely missed her toe, then rolled the opposite way it was supposed to.

Katie giggled, covering her mouth with her hand. "Sorry."

Spencer had his lips clamped together, the corners of his mouth trembling.

Cheeks burning, Liv bent down to pick up her ball. "Well, that didn't go like I expected it to."

Spencer shot her an encouraging smile. "It's okay; we'll try again."

She put her fingers in the holes and faced the lane. Spencer stepped up behind her. He put a hand on her hip, and her stomach jumped into her throat. He slid his other hand down her arm and gripped her wrist. She felt his breath on her cheek when he spoke. "When I say to drop it, you let go."

With his arms around her, she could hardly breathe, much less think about a stupid bowling ball.

But since she didn't want to make a fool of herself again, she forced herself to focus.

"Swing it like this . . ." Spencer guided her arm back and then pushed it forward. "Drop it."

Liv dropped the ball. It slowly rolled down the lane. Veered to the right. And took out three pins.

Grinning, she twisted toward Spencer and found him smiling, too. Their eyes met and his grip on her waist tightened.

Her heart felt like it was trying to make an escape from her chest as she leaned in to him.

"Good job, Liv!" Katie said, throwing her hand up.

Spencer took a giant step back.

Working to hide her disappointment, Liv turned to Katie and gave her a high-five. "Thanks, Katie."

"Now you go again." Katie grabbed Liv's arm and tugged her over to retrieve the bowling ball the machine had spit back out. "And it'll get easier every time."

Liv watched Spencer sit down and retie one of his shoe-laces. Hopefully, bowling wasn't the only thing that would get easier every time. Because now that she'd experienced how it felt to be right next to him, all she wanted was to get back to that place and linger for a while.

Katie was right about how good Spencer was—he got strike after strike, and when he didn't get a strike, he almost always picked up his spares. And Spencer was right about Katie being chatty. She talked nonstop, explaining the ins and outs as they played. But she didn't mind; Katie's enthusiasm was catching, and there was something comforting about the constant chatter.

Once in a while, Liv would look at Spencer and think about the fact that he'd been arrested. But then she decided that whatever had actually happened that night, it didn't matter. The way he talked to his sister and the way he encouraged her instead of making her feel stupid—he was a good guy. That was all there was to it.

At the end of the game, her score was the lowest. By a lot.

Spencer draped his arm over her shoulders as they looked at their scores. "Not too bad for your first time. Not too great, either."

"Rude," Liv said, jabbing her elbow into his gut.

They were laughing when Spencer's face suddenly fell.

"Spencer," a man said as he approached. He was holding hands with a lady who looked quite a bit younger than he was, but too old to be his daughter. "Angel! You're here, too. What a nice surprise."

Katie ran up to the guy and gave him a huge hug. "Hi, Daddy. I was just talking to Spencer about how we used to come here all the time."

The man's attention turned back to Spencer, then landed on her. "New girlfriend?"

The serious expression Spencer wore way too often was back on his face. "Katie, get your shoes on. We're going."

"Why don't you kids stay and play a game with us?"

Spencer turned away from his dad without answering, leaving Liv standing there. Unsure what else to do, she changed out of her bowling shoes, back into her flip-flops. Then she gathered Katie's and Spencer's rental shoes and took them back. By the time she'd done that, Spencer and Katie were near the door waiting for her.

Liv glanced back at Spencer's dad, who was staring at them. "If you want to stay—"

"I don't." Spencer put his hand on her back and practically shoved her out the door.

"I do," Katie said. "We never see him."

"Just get in the car, Katie. We need to drop off Liv and get back home."

As they rode through town in silence, Liv slumped down

in her seat, thinking that no matter how good a night with Spencer started out, it always seemed to end in a quiet, awkward car ride home.

19

Looking out the passenger window, Liv's eyes fixed on the red Ford truck parked in front of the tiny, run-down house. "Oh great. She's got company. Again."

When she turned away, her bangs fell into her face. She started to brush them back, then held them up for a better look. Blond. *Glancing down, she saw not a cheerleading uniform, but a bright pink top, tight jeans, and silver heels.*

A hand wrapped around hers. "I'm sorry, baby. I know how much that bugs you."

Jace was the only one who knew what her life was really like, and even then, she hid things from him, too. She glanced at the truck again. She didn't want to talk about it or even think about it. She wanted a distraction from the anger. From the shame. She slid her hands behind Jace's neck and pressed her lips to his.

His arms encircled her, pulling her onto his lap. She pressed her body against his, soaking in his kiss, his warmth, wishing she could stay in his arms all night.

Liv reluctantly broke away and looked at the clock. "I better get in there. She's been riding me about curfew lately. Heaven forbid I don't come home in time to meet the man of the night."

Jace gave her another quick peck on the lips. "I'll call you later."

Liv got out of the car and walked up the driveway, each step bringing her closer to the last place she wanted to be. Gripping the door handle, she turned it slowly, hoping to sneak in unnoticed. She slipped inside, soundlessly closed the door, turned . . . and made eye contact with a woman with sandy blond hair—the older version of herself—coming out of the kitchen, two beer bottles in hand.

Mom set the bottles on the hall table. "Didn't I say eleven?" Her words slurred together. "You're late."

"Fifteen minutes," Liv said. "Give me a break."

"I don't want you out with that boy every night, getting yourself into trouble. The last thing I need is a knocked-up daughter."

Liv glanced at the strange man on the couch. Dozens of empty beer bottles filled the coffee table. "At least I stick with one guy."

The slap was hard enough to send her head in the opposite direction.

Cheek burning, Liv clenched her teeth and glared.

"Don't you ever talk to me like that! I'm trying to keep you from making the same mistakes I did."

"Like having me when you were sixteen? I love being referred to as a mistake, by the way. But thanks for all your help. Your World's Best Mom trophy is in the mail."

Mom shook her head and pointed down the hall. "Go to your room."

"No problem." Liv patted her thigh. A large golden retriever appeared by her side. "Come on, Duke. Let's give Mother her privacy."

Liv walked down the hall, entered her room, and closed the door behind her. She kicked off her shoes and sat on the bed. Duke jumped up, resting his head in her lap. As she scratched his ear, the silver charms on the bracelet Jace gave her rattled.

She let go of the tears she'd been trying to hold back. Her cheek still burned from the slap. Mom had probably felt bad for all of two seconds before taking those beers to tonight's one-night stand. In another few minutes they'd be in Mom's room. After they were done, he'd get in his truck, leave, and never come back.

Duke whined, like he'd been able to hear her thoughts. "Don't worry, boy. I'd never leave you with her. You're going to come with me."

She planned on getting out of this house as soon as possible. She'd been working hard—getting good grades and picking up double shifts whenever she could. Saving her money wasn't easy—especially while trying to keep up appearances for school—but she was slowly making progress, and hopefully with a scholarship, it'd be enough. After graduation, she and Courtney were going to move to Minneapolis, and Jace was hoping to play baseball for the University of Minnesota. They'd all leave this place behind. She couldn't wait for that day, when she'd be able to start her real life.

If only it wasn't two years away.

Pain shot across her head as she sat up in bed. The images from her nightmare were etched in her mind, sending a sick feeling through the pit of her stomach.

Liv lifted a hand to her cheek, feeling the ghost of the slap burned into her skin. Unexpected tears sprang to her eyes and she blinked them away. *It was just a dream. An awful, horrible dream.*

She got ready quickly, the pain in her head making it hard to focus on anything but that, then grabbed her backpack and headed downstairs for breakfast.

Mom stood in front of the stove, making scrambled eggs. Liv walked up behind her and threw her arms around her. After the dream she'd had, dealing with an overprotective mom who occasionally corrected her grammar didn't seem so bad. She still wanted to cry every time she thought about that slap.

Mom set down her spatula and twisted to face her. "What was that for?"

"I'm just glad I have you for a mom."

Tears formed in her eyes. "So you think I'm doing okay?"

"More than okay."

Mom put her hand over her heart. "That's so good to hear. I do try, but some days I feel as if I get everything wrong." She tucked Liv's hair behind her ear. "I'm lucky to have you. It's easy to be a decent mother when you're blessed with such a lovely daughter."

"I know I forget to say it, but I appreciate all you do for me."

"Well, you're welcome." Mom moved the skillet off the burner. She wiped her hand on the dish towel hanging from the stove, then pointed to a file on the counter. "I jotted down some information for you, for that paper you have to write. All the general facts about when and where you were born and other things I thought you might want to know. Such as how your middle name is Francesca because mine is, as was my mother's."

"I didn't know that. That's kind of cool. What else?"

Mom pulled three plates out of the cupboard. "Well, it was raining cats and dogs the night you were born." She dished out the eggs. "As for traditions, I suppose ours aren't that exciting. Since your father and I always had hectic work schedules, we mostly went to dinners at nice restaurants for birthdays. Christmas morning after all the presents are opened, we have a big brunch."

The timer on the oven beeped. Mom grabbed two pot-holders and pulled out a tin, filling the kitchen with the scent of blueberry muffins. She closed the oven door with her hip. "Anyway, it's all organized in that folder. Sorry it took so long. I'm finally getting adjusted to life here. It's nice to live at a more leisurely pace, and I'm quite enjoying my cooking class."

Sometimes she worried Mom was unhappy here. She spent most of her time at home buried in medical books, and she'd occasionally say something about her job at the hospital with such longing behind her words. "You don't miss your old job too much?"

Mom pursed her lips together, tipped her head one way, then the other, like she was mentally weighing her answer. "Once in a while I do. It was what I dedicated my life to for so long. But I was always working nonstop, and having a break has allowed me to get into things I never had time for as a surgeon. And I can always watch old surgeries when I start to miss it."

Liv held up her hand. "Don't remind me."

Mom laughed. "Okay, I'll save the medical talk for your father. Can you go tell him breakfast is ready?"

"Sure." As Liv walked into the living room, her gaze landed on the coffee table.

She closed her eyes, seeing all the empty beer bottles from her awful dream. Suddenly she saw a man there, too, sitting on the ratty brown couch behind the messy table, pulling on his boots.

The grin he gave her sent chills down her spine.

"Guess good looks run in the family," he said.

A growl came from next to her, and the golden retriever stepped between her and the man.

Liv's thighs hit the lamp table as she backed away. "You should go. Now."

"Relax, sugar. I's just paying you a compliment." *He stood, tipped his head at her, then opened the door.*

Liv could smell the morning air, feel the breeze on her skin.

"Livie, are you okay?"

She opened her eyes, the trashed living room, dog, and creepy man fading away. The cold filling her body didn't. Images from her dream flashed through her head: the red truck; the man on the couch; the slap; the comfort she'd taken from the dog afterward. She thought of the dog she'd met on the trail. The calm she'd felt when she ran her hands over his coat, the exact same calm she'd felt in her dream.

You know there's something more to the dreams. The hallucinations. A knot formed in her stomach, and her lungs stopped working the way they were supposed to. *No I don't,* she tried to tell herself, now on the verge of tears.

For a long time, she'd wished they'd stayed in Minnesota, thinking it could've somehow unlocked her memories. But right now she felt strangely happy they'd left, the echo of the blond cheerleader's desire to get away going through her.

"Livie?" Dad stood in the open doorway, paper tucked under his arm, brow furrowed. "What's wrong?"

"Nothing." Her voice came out raspy and choked with tears. Because the answer was everything. Everything was wrong.

⤙✦⤛

"You look like you're deep in thought this morning," Spencer said, stepping up to Liv as she walked down the halls of the school.

"That's me. Always deep in thought." She'd tried to make it sound like a joke, but it didn't come out right, and from the look on Spencer's face, he'd noticed.

He grabbed her arm, pulling her to a stop. "What's going on?"

She was going to say "nothing," but she needed someone to talk to, and Spencer was the only one who knew about her accident. "Every time I make progress with my parents, something happens that makes me wonder if they're being completely honest with me."

"That's parents for you. You're required to tell the truth all the time, but them," he said, the muscles along his jaw tightening, "they can do whatever they want and you're just supposed to accept it."

She remembered how uncomfortable their encounter with Spencer's dad had been. "Sorry. I didn't mean to bring up a sore subject. Last night I got the vibe that you and your dad don't exactly get along."

"Yeah, well, he left my mom to be with that woman. Now he's only a dad when he wants to be. He acted all hurt we didn't stay at the bowling alley, but it's not like he's made an effort to spend time with Katie or me."

"I'm sure he misses you guys, though."

"I don't know. Maybe in time we'll . . ." Spencer scuffed the tile with his shoe, then looked back up at her. "So what makes you think your parents are lying to you?"

Was she really going to do this? Admit out loud—especially to Spencer—some of the disturbing thoughts she'd been having lately? She bit her lip. "Any time I ask them about Minnesota or the wreck, it's like this barrier goes up. I just know that they're not telling me everything. And doubting them makes me feel like a bad person, because I know they love me and I know they sacrificed so much for my recovery, but they left jobs at one of the best hospitals in the nation to come *here.* Really?

"No offense," Liv added as an afterthought when she realized she'd sort of slammed Spencer's town.

"Hey, it wouldn't be my first choice, either." Spencer shrugged one shoulder. "We do get all these old people who don't want to deal with snow. But I guess that's probably not something your parents would keep a secret."

Frustration rose up in her at the thought of all she couldn't tell him. Voices. Hallucinations. Memories that obviously weren't hers. "They're constantly whispering behind closed doors, shutting me down if I dare to ask about anything in Minnesota. Then they give me these strange looks that make me feel . . . I don't know. Like they expect me to fall apart at any moment. And it's not like they planned to move here and took months to do it. It was like the second I was out of the coma, we were driving across the country, scrambling to get here as soon as possible."

Spencer's posture tensed.

She stared at him, wondering if he'd somehow figured it out already. "What?"

"Thinking of you in a coma. It's . . ." His eyebrows drew together and he shook his head. "I don't like it."

"It's not my favorite thing, either." It also made her feel like she needed to experience as much of life as she could, here and now. With Spencer. She'd come too far with him, and now she was worried she was ruining things with talk about her screwy life. "We should figure out what we're crossing off the list today." *Please tell me you still want to do something with me today.*

Spencer rested a hip on the wall next to her. "I wasn't saying we couldn't talk about the coma thing."

"I know. But I need a break from thinking about it, or I'll go crazy." *At this point,* crazier *is probably the better word.* "How about we do something low-key? I know this is going to make me sound like a wimp, but my arm's kind of sore from bowling."

"You're right," Spencer said, shooting her a devilish grin. "That *does* make you sound like a wimp."

Liv smacked his chest, glad they were joking back and forth again so quickly.

He rubbed the spot she'd hit. "Apparently your arm's not too sore to abuse me." His eyes met hers, and even though she was getting more and more comfortable around him, it still sent a thrill through her stomach. "Hmm. What to do with you?"

I definitely have a few ideas. And most of them involve your lips pressed against mine. Heat crept up her neck as she thought about kissing him. And before she realized what she was doing, she'd put her hand on his arm, just above his elbow, and leaned in, pressing herself against him.

His eyebrows shot up and his posture tensed. "Um . . ."

Cheeks on fire, she took a step back. "I . . . uh . . . we were talking about what to do tonight."

"Tonight. Right." He swallowed hard, like it took great effort. "Well, it is Friday night. You want to go to a movie? We'll do the whole theater experience and everything."

"Sounds like fun," Liv managed to say, although her voice came out all breathy. As embarrassed as she felt over her boldness, she couldn't stop thinking about how much she wanted to be that close again.

And how a dark theater might be just the right place for it.

❧❦❧

Spencer pulled his car into the parking lot of the strip mall. "Compared to the theaters in big cities, this one kind of sucks, so it's a good thing you don't know any better."

"Awesome by default," Liv said. "Hm. Maybe that's why I think you're so fun to hang out with."

"No." Propping his elbow on the armrest, he leaned in and flashed her his charming smile. "That's just because I am."

The memory of how it felt to be pressed against him hit her, and her heart picked up speed. Maybe she'd have to try it out again. Except if she thought about it too much, she'd probably end up making a fool of herself.

Hopefully, he'll do the initiating this time.

His gaze ran down her, and the temperature in the car rose. Then he straightened and she swore he was flushed. "We, um, better hurry or we'll have to sit in the crappy seats."

As they walked toward the tiny theater, Spencer put his hand on her back. Butterflies fluttered through her stomach, her skin felt tingly from his touch, and she scooted closer, getting a whiff of his soapy-clean scent.

Just short of the theater, he came to an abrupt stop.

Following his line of sight, she saw a big group of kids from school: Sabrina, Candace, Taylor, Keira, Clay, Austin, and Jarvis—the who's who of the popular crowd. Jarvis was standing close to Sabrina, his arm over her shoulders.

Spencer's muscles went rigid, his expression pinched. "Looks like this place is too crowded. Let's go do something else."

"Can't we just sit away from them? They might not even notice us."

"They'll notice us, and they'll be obnoxious about it."

An unwelcome thought entered her mind, and as much as she hated to ask, she had to know. "Is it because of Sabrina?"

She held her breath, terrified of the pain she'd feel if he said yes.

He took his hand off her back and ran it through his hair. "It's because of all of them. And I'm not in the mood to deal with it."

Liv nodded. "Okay."

Keeping up with Spencer as he walked to the parking lot was a struggle. She practically had to jog. When she was back in his car, she looked at him, wondering why he'd had such a strong reaction to seeing the other people from school.

"Any ideas?" Spencer asked.

Oh, I've got lots of ideas. I just wish you would tell me which one was right. "We can always finish the movie we started the other day."

"That works." He glanced at her. "Thanks for being so cool about everything."

"That's me. Super cool."

The smile he gave her was weak, but at least it was a smile. He started the car, pulled onto Cottonwood Street, and headed toward his house.

If he's hung up on someone else, lose him now. It's so not worth getting your heart stomped on.

No way. You can make him forget all about Sabrina. If I don't get some lip action soon, I'm going to forget how.

Too late. I've already forgotten how, Liv immediately thought, then frowned. According to Mom, she'd never had a boyfriend, so there would be nothing to forget. Unless Mom was wrong. Or didn't know.

Turning up the volume on his car stereo, Spencer said, "What about this?"

Liv sat back and focused on the music, letting it drown out the noise in her head. Heavy drums, electric guitar, and a male singer who belted out the lyrics with power but without screaming. "I like it. A lot."

"Okay, so even though you've got questionable taste, if we mix in some Metallica, then I'll forgive you for the rest." Spencer pulled into his driveway and shut off the car, leaving them in silence. "Let's go finish our movie."

When they got inside, a woman with shoulder-length dark hair glanced up at them from her seat on the couch. "I thought you were going out."

"Changed our minds. We decided to watch a movie here instead, but if you're using the TV we can—"

"Go ahead." She stood and gave Liv a warm smile. "You must be Liv. Katie's been talking about you nonstop. According to her, you're the coolest."

"Well, I feel the same about her," Liv said.

The woman put a hand on her chest. "I'm Lori, by the way."

"Oh, sorry." Spencer motioned to his mom. "That's my mom, Lori. Mom, Liv."

"Nice to meet you." Liv looked around the room. "Where is Katie, anyway?"

"She and Hailey made up, so she's over at her house. I think I'll take advantage of the quiet and go read a book." Lori handed the remote to Spencer, then squeezed his shoulder. "You okay?"

"I'm good." He looked at his mom in this protective, concerned way that melted Liv's heart. "What about you? How was work?"

"Long. But you two don't want to hear about my boring day. Go ahead and make yourself at home." She gave Spencer's shoulder another squeeze, then walked out of the room.

Spencer and his mom's interaction had been quick, but there was something about it. The natural, unstrained way they talked. The way she knew him well enough to know something was wrong, even if she didn't press him for more.

Liv knew Mom and Dad loved her, but sometimes it felt like they didn't really know that much about her.

I wonder if I'm different than I used to be. If the wreck changed my personality. Maybe that's why they give me those odd looks all the time.

This wasn't the time or place to figure that out, though. Turning her thoughts back to the present, she followed Spencer into the living room. As soon as Spencer got the movie playing, he sat next to her on the couch, leaving plenty of space between them. She thought he'd notice and scoot over, but he remained there, and since it seemed like he'd done it on purpose, she couldn't bring herself to move closer.

Once in a while she'd glance at him, wondering what exactly they were doing. Yesterday in the bowling alley he'd been close to making a move. Just thinking about the look in his eye and the way his hand had gripped her waist sent her heart racing.

Then today in the hall, she'd been the bold one, and while he'd seemed shocked, he hadn't seemed totally unreceptive. Even in the car she'd sworn they were about to cross into the more-than-friends place she longed to be.

Now they were sitting far apart, and his full attention was on the TV, like it didn't matter if she was in the room or not. The instant he'd laid eyes on Sabrina, his entire mood had changed.

Even though he denies it, what if there's still something between them?

If that was the case, Liv decided she should try not to get too attached.

Problem was, she knew it was already way too late.

20

"All that buildup and we're going to the grocery store?" Liv twisted to face Spencer as he turned his car into the Safeway parking lot Monday after school. At lunch, he'd said he was going to take her somewhere special but refused to tell her where. "I've, um, already experienced that, and while it kind of freaked me out at first, I've got it down now."

"I work here, so I . . ." He parked the car, then looked at her, brows lowered. "The grocery store used to freak you out?"

"You work here? I've never seen you." *And I hope you haven't seen me, considering the first time I came I had a mild panic attack in one of the aisles.*

"Mostly on the weekends. Now go back to the getting-freaked-out-by-the-grocery-store part."

She pulled at a stray thread on her jeans. "After only being around my parents for months, it took me a while to be normal with other people."

Her confession hung in the air, and she glanced at him, afraid he'd be looking at her like she was a freak.

"So . . . wait." One corner of his mouth turned up. "You think you're normal now?"

She shot him a dirty look. "Very funny."

He reached across the gear shifter and squeezed her hand,

causing her stomach to do a somersault. "Sorry, I couldn't resist."

"You have no idea how frustrating it is to not be able to deal with daily life. It took a long time for me to stop flinching whenever people got close to me." The fear those first few outings caused had been brutal. But now . . .

Well, now she was sitting here in a car with a boy whose warm, slightly calloused hand was on hers, her rapid heart rate from his touch instead of from fear. "So since I've got going to the grocery store down, I'm thinking maybe we choose a different 'somewhere special' to go."

Somewhere we'd be alone.

"Have a little faith," he said, squeezing her hand again. "I've got something bigger planned, but we need to go in and stock up on supplies first." He let go of her hand, and they got out of the car.

Cool air hit her as they entered the store, the sensation of going from hot to cold sending goose bumps across her skin. Spencer grabbed a small basket and walked down the aisles. She couldn't help staring, taking in everything about him. His shaggy hair, the glasses, the way the muscles in his arm moved as he twisted the basket.

"Think fast," he said, tossing a bag of marshmallows at her.

The bag hit her shoulder and fell to the ground.

"Looks like we better move 'catching' up on the list."

"Maybe if you gave me more of a warning . . ."

"That's not exactly the point of 'think fast.'"

She picked up the bag and chucked it at his head.

His hand shot up, catching it before it hit his face. "That's right. I got skillz for the billz."

Liv laughed. "I don't know what that means."

"It means I'm awesome." He tossed the marshmallows in the basket with the graham crackers and hot dogs and then grabbed a giant Hershey bar. "Okay. We've got everything we need."

"Now will you tell me where we're going?"

He brushed her hair behind her shoulder and ran his fingers down her arm, leaving a tingly wake in their path. "You're going to just have to wait and see."

Spencer drove past a sign that said Dead Horse Ranch State Park and started throwing out random facts about the park. The name made it sound like the least romantic place ever, but there wasn't a cloud in the sky, the plants were greener here, and there were all these cute little orange-and-brown birds Spencer called cactus wrens.

He slowed and maneuvered around the deep grooves in the road, the car rocking back and forth with the bumps. "Once you get the hang of a bike, we'll come here and ride some of the trails."

"I don't think I'll ever be that good," Liv said.

"Not with that attitude, you won't."

She tucked her leg under her, shifting to face him. "As you've so nicely pointed out, I'm clumsy. And I can't catch."

"You'll get over it."

"Wow. That's very inspirational. You should make posters like the ones hanging in the classrooms."

"Someone's feeling feisty today." The car slowed to a stop, and Spencer pointed out the window. "This is the Verde River. I used to come here all the time, but it's been a while."

They got out of the car and Spencer grabbed a blanket from his trunk. He spread it near the water's edge, in the shade of a tall cottonwood, sat, and patted the place next to him. Crossing one leg over the other, she sat next to him and gazed at the river.

For several minutes they stayed like that, listening to the water rushing by. It felt like they were the only two people for miles. And they probably were.

"You're the first girl I've ever been around who doesn't talk nonstop. Most girls can't stand the silence." He looked at her. "Or are you constantly holding back?"

"I don't have a lot to say, I guess. My house is usually quiet, and besides, I think you know everything about me already."

"I doubt that."

"Well, you're still plenty mysterious."

Spencer lay back on the blanket, so she did, too.

She was dying to know if he'd really been arrested, and if so, why. But every time she opened her mouth to ask, she just knew it would ruin the moment. And this moment wasn't one she wanted to ruin.

The sun dipped lower as the minutes passed, its glow dimming as sunset approached, and Spencer announced it was time to build a fire. They gathered branches and sticks and put them in the fire pit.

Spencer crouched down next to it. "Okay, so you've got your kindling, and the wood stacked just so . . ."

Liv shot him a sidelong glance. "Is there going to be a quiz later?"

"You need to learn how to start a fire."

"Where am I ever going to be that I don't have someone to help me start a fire?"

"I think I liked it better when you didn't say anything."

She shoved him, and he had to put a hand down to keep from tipping over. "I can't believe you said that," she said.

"I'd give you the silent treatment, but you'd probably like it."

"If you don't let me start this, we're not going to eat." The corners of his lips twitched as he fought to keep up his serious facade. "Now, pay attention." He held the lighter to the kindling. The flames licked at the bark, then finally caught hold. Bending close, he blew on it. The fire spread, glowing brighter with each new piece of wood it claimed.

"And that is how it's done." Spencer's eyes lifted to hers. "I wouldn't like the silent treatment, you know. Even if the only time you talk is to give me a hard time."

"Around everyone else I feel like I have to constantly be on alert, in case I slip up and don't say the right thing. With you . . . well, since you know about my lost memories, I can relax." She smiled. "The insults just pop in there."

"How lucky for me." The warmth of his grin echoed in his voice.

They sat back on the blanket again, watching the fire grow. There was something hypnotic about the flames, the way they danced and swayed as they burned through the wood. Smoke drifted over to her. The smell reminded her of something, but she couldn't figure out what. She took a deep breath—

Pain sliced across her head and she pressed her fingertips to her temples.

"You okay?" Spencer asked, twisting to face her.

"Sometimes I feel like there's a memory locked away, but I can't reach it. The harder I try, the worse of a headache I get."

"Maybe you should stop trying to remember."

She lowered her hands and tilted her head. "If you lost all your memories, wouldn't you want them back?"

He blew out a long breath. "I'd be glad to erase my past and start over."

"What's so bad that you'd want to erase it?"

Pain crept into his expression. One side of his face was in shadows; the fire lit up the other half. "If you knew the kind of person I used to be, you'd never want to hang out with me again."

Unsure what to say to that, she simply stared back. Finally, she found her voice. "The past is done, and we can't change it. All we can do is try to be better. What really matters is who you are now."

Jaw set, Spencer shook his head. The sorrow in his eyes made her want to do something, anything to make it go away. She reached out and put her hand on his heart. "You're a good person. Nothing will convince me otherwise."

"Thanks." He took her hand in his, lifted it, and kissed the palm.

Then his posture stiffened, and he dropped her hand like it had burned him. "Um, I'll grab the hot dogs and we'll get cooking."

He shot up, leaving her alone by the glowing fire, dazed and confused.

Liv pulled the front door closed behind her. *I think I could do that every night and never get sick of it.*

Even if it didn't turn out exactly like I wanted it to.

"Olivia, why didn't you answer your phone?" Mom stood in the living room, fists on her hips. "You know I worry about you. Then I couldn't get hold of you, and I started thinking the worst."

"I didn't hear it ring." Liv reached into her bag and pulled out her cell. "Oops. I forgot to turn it on after school. But as you can see, I'm fine."

Mom sniffed the air, then bent closer. "You smell awful."

"It's just campfire smoke. We built a fire and cooked hot dogs. It was really fun."

Mom wrinkled her nose. "Hot dogs? You're skipping my dinner for hot dogs?"

"Hey, Livie," Dad said from his seat on the couch. "You're home pretty late."

"I didn't really think about it. It was just so peaceful, being out in nature. The river was pretty, the weather was warm but not stifling. Then when it cooled down, we made a fire, roasted hot dogs and marshmallows, and I didn't realize how late it had gotten."

Dad came over and put his arm around Mom. The look he gave her made it clear something was up. "While you were gone, Victoria and I were talking about how much time you've been spending with this Spencer fellow . . ."

Dread crept into her chest. If they told her she couldn't hang out with him anymore, she was going to freak.

"We want to meet him," Dad said.

"I'm making pot roast tomorrow for dinner," Mom said, "and he's welcome to join us."

Liv stood there, trying to come up with an excuse for why that wouldn't work. But as she studied her parents' expressions, she knew they'd made up their minds. "I'll ask him."

A smile spread across Mom's face. "Good. Now why don't you go get cleaned up and start on your homework, and I'll be there in a little while to talk to you about a couple of things."

Mom walked into Liv's room and sat on the end of the bed. The way she was wringing her hands, looking around but never settling on anything, sent Liv's nerves on alert.

Something is seriously wrong. First they want to meet Spencer, and now . . .

Oh geez, how much worse can it get?

Then it hit her. There was only one reason Mom would be so nervous. *She's going to tell me what happened in Minnesota. They finally think I can handle the truth.* She scooted forward. All this time she'd been wondering about it, but now that it was here, her stomach was churning and her throat was dry, and she almost wanted to yell, *Wait! I don't want to know anymore.*

What if I can't handle it? What if it sends me over the brink?

"I probably should've said something earlier." Mom took a deep breath and she braced for the rest. "But I think it's time we have a talk about boys."

21

Liv took her tray of food and sat across from
Spencer. All day, she'd had trouble even looking at guys. Just
remembering the extremely detailed anatomy lesson Mom
had given her made her blush.

"So, I'm thinking that today . . ." Spencer's eyebrows drew
together as he studied her. "What's up with you?"

"Nothing." The questioning look was still on his face, so
she tried to get back to the subject. "What were you saying
about today?"

"I was thinking we should play volleyball. It's a good sport
to start on. Then once you get the hang of it, we'll work up to
basketball, baseball, and bike riding."

That reminded her of the other bomb Mom had dropped
on her yesterday. She was supposed to invite Spencer over.
"You know how I told you my mom's kind of overprotective?"

Spencer nodded. "Yeah, but don't worry. Volleyball's not
much of a contact sport."

"It's not that. It's . . . I forgot to turn on my phone yesterday and my parents called and since I didn't answer they
got all worried, and then we got home kind of late, and since
I've been spending all this time with you . . ." She took a deep
breath, then got to the point of her rambling. "They want
to meet you. I'm supposed to invite you to dinner, and you

don't have to stay, but if you could at least come in for a few minutes and meet them, then that's all they really want."

Looking at Spencer's scrunched-up expression, she knew he was about to say no.

"Are they going to ask me a ton of questions?" he said.

Liv shrugged. "I think they just want to see who I'm spending time with. We can even watch a movie or something like that, although if you have to meet them, you might as well get dinner out of it. My mom's a good cook."

He pushed the peaches around his tray with a fork. "Okay. We can spend this afternoon broadening your musical horizons."

"Really? You'll come?"

"You thought I'd say no?"

"I kinda did. I didn't think hanging out with me would be worth the hassle."

"In case you couldn't tell"—Spencer swept his arm across the empty space around them—"you're my only friend."

"I thought you liked being a loner, though."

His eyes lifted to hers. "Before it wasn't a big deal, but now that I've gotten used to talking to you, I think I'd miss it."

Liv smiled. But then she realized that meant he was coming to dinner.

With her *parents*.

"My mom was pretty horrified when I told her I had hot dogs," Liv said to Spencer as he walked her to chemistry. "I don't see why hot dogs aren't okay but sandwich meat is."

"Probably because hot dogs are all the leftover meats of every animal shoved into tube form."

She stopped walking. "That's a joke, right?"

"Does it matter? You said you liked them."

"I did, but for future reference, there are some things I'd rather not know."

Spencer's mouth turned up in a mischievous smile. "Then I guess I better not mention the animal fat they inject in marshmallows to make them puffy."

"Ugh. That is seriously sick."

He laughed. "I'm just giving you a hard time. Marshmallows are mostly sugar."

She smacked his chest with the back of her hand. "You're so mean. Taking advantage of my memory problem."

"But it's so easy. And so much fun." He glanced down the hall. "I better get to class. See you in a few."

Liv watched him walk away, then turned around and almost ran into Sabrina. Instead of sneering like she'd come to expect, Sabrina's expression stayed neutral. "So Liv, I think I overreacted a bit."

Liv looked at her, waiting for the follow-up insult.

"Like I said, Spencer and I used to date, and honestly, I was a little jealous because I thought you guys had something going on. But when he and I were together, he always held my hand or kissed me good-bye, and I can see that he doesn't like you like that. Guess I got worked up over nothing." She raised her perfectly shaped eyebrows. "So what do you say? Can we go back to being friends?"

The words took a few seconds to register. And it was hard to focus on Sabrina's question, since she'd just informed her that Spencer had no more than friendly feelings toward her. She wanted to deny it—she knew there was something there. But any time they got close to taking their friendship a step further, he pulled away.

Her heart dropped. *What if she's right?*

"Liv?"

She pulled her attention back to Sabrina. "Oh, um. Sure. We can try the friends thing."

Sabrina smiled. "And you and Spencer can totally sit by us at lunch."

"I don't think he'll want to, but that's a nice offer."

"I'm sure you could convince him, though."

Convincing Spencer to join the cool crowd for lunch wasn't at the top of her to-do list. "I'll talk to him," Liv said, "but right now, I think we better get to class."

Sabrina gestured toward the door. "After you."

Liv hesitated, not sure she trusted Sabrina's sudden niceness. *Better not turn your back on her.*

Sabrina smiled again, but it did look a little calculated.

Even supposed friends kick you when you're down, the usually perky voice added, a cold edge to her words. *Then you end up all alone, crying in the rain.*

Liv tried to follow the memory tickling her mind. She got flashes of pouring rain, felt the sensation of water running down her hair and soaking through her clothes. Grief slammed into her, so strongly it felt like her chest might split from it. Then as quickly as it had come, the memory was gone, too slippery to hold on to, leaving only an aching heart and a throbbing headache in its place.

"I'm so excited," Keira said as she loaded her books into her locker. "We can all be friends again!"

Liv closed her locker and turned to Keira. "So Sabrina and Spencer went out for a long time, right?"

"Yeah."

"Were they, like, a snuggly couple?"

"Oh, yeah. Teachers were always after them for kissing in the halls."

Great. Just what I wanted to hear.

Maybe he just appreciates that you're a smart person, so he talks to you more.

Yeah, that's what guys always go for. Intellectual conversation.

"They had their fights, too, like any relationship," Keira continued, obviously not noticing how upset the news was making her. "I certainly thought they'd be together at least until graduation, and I know Sabrina's gone out with other guys, but she's never quite gotten over him."

The thought of the two of them together made her physically ill. "I don't think she really wants to be my friend. I think she's just trying to get close to Spencer again."

Keira shrugged. "Well, right now, you know Spencer better than anyone else. Do you think it'll work?"

"I don't know." *But I hope not.*

"Heads up," Keira said, looking over Liv's shoulder.

Spencer approached, and while he didn't grab her hand or kiss her, his smile seemed to echo the happiness she felt whenever he was around. He gave Keira the nod, then put his hand on Liv's back. "I've already wrapped up everything I need to here. You ready to go?"

She nodded and walked with him out of the school.

"So," she said as they neared the parking lot, "Sabrina informed me she wants to be friends now."

"Oh?"

Liv studied his reaction, but he didn't give her much to go on. How did one look when he was hung up on someone else?

That should be easy enough to figure out. I'll just think of

Spencer and look in a mirror. "She said we're welcome to sit with her and the rest of the group at lunch."

His expression seemed guarded. "I'll be sticking to my usual spot, but you can sit by them if you want to."

"I'd rather sit with you." She bumped her shoulder into his. "How else am I going to find out everything I never wanted to know about my food?"

Spencer shot her a smile. "I strive to please." The door to his car opened with a squeal, and Liv sat down. After he closed the door behind her, he got in and turned up the music, a comfortable silence falling between them. As she stared out the window, her thoughts drifted back to that memory she had earlier that she couldn't quite hold onto. She closed her eyes, trying to focus on it again. This time, she didn't see or feel rain. She felt the motion of the car under her, saw unfamiliar tall buildings blurring past, then heard a soft female voice, drifting to her from the front seat of the car.

"You're going to have to take it easier," the woman said. "The medication will help, but . . . you scared us, sweetheart. You've got to pay better attention to how you're feeling before it gets to that point. I can't go through such a scare again."

A hand squeezed hers. Liv glanced down at the Easter-egg-purple nails, then up to Elizabeth's face. "I'll do your chores for you if you need me to. Just don't pass out again."

"I didn't pass out." Liv could still feel the throbbing knot on her head where she'd hit the tile floor. "My heart's just a dud."

Elizabeth's eyes widened and her chin quivered, like she was going to cry.

Liv patted Elizabeth's hand. But I'll keep taking the medicine, *she thought,* and it'll all be okay. Somehow.

"Liv?"

Liv jerked her eyes open and looked across the car at Spencer, doing her best to act like she wasn't in the middle of a weird . . . whatever it was. Her breaths were coming too fast, though, and she'd broken out in a cold sweat.

"What?" she asked, and the lump in her throat made the word sound squeaky.

"We're here."

She glanced out her window and sure enough, they were at her house. All the nerves from earlier that day hit her again, adding to the mess of emotions already crashing through her. For one terrifying moment, she thought she might puke in Spencer's car.

She put a hand over her stomach and took a couple deep breaths. "Before we go in, I should probably warn you that my parents are a little . . . different. I'm not really sure how most parents are, but I doubt many mothers carry books around about the human brain or watch surgeries in their spare time." *Especially not while cooking.*

Spencer pulled his keys out of the ignition. "She must be really smart."

"She is. They both are. Sometimes I wonder how they can even be my parents."

"I think that's how everyone feels at one time or another." He reached over and squeezed her knee. "Relax. I'll be on my best behavior."

"It's not really you that I'm worried about." Liv exhaled and got out of the car. She paused at the end of the sidewalk and spun to face Spencer. "You know how I told you my parents lie to me?"

"Yeah," Spencer said, drawing it out.

"What if *you* brought up them working at the Mayo

Clinic? And then you can ask why they chose to move here. They won't expect it, and then you'll be able to see for yourself how weird they get."

"I don't know, Liv. I don't want them to hate me."

Her momentary excitement faded as soon as it had come. She wanted answers, even more after what had happened on the drive over. "I'm never going to figure out the truth." *I'll just be messed up forever.*

Spencer glanced at the house, then back at her, and he heaved a sigh. "I'll try to work it in somehow."

The stress filling her slowly leaked out of her body. "Thank you," she said, again wishing she had the guts to hug him. For a moment, they stood there, the hot sun beating down on them. She took another deep breath, walked the rest of the way to the house, and opened the door. "Mom, I'm home. And Spencer's with me."

Mom appeared at the top of the stairs. "I'm so glad you came," she said as she made her way down. "I'm Victoria Stein. It's so nice to finally meet you."

"Spencer Hale. It's nice to meet you, too."

"Go ahead and make yourself at home, and we'll have dinner in a little while." Mom smiled, then looked at Liv. "I'll be cooking if you need anything."

Liv waited for more, but Mom simply turned and headed into the kitchen.

Well, that wasn't so bad. Of course, there was still plenty of time for it to sway that way.

Over the next hour and a half, Liv and Spencer sat in the living room, sharing his headphones as they listened to the playlists on his iPod.

"I can't believe you don't like 311." Spencer shook his head, like it was the most tragic thing he'd ever heard.

"What's to like?" she asked.

"You didn't give them a chance."

"Four songs was their chance, and they blew it."

His mouth dropped.

Footsteps sounded across the entry and Dad stepped into the living room. "Hey, Livie." He nodded his head at Spencer. "Spencer, I assume."

Spencer started to stand, then got yanked back by the cord still hooked to the iPod and Liv. The earphone popped out and he straightened, extending his hand. "Uh, nice to meet you, Mr. Stein."

Dad shook Spencer's hand, then they stood there, neither one looking sure what to do next.

Mom walked in and broke up the quiet. "Oh good, Henry, you're home. Forty minutes later than you said you'd be, but at least you made it in time for dinner."

"Had to follow up with a couple of patients," Dad said. "I was going to call, but—"

"Don't worry. I remember what it's like to have patients who need checking up on."

Wanting to distract from the tension suddenly filling the room, Liv said, "So do you need any help bringing in the food, Mom, or should we sit at the table?"

"You and Spencer have a seat. Henry and I will be right in."

Liv grabbed Spencer's arm and tugged him toward the dining room, praying that Mom and Dad would fix whatever was going on between them before dinner. She was already nervous enough about having them in the same room with Spencer—and that was when they were being their versions of normal.

The table was set with cloth napkins and the gold-rimmed china she was no longer allowed to carry in case her bad arm acted up. She pointed Spencer to a chair, then sat next to him. She drummed her fingers on the table, trying to think of something to say.

"Relax," he whispered, placing his hand over hers. "You're making me nervous."

"It's just that . . . they're usually not . . . But sometimes when it comes to work stuff, my mom seems—"

Mom entered the room, carrying steaming platters, Dad following behind her, his hands full as well. They set the food on the table and took their seats. The first few minutes of the meal ticked by with little conversation; Liv couldn't tell for sure, but she thought that Mom was probably giving Dad the silent treatment, and in return, he was keeping his mouth shut to avoid making her angrier.

Oh my gosh, this is so uncomfortable. I shouldn't have asked Spencer to stay for dinner. A spike of panic tore through her. *Or told him to ask about Minnesota.* She'd gotten so caught up listening to music and being close to Spencer that she'd forgotten they'd made a plan. A plan that was a really bad idea now that Mom was so pissed off. She turned to whisper to him to abandon it, but then Mom spoke up.

"So Spencer," she said. "Olivia told you about the accident she was in and all the surgeries she had to have." Mom hadn't exactly been happy that he knew, but Liv was worried it would come up and confessed that Spencer knew about the accident.

"She told me a little about it, yes," Spencer said. "She also mentioned that after she recovered, you guys moved here pretty quickly. I'm surprised you wanted to leave Minnesota behind for Arizona. Especially the Mayo Clinic." He looked at Dad. "I hear that hospital is hard to get into, since it's one of the top in the nation. I'd think you'd be bored at the dinky clinic here after working there."

"Practicing at a big hospital can be very taxing." Dad placed a hand over Mom's, and to Liv's surprise, Mom didn't pull away. "Victoria and I felt it would be better for our family to move here so she could take some time off, I could work normal hours, and Olivia could continue her recovery in a smaller, safer community." He smiled at Mom. "It's been one of the best decisions we've ever made."

What. The. Hell.

No weirdness. Totally calm. Nothing like when she asked about the move.

Spencer glanced over, giving her a *want me to keep going?* look. She felt stupid and frustrated and totally confused.

Maybe I really am going crazy. Paranoia was listed as a symptom for both bipolar disorder and schizophrenia.

"Now, back to what I was saying about Olivia." Mom leveled her gaze on Spencer. "Obviously, she has to be careful."

Liv wiped her sweaty palms on her jeans. "Mom, we don't need to get into this. He knows about all that stuff. We'll be careful."

Dad opened his mouth like he was going to say something, but Mom shot him a look and he returned his attention to the food. Apparently their warm fuzzy moment with holding hands and talking about their wonderful move was over.

"She's already been in one car accident," Mom continued in that stern, on-a-mission tone. "Her recovery was a long process and she has to take medication on a daily basis. If you're going to be spending time with her, I think you should be aware that not only does she need to be careful about germs and what she eats, but also that drinking or drugs could be extremely hazardous to her health."

The temperature in the room was rising by the second. *After being lectured by Mom, he's never going to want to go anywhere with me again. And let's not forget the fact that I asked him to interrogate my parents and they passed with flying colors.*

Spencer set down his fork and looked across the table at Mom. "I understand, Mrs. Stein, and whenever she's with me, I'll take care of her."

Mom studied him for a torturous, heart-attack-inducing eternity. Then her expression softened and a small smile touched her lips. "You have no idea how glad I am to hear that."

Liv was glad to hear it, too. But her joy faded as she wondered if Spencer only looked at her as a good friend. One who needed to be taken care of.

I didn't want to believe Sabrina, but Keira pretty much confirmed what she said. If he was *interested, he would've made a move by now.*

A heaviness centered in her chest. Because she'd been hoping for so much more than chivalry.

Liv picked up Spencer's iPod off the coffee table. She wadded up the headphones and handed it to him, along with his notebook that held the list. "311 aside, I enjoyed the rest of the music."

"You're going to like them one day." Spencer dumped his stuff in his backpack and zipped it up. "Just give it time."

"Only if you admit you like Katy Perry." She held up her fingers and pinched them together. "Just a little bit."

"Never going to happen."

Liv opened the front door. "I guess I'll see you tomorrow." Leaving the door ajar, she took a few steps outside with him. "Thanks for being cool about this. Coming over to dinner and meeting my parents." *And please tell me it's because you want to be more than just friends.*

"Honestly, I was a little worried, but it was fine. And dinner was good. But tomorrow, we're working on your coordination—as safely as possible, of course. I don't want your mom coming after me."

"I'm not as fragile as she makes me out to be, you know." She lifted her chin and put conviction into her voice. "I can take care of myself."

One corner of his mouth turned up. "Yeah, I can tell by how you act whenever you think you might be bleeding." He put his hand on her shoulder. "But don't worry, the last thing I'd call you is fragile."

She didn't know if that was a good thing or a bad thing.

He gave her shoulder a light squeeze. "I'm glad you gave me a chance even though I was a jerk. Being a loner kind of sucked."

"Well, you weren't a complete jerk. You did help me gather my papers on the first day of school." She took a tentative step toward him. "And everything after that has more than made up for the beginning."

He leaned closer, his lips moving toward hers. Her heart raced, and she automatically leaned into him.

Then he gave her a hug so short she didn't even know if it counted, and he stepped back. "See you tomorrow."

Before she could get out a word or try to put together what had just happened, he was halfway down the sidewalk. She'd been so sure he was going to kiss her, but she didn't have enough experience to know for sure. His feelings toward her were a mystery; the ache she felt as he drove away, on the other hand, told her all she needed to know about how much she cared about him.

22

Liv sat at the edge of the pool, her feet dangling in the water. "Stick to where you can touch," she said to Elizabeth.

Elizabeth splashed her. "Come get in with me."

"I'm working on my tan. Stop splashing."

"You're working on getting Andrew's attention."

Liv leaned toward Elizabeth. "Shh. Not so loud." She shook her head. "I should've never let you come with me."

"Then you'd just be the sad girl who came to spy on the lifeguard all alone."

"That's already who I am. You're way too noisy to be a good confidante."

"Is that how you treat your friends?" Elizabeth asked. "No wonder you don't have any."

Liv kicked her foot, sending water over Elizabeth. She laughed as Elizabeth shrieked.

"Oh, look how cute," a snide voice said.

Even before she turned, she knew it would be Jackie. As always, Amy and Sarah were standing with her.

Jackie tucked her blue stripe of hair behind her jewel-and-ring-adorned ear. "The snitch has no friends so she has to hang out with her little sister. How pathetic."

It wasn't like she'd called the cops or reported Jackie's drug use; she'd simply told her that she wasn't going to take part in *something that could ruin her future. Jackie had been calling her a snitch ever since.*

Jackie glanced up at the lifeguard tower, where Andrew sat, looking cute as usual. "You still thinking you have a shot with him? That he'll want to go out with a snitch?"

Sick and tired of Jackie and all her crap, Liv stood. "You're the pathetic one. You think you're cool because you party? If I had a personality like yours, I'd probably need to get wasted all the time, too."

Jackie sighed. "It's exhausting always having to listen to you preach about purpose and change and how we should try to make a difference in the world." She stepped closer. "That's why you didn't have friends before I let you join my group, and why you won't ever have any again. It's also why Andrew will never go for you."

Jackie tilted her chin toward Andrew. "He's into girls who know how to have a good time." A cruel smile curved her lips. "I showed him one last night while you were sitting at home with your family."

"You're such a liar," Liv said.

"Andrew!" Jackie yelled. When he looked their way, she waved. He grinned. The kind of grin she'd been hoping all day to get from him. Jackie looked back at her. "Gotta go. Unlike you, I have a life."

Jackie and her followers walked away. Mom had always taught her to stand up for herself; she failed to mention that sometimes making the right decision ends up making your life a living hell.

I can't believe I used to be friends with her.

Feeling depressed, she turned to tell Elizabeth it was time to head home.

But she wasn't where she'd been a minute ago.

"Elizabeth?!" Panic tore through her as she looked around. Her heart beat faster and faster as she searched the edges of the pool and still didn't find her sister.

Crouching down, she peered into the water again. Then she saw the pale skin and dark hair, arms and legs thrashing under the water. Sheer black horror took hold of her. Gaze on Elizabeth, she dove in. She gripped her sister around the waist and pulled her out of the pool.

Elizabeth sputtered and coughed.

"Are you okay?" Liv asked, wiping Elizabeth's hair off her face.

Elizabeth coughed again. "I slipped, then I couldn't get up, and I thought I was going to die."

"I'm so sorry. I just turned for a minute."

Andrew ran up and squatted across from Elizabeth. "Are you okay?"

Liv shoved him. "You should stop flirting with girls and pay attention to the pool. She could've drowned."

"I saw her right before you dove in." Andrew put his hand on her shoulder. "You did a good job getting her out." He returned his attention to Elizabeth. "Feeling better?"

She coughed again, nodded, and looked at Liv. "Are you going to say something or should I?"

"Thanks for your help, Andrew, even though you were too late." Liv eased Elizabeth to her feet and wrapped a towel across her shoulders. She put her arm around her little sister, thinking she'd never take her for granted again, and headed toward the locker rooms.

Elizabeth shook her head. "You finally had your chance and you yelled at him."

"That's because I found out he's an idiot. Besides, you're more important."

"Really?"

"Really." Elizabeth's puzzled expression caused her to add, "Plus, he and Jackie have something going on. There's no reason to chase after a guy who's obviously not into me."

Elizabeth put her arm around Liv's waist. "Any guy who doesn't see how great you are is an idiot."

"Thanks. I needed to hear that." She sighed. "You know, you're very mature for your age."

"That's because I hang out with you. And since we're being honest, I got that line off a movie I saw on TV the other day."

"Well, it works."

"I may be little, but I got your back."

Liv grinned. "I got yours, too, sis."

Liv smiled as she opened her eyes. *My sister can be a pain, but she always comes through when I need her the most.*

But then the last of her dream evaporated, bringing the painful reminder that Elizabeth was just a figment of her imagination.

Unfortunately, the building headache and the hollow feeling in her chest weren't.

Liv showered, dressed, and went downstairs, following her typical morning routine. Mom already had breakfast out— oatmeal and orange juice today. She told her good morning as she stuck two pieces of bread in the toaster.

Ask her about your sister.

I can't. I don't have a sister.

Liv picked up her spoon. Her fist clenched, the handle digging into her palm. *You know something's not right. Stop hiding from the truth and ask her!* The voice echoed through her head, making it impossible to ignore. It was the voice that usually preached about being smart and bold and independent, but it had never had such strong control over her before. Her fingers wouldn't uncurl, like her body had decided not to budge until she confronted Mom.

The toast popped up, and Mom grabbed it and placed it on a plate.

Liv licked her dry lips. "Why didn't you guys ever have another kid?" It was one of those questions that was rude to ask, she knew, but it was also rude to lie to someone with no memory.

Mom dropped the plate. It clattered against the counter and fell into the sink. From the crashing noise she knew it had broken.

"Oh, drat," Mom said, her voice shaky as she peered into the sink. "I better clean up this mess."

Liv was on her feet before she knew she was going to stand. *Don't let her ignore the question.* "Well? Why?"

Mom leaned her hands against the counter and her shoulders slowly deflated. "I told you that the doctor said we couldn't . . . It's a miracle we have you. That's enough for me. For me and for your father."

"You never thought of adopting?"

Still, Mom wouldn't look at her.

"Mom. Come on. We must have talked about this before the accident. I want to know more about our family."

"I'm happy with the family I have now. Aren't your father and I good enough?"

Guilt mixed in with determination, and she faltered now that the voice wasn't driving her forward and her body seemed to be her own again. "Of course you are. I just . . ." She didn't know how to finish, so she let the words hang in the air.

"You're going to be late if you don't hurry." Mom took Liv's pillbox off the counter, dumped Wednesday's contents into her hand, and extended them to her.

Liv hesitated, looking at the mix of shapes and colors. She recalled one of the first dreams she'd had with Elizabeth, when there'd been a similar pillbox on the dresser. She'd taken the assortment Mom was holding as long as she could remember, never questioning exactly what they were for.

In researching mental diseases, it talked about medications. Maybe some of these pills were supposed to treat bipolar disorder or schizophrenia. *If they are, they're so not working.*

"What's this gray pill for?"

"It's Neoral," Mom said. "Your immunosuppressant."

"So it would suppress my immune system? I thought my immune system was already weak."

"It helps after surgery, with . . . It's important to take."

"What about this red-and-yellow one?"

"It's an antibiotic. To help with the weakened immune system."

"And this circular white one?"

Mom sighed. "We don't have time to go over all your medications right now, Olivia. Just take them and finish your breakfast."

"But—"

"But nothing. You better be ready to go in five minutes, or you'll be grounded, and that means no spending time with Spencer or anyone else." Mom stormed out of the kitchen, leaving the shards and toast in the sink.

It was unlike her to leave a mess.

The evading, though . . .

Mom was a pro at that.

23

Clay stepped next to Liv as she headed for the doors of the school. "Long time no see. I mean, I've seen you, but I haven't really talked to you."

"I guess Sabrina lifted the ban, so now people can talk to me again."

Clay gripped her arm and gently turned her to face him. "That's not why I wasn't talking to you. I couldn't care less what Sabrina says. I just thought you and Hale were a thing. But I heard you guys are just friends."

"Well, if that's what you heard, it must be true."

"Is it?"

She hesitated a moment, then nodded. "Yeah. Spencer and I are just friends." *Unfortunately.*

"But why'd you choose to start hanging out with him all the time instead of, let's say, a nice, funny guy who tells great knock-knock jokes?" Clay grinned. "That's supposed to be endearing, not conceited, by the way."

Liv smiled back at him. "It came across as a little conceited."

"Dang it," he said, snapping his fingers. "I'll get right to the point, then. You and I should go out on Friday."

"Friday?"

"You have other plans?"

"I'm not sure."

His face dropped, making her chest squeeze.

Why am I saying no? Obviously Spencer's not interested, and Clay is. He's cute, and he made it clear he actually wants to go out with me.

And I'm dying for some lip action.

She could feel her cheeks flush. *Okay. Weird random thought.* But now that she was picturing kissing Clay, she wasn't totally opposed to it. A small voice inside her head whispered, *Just say yes.*

"Can I get back to you?" she asked. "I've got to talk to my parents first."

"Sure thing. Just let me know."

Spencer stepped up on the other side of her and put his hand on her back. "Hey."

"Oh, hey," she said.

Clay looked from Spencer—who was putting out an icy vibe, eyes narrowed—then back to her. "I'll see you later, Liv."

"Later." She waited until he'd gone a few steps, then twisted to face Spencer. "What's up?"

"We either have to reschedule our plans for after school, or Katie's got to come."

"Uh-oh. Are she and Hailey fighting again?"

"I think my mom's worried about sending her to the neighbors' house all the time. I told her I'd take care of her. Honestly, Katie's a pretty good little athlete."

"I like spending time with Katie. She . . ." Liv stopped herself before she said, *reminds me of my sister.*

"She what?"

"She should definitely play with us," she said quickly, trying to recover from the stinging reminder that she didn't have a sister.

Spencer stuck by her side. "Something's bugging you. What's up?"

"It's nothing," she muttered.

He draped his arm around her shoulders and pulled her in close. "What was that?"

Looking up at him, her thoughts changed to the mystery that was Spencer. One minute he was distant, then suddenly he was inches away, wearing an expression of concern, focusing all his attention on her.

"It's nothing I want to get into right now."

Spencer studied her for a moment.

Self-conscious, she dropped her chin and pulled her hair forward. If Spencer had any romantic feelings for her, she wouldn't think about Clay. But if friends were all she and Spencer were going to be, she needed to keep herself from falling any harder for him.

It was starting to make her crazy. And the last thing she needed was one more thing to make her feel crazy.

⸙

Liv's body was warm from the sun and the exercise. Playing volleyball with Spencer and Katie hadn't been as much of a disaster as she'd thought it'd be, so she was feeling pretty happy about life, too.

On their way inside, Katie surprised her with a huge hug. "Spencer's so much happier when you're around. He was *so* grouchy for-*ever*. But now he's almost back to normal."

Liv smiled and squeezed her back.

Spencer shook his head. "Katie, do you remember how we talked about things we should keep *inside* our heads? Especially when other people are around?"

Katie made a zipping motion across her lips. The invisible

zip only lasted a few seconds, though, and then she was talking nonstop again. On their way to the kitchen, she managed to cover a story about her friend Hailey and some show she'd seen on TV last night. She opened the fridge door and handed Liv a cold root beer.

"Thanks, Elizabeth," she said.

Spencer froze, his hand on a soda; Katie stared. Both of them wore confused expressions, and she hurried to correct her unconscious mistake. "Katie. Sorry. I'm not sure why . . ."

But she knew why. And it made tears lodge in her throat. She forced a smile onto her lips and silently chanted, *Don't cry, don't cry.*

Without a word, Spencer put his hand on her back and led her down the hall.

He opened the only door on the right, set his soda on the nightstand, and then tugged the navy blue comforter on his bed up over his pillows. "Have a seat."

Liv sat on the foot of the bed, and he walked over to his dresser and put his iPod in the docking station.

A pile of crumpled clothes was in the corner of the room; the wall opposite the bed had a bright orange poster. A basketball with flames was centered in the middle, and black names and numbers were scribbled across it.

Soda in hand, she gestured to the poster. "You're into basketball?"

"My dad took me to a Suns game a couple years ago and we got the poster signed by some of the players. I used to play a lot when I was younger. Not so much anymore."

"That explains your quick marshmallow-catching reflexes. So are you going to play for the school once the season starts?"

"Nah," he said, continuing to mess with his iPod. "Even

if the coaches were impressed by my mad grocery-catching skills, I'd rather be at school as little as possible."

"Then why do you stay after every day?"

"I just have to take care of some stuff." The music started and he turned the volume up. "Today, we're going with Green Day."

Spencer walked across the room and sat next to her. "Time to start talking. Earlier today you seemed down, then just now with Katie you looked like you were about to cry."

Liv sighed. "It's hard to explain."

"Try."

"Why should I?" she asked, crossing her arms. "You never explain anything to me."

"Um, hello? Volleyball, the art of building a fire, how to get to the slide in McDonald's . . . should I keep going?"

"I mean personal stuff. And my thing, well . . . it's going to sound completely crazy."

"Okay, now you *have* to tell me." Spencer covered her hand with his and squeezed it. "What's going on?"

She mentally weighed her answer, going back and forth on how much to tell him. She'd already made herself look crazy enough last night at dinner. But Spencer was the only person she could confide in, and not talking about Elizabeth felt almost like a betrayal to her, somehow.

"Katie . . . she reminds me of someone. I have these dreams . . ." Liv blinked away tears, hating that they came so easily. "The dreams seem so real. There's this little girl—in my dreams she's my sister—and her name is Elizabeth."

"Oh. So when you said Elizabeth . . . ?"

"Yeah. I slipped and called Katie the wrong name. When I see Katie, when I see any brunette girls around her age"— she shook her head and forced out the last few words—"I miss her. I miss Elizabeth."

Spencer didn't say anything.

Knowing how crazy she sounded, she dropped her gaze to her lap. "I thought maybe it was just a girl I knew—maybe babysat for or something like that—but my mom says I didn't know any younger girls named Elizabeth. She thinks my brain came up with the images when I was in the coma. Like a way to keep going."

"Well, she does know a lot about how the brain works."

"I know. But the dreams . . . they feel so real." Her emotions were high, and she was afraid she was about to burst into tears. She clenched her jaw, trying to keep them back.

"I'm not saying she's right. I'm just thinking out loud here, trying to sort out the details."

"I don't know if it helps, but in the dreams, it's like sometimes she drives me crazy, yet we've got each other's backs, and I love her so much I'd do anything for her. Or would. If she was . . ." She swallowed and the ache traveled from her throat to her chest. "If she was real."

"That sounds like a sister, all right. Pain in the butt half the time, winning you over with her rambling the next." He shook his head, a half smile on his face, and she could tell he was thinking about Katie.

The way he describes it is exactly how it is when I think about her. How would I know that if there wasn't something to it?

"The dreams," Spencer said, lowering his eyebrows. "That's why you're so sure that your parents are lying to you?"

"They're a big part of it. But it's more than that. I know they acted calm when you talked to them about moving, but when I ask about things . . . Something bad happened; I know it did. I feel like the dreams are trying to tell me to look deeper, which I know sounds weird, but what if my wreck was a result of whatever really happened? Like maybe I fought with my parents right before I crashed and that's why they don't want to tell me. Maybe we had a fight over pink hair or . . . I don't know . . ." She thought of her dreams with Jace. "Maybe I was hiding a boyfriend from them or something, and they found out."

"A boyfriend." It seemed like he was trying not to sound skeptical, but he didn't quite pull it off. She wasn't sure if it was her theory or her having a boyfriend that was so unbelievable.

She shrugged. "Or maybe I found out something they didn't want me to know, or . . ." She shot up. "What if I did have a sister, and something happened to her, and that's why I was driving so fast?" Her mind spun over the possibility.

Spencer arched his eyebrows but didn't say anything.

"Or maybe I just have an overactive imagination." She slumped back against the wall. "But a large chunk of my life is missing, and no matter how much I try to tell myself it doesn't matter, it does."

"I never said it doesn't matter. I want to help you, Liv. We'll figure it out, okay?"

The *we'll* made her heart squeeze. Like they were a team. Like she wasn't completely alone. A spark of hope was even threatening to break through. She let out a long breath. "Okay."

For a moment, only the sound of the music filled the room.

"I really like this group. They definitely go on the good list," she said, wanting to change the subject.

"Yeah, they're one of my favorites. Okay, since you like Green Day, I'll give you back the cool points I took away when you dissed 311."

She tucked her leg under her as she twisted toward him. "And why do you get to award the cool points? I think I should be in charge of those."

"Hm." He studied her, his lips moving to one side, then the other. She tried not to squirm under his scrutiny, but her face felt hot and her heart relocated to her throat. Grinning, he shook his head. "Sorry. Cool points are a big responsibility, and you're just not ready."

Liv rolled her eyes. "You think you're *so* funny. Well, I have some news for you, Spencer Hale." She raised an eyebrow and leaned closer.

He lifted his hand and ran his fingers through her hair. She shuddered as his fingertips grazed her cheek. She tilted her head up, waiting for his lips to meet hers.

"Must've gotten this when we were playing volleyball." He pulled a dried leaf out of her hair and tossed it on the floor.

Liv froze in place, not sure what to do or say next. It was becoming painfully clear he was never going to make a move, and now she felt stupid and disappointed. For, like, the hundredth time. He was still staring at her, too, this unreadable expression on his face. "You okay?"

No. I thought you were going to kiss me. You just lost one hundred cool points.

"I'm fine. In fact, I'm going to be completely normal for the rest of the day, no more talk of drama or weird dreams. I'm just going to enjoy the here and now."

"Completely normal?" His expression showed how unbelievable he thought that was.

Liv smacked him. "Hey. Have a little faith in me."

He ran a finger along her jaw. "I have a lot of faith in you."

She was afraid to even hope for more because she'd been disappointed too many times, and she didn't think her heart could take it. But as she stared into his eyes, she noticed a hint of vulnerability.

Then her phone rang, loud and shrill in the quiet. Spencer sat back, and she hesitantly dug out her cell, cursing whoever was calling.

Mom. Liv stared at the display for a moment, still frustrated and angry over their conversation this morning.

"I think you've been spending too much time away from home," Mom said the second she answered, not bothering with a greeting. "I want you home for dinner."

She was tempted to say, *There are a lot of things I want, too. Why do you always get to pick and choose?*

But she remembered Mom threatening her with grounding her from Spencer, and she couldn't lose the one thing holding her sanity together, even if he also drove her crazy. "I'll be right there." She hung up and looked at Spencer, wondering if they'd had a few more minutes, if something might've happened. "I've got to go home."

24

Dishes clanged together, a loud slam echoed through the air. "I understand that you're tired, but you don't ever listen to me anymore."

Uh-oh. Mom sounds upset.

"I only zoned out for a minute, darling," Dad said. "I'm sorry, but if you'll tell me again—"

Another loud slam. "Forget about it! I guess I'll call one of my friends and tell her. Oh wait, I don't have any here."

Liv wasn't sure whether to run into the kitchen and try to fix things, or run to her bedroom so she couldn't hear her parents arguing.

"I've told you dozens of times that if you want to get a job at the hospital, then I think—"

"It's too important to *think*, we have to *know*. They'll want to talk to my co-workers, and they'll want to know why I quit the Huntington's trial. If anyone digs too deeply . . . We can't risk that, Henry. Besides, Olivia is my top priority, and I'll keep trying. Because unlike you, who gets to be the easygoing one and wins her love so easily, I have to work at it."

Liv didn't want to hear any more. She walked back to the front door, opened it wide, and then slammed it shut. Putting as much volume as she could behind her voice, she called out, "I'm home!"

The house fell silent and she made her way to the kitchen. Moments ago, she was so frustrated with Mom and Dad she didn't think she could even talk to them, but right now, she only wanted to fix everything so she didn't have this awful feeling churning in her stomach.

"I thought I'd come help with dinner." She smiled at Mom. "What do you need me to do?"

"Dinner's already made. Why don't you ask your father how I made it? He's very interested in that kind of thing." Mom grabbed dishes out of the cupboard and stormed into the living room.

"She's a little mad at me," Dad said.

Liv raised an eyebrow. "You don't say."

Mom walked back into the room, yanked the silverware drawer open, and grabbed forks, knives, and spoons. "Are you two going to just stand there, or are you going to come eat?"

Afraid to say anything, Liv headed into the dining room and took her usual place at the table. The entire meal was tense. The few times Dad attempted to talk over the blaring classical music, Mom glared at him.

When dinner ended, Dad stood and started clearing the table.

"Don't bother. This is my job now." Mom grabbed the plates from him and took them to the kitchen.

"Olivia and I always do the dishes," he said as Mom came back into the room.

"Just go for your walk."

"Come with us. Then I'll take care of the dishes after we get back." Dad stepped forward and put his hand on Mom's waist.

She stepped out of his grasp. "Just go. Before I get really upset."

If she's not already really upset, I don't even want to know what that looks like.

Mom disappeared into the kitchen, and the slamming cupboards and dishes banging together resumed.

"Let's go for our walk," Dad said.

"Are you sure we shouldn't . . . ?" Liv motioned to the kitchen, then lowered her voice to a whisper. "Stay and help?"

"Trust me, you don't want to go in there right now."

"So, what happened to make Mom so mad?" Liv asked as she and Dad walked down the block.

"She was telling me about what she'd learned in her cooking class, but I had a long day at work, and I zoned out in the middle of her story. She's given up a lot, and I think she feels underappreciated."

It wasn't that she didn't appreciate Mom; she just hated how neither one of her parents could give a straight answer about the past. Part of her wanted to let it go and keep on pretending she was part of a happy, stable family. But she couldn't. Not with everything inside her unraveling more and more, all her instincts screaming something wasn't right.

She stopped walking and grabbed Dad's elbow. "Mom said that I just love you, but that she has to work at it. That's not true. I mean, I do love you. Both of you."

"We love you," Dad said.

That much, at least, she knew. Which made it hard to push forward. "Both of you get so upset when I ask questions. Like this morning, I wanted to know about my medications, and that upset her." She waited a beat to see if he would say anything, but he remained quiet. "She also got upset when

I asked her why I don't have a brother or a sister . . ." She watched Dad's face, wanting to see his reaction.

He flinched, like the words hurt him.

Liv stared, her heart beating faster and faster, the rush of her rapid pulse filling her ears. *Say it. Tell me Elizabeth's real. I know she is.*

Dad pressed his lips together and sorrow flickered through his eyes. "She tried so hard to get pregnant. She suffered through tests and hormone treatments . . . She was depressed; her moods were up and down. We didn't think we'd ever have a child."

Liv wasn't sure what was worse: the fact that she'd been wrong about Elizabeth or that she'd pushed Mom on a painful subject. "I didn't know," she said, but then she remembered Mom crying about the torn picture in the photo album. She *should* have known.

Dad gently patted her cheek. "I know you wouldn't purposely hurt your mom."

Inside, her emotions were raging. Let it go, or push while Dad was talking? "I don't want to be kept in the dark," she blurted out. "I want to know what happened in Minnesota."

Dad glanced at the sidewalk, then back up at her. He swallowed, hard, and his voice came out shaky. "Your mother and I found you the night of the wreck. When you . . . hit the tree. The car was destroyed. You were . . ." He shook his head. "There was so much blood. It was awful. We did the best we could with our skills. I didn't think . . ." He swallowed again. "You're lucky to be alive."

Dad took a step closer, his eyes locking on her. "All we wanted was for you to live. We wanted you to have a normal life, but with all the injuries . . ." He covered his mouth, looking like he was fighting tears, then hugged her tightly.

She patted his back. "It's okay, Dad. I'm okay." Now she wanted to cry. She wasn't exactly okay, but she was alive. She imagined the roles reversed, coming across someone she loved who was injured and bleeding. No wonder they didn't want to talk about it.

"If you'd like to go through all your medications, I'll be happy to tell you about them. You have other questions, come to me. But please don't press your mother about babies or her work. At least not right now, when she's still adjusting and feels like she's losing you and me."

"Okay."

"And you know your mother and I would do anything for you, right?"

"I know." The second she said it, she knew it was true. It made her feel even guiltier for questioning them when they'd done so much for her. The joy on Mom's face had been one of the first things she'd seen when she came out of her coma.

I wonder how long she took care of me, watching and waiting for me to wake up. All those months of constant care, having to teach their sixteen-year-old daughter basics all over again.

She and Dad turned around and headed home, taking the rest of the walk in silence. By the time they got back in, the dishes were done and the kitchen was empty. Liv headed upstairs to do homework. But when she sat back on her bed, she caught sight of the pink pony on her nightstand, and then all she could think about was Spencer.

Oh no, Liv thought. *Not this girl.*

Liv's blond version walked down the hall with Courtney.

Courtney looked at her, eyebrows raised. "Remember how Beth was staring at us during the assembly?"

"The assembly where we had to watch that stupid film on how Goth kids have feelings, too?" Liv asked.

"I think the point was diversity, but yeah. So anyway, during last class she wrote Jace a note saying he shouldn't be with you, he should be with her."

"Like he'd go out with her. She's plain. And chubby."

"I was thinking we get her back." A wicked smile spread across Courtney's face. "Someone needs to show her not to mess with us."

"It's not a big deal. She can dream."

Courtney nudged her. "Don't be lame. Just go with me on this."

The two of them walked down the hall toward Beth.

"Beth, hi," Courtney said.

The girl turned to them and her eyes widened. "Um, hi."

Courtney elbowed Liv.

She hesitated, glanced at Courtney, then turned on Beth again. "I hear you think you'd be a better girlfriend than me."

Courtney took a huge wad of pink gum out of her mouth and put her arm around Beth. "What's that all about?"

Beth looked from Courtney to her, panic clear on her face. "He and I used to be friends. I didn't mean ... I just ..."

Liv stepped closer. "You just what?"

Determination replaced the panic as Beth stood taller. "I thought he should be with someone smarter, someone who doesn't only care about looks and popularity. Someone who's not a follower."

"It's so cute how you think you and Jace are still friends. Turns out looks do matter to guys. So you can write all the

notes you want, he'll still be kissing me at the end of the day. He's always going to choose me."

When Beth turned to go, Liv saw the pink wad of gum in Beth's hair.

Courtney grinned. "Nice. I knew you were in there some-where." She shook her head. "Trying to act like getting revenge isn't fun."

The gum in Beth's hair, the look on her face—it made her feel horrible. She wanted to go tell Beth that she was sorry and help her get the gum out. But she couldn't do it. Not with Courtney standing right beside her. Beth didn't understand, though. Without Courtney and Jace, she had nothing. So she'd do anything to keep them happy.

That's when it hit her: Beth was right. She was *a follower.*

Liv snaked her arm out of the covers and felt around for her alarm clock. She hit the off button and lay there for a minute. She wanted to cry for the girl she'd been mean to.

I'm not a follower. I'm not a mean person.

It's okay. That wasn't me.

But the memory and the guilt felt real.

25

Liv walked up to the two Goth girls. "Hi."

They stared at her.

"I know I don't really know you, but I wanted to step out of my comfort zone and say hi to new people."

One eyebrow cocked higher than the other, the short-haired girl crossed her arms. "Are we supposed to feel lucky?"

Liv shrugged. "I just wanted you to know that I think it's cool you guys have your own style and stick to it, no matter what people say. So anyway, there's that, and I guess I'll see you around."

Okay, it wasn't enough to make up for throwing gum in someone's hair, but it was a start. Today her goal was to be kind to everyone. Even Sabrina.

Wanting to make sure she started off on a good note, she headed for Spencer's locker to get her daily dose of his cute face.

Then she saw him. Talking to some girl. It wasn't Sabrina. It wasn't a girl she'd seen before. The girl was short and wore her hair in a choppy blond bob.

Liv's heart dropped. *I thought he didn't talk to anyone but me.*

Blondie leaned in close, grinning up at Spencer. In order to keep her being-nice-to-everyone goal, she decided to head the opposite direction. It's not like Spencer couldn't have other friends; she just thought he didn't.

She reached her locker and tossed her backpack in. When she turned around, Clay was right behind her.

"So what did your parents say about tomorrow night?" he asked. "I've already seen the only movie playing and it was lame. There's not much else to do here, so I'm thinking we'll head to the party."

Going out with Clay had completely slipped her mind. "About that . . . my mom was in a wretched mood last night, so I didn't get a chance to ask."

"Oh." His blue eyes met hers, and she noticed again how good-looking he was. The only thing stopping her from agreeing to go out with him was her feelings for Spencer.

Except I don't even know how he feels. Maybe he likes the short blond girl.

"So the party? Is it always at the same place?"

"Usually we have it at The Gulch. We light a bonfire and just hang out."

"Sounds like an adventure."

"It depends on who comes." Clay pulled a pen out of his pocket, grabbed her hand, and wrote a phone number across it. "So you can call and let me know."

"I'll definitely give you a call. Either way." The halls had cleared and her class was on the other side of the building. "I better get going, but I'll see you later." She shot him a smile and headed down the hall.

But halfway there, she noticed she'd grabbed the wrong book. She was debating whether to head to class without it or go back to her locker when the bell rang.

I'm already late anyway. Might as well get the right one.

The dream she'd had popped into her mind again. All

morning she'd been bothered by it. In the few weeks of
school and hanging out with Spencer, she'd felt like her life
was clicking back into place. But every time she had one
of the strange dreams that were hard to distinguish from
reality—or, well, she didn't want to say hallucinations, but it
was hard to deny when she kept hallucinating—she couldn't
help feeling like something was majorly wrong with her.

A giggle brought her back to the present.

The short blonde and Spencer stood in the hall.

Spencer glanced up as she got closer. "Liv. Hey."

"Hey back," she said, trying to keep the irritation out of
her voice.

"What are you doing?"

She lifted her book. "Grabbed the wrong one."

The blond girl pursed her lips and crossed her arms, looking
put out by the interruption. She was much prettier than Liv
would've preferred. Tiny waist, clothing that showed she was
into fashion, and big blue eyes.

I wouldn't mind if a giant wad of gum landed in her *hair.*

Shoot, I'll help you put it there.

"Natasha and I are headed to the library," Spencer said.
"We've got this project in US history. Any ideas what subject
we should attack?"

"You know me. I'm not the greatest with history." What
she really wanted to know was how much of a history he
and Natasha had. Most mornings he came and talked to her
before class; today, he'd chosen Natasha.

Well if he wants a stupid girl, he can have her. I've got other
options.

She thought about the way Clay had grabbed her hand
and written on it. How he was always smiling and confident.

Other very cute and charming options, thankyouverymuch.

Natasha tugged on Spencer's sleeve. "We better get going."

Options or not, that girl bugged her. The day had barely begun and her goal of proving she would never be mean to anyone was already starting to crack.

"I need to go, too. I'm late enough as it is." As fast as she could move without actually running, she headed for her locker. She told herself if Spencer got a girlfriend—a girl-friend who wasn't her—she'd survive.

Somehow.

You've got to be kidding me, Liv thought as she walked into the cafeteria.

Natasha and two other girls were seated by Spencer. As Natasha talked, she gestured wildly with her hands.

I can't deal with this right now.

First period she'd gotten in trouble for being late; second period she'd been preoccupied thinking about Spencer and missed an easy question; and now—well, now that Natasha girl was starting to piss her off.

Sabrina stepped up next to her. "That's Spencer for you. One day it's you, the next there's someone else."

"He and Natasha are working on a history project together," Liv said, burning jealousy churning in her gut.

"Yeah. That's what it looks like." Sabrina tilted her head toward her normal table. "Care to join us?"

Liv sighed. "I think I will."

Sabrina offered a smile—one that actually seemed sincere.

I'm in Opposite World. Spencer's surrounded by people, and Sabrina's being nice.

"Isn't this a pleasant surprise," Clay said as she sat next to him. "I knew you weren't as immune to my killer good looks as you were pretending to be."

Liv shook her head, but she couldn't help but smile. "Keep that attitude up and I'm not calling you at all, just to teach you a little humility."

He grinned back. "Who knew there was such a sassy girl underneath that sweet face?"

"Is that a compliment or an insult?"

Clay leaned closer, eyes fixed on hers. "It's definitely a compliment."

The flirting thing was pretty easy once she got started. Clay didn't hold back; he told her exactly what he was thinking. And it was nice not to have to decode everything. Now and then she'd glance in Spencer's direction, but every time, Natasha's mouth and arms were moving.

Spencer didn't exactly look happy. His eyes were glazed over, and the more minutes passed, the farther his shoulders slumped.

Liv caught the tail end of Sabrina's story. "...told my mom that as long as she keeps ruining my clothes, she's going to have to spring for more. Usually they're just faded or she puts them in the dryer too long and they shrink. But this time, there was a big bleach stain across the back of my favorite shirt."

"The red one?" Candace asked.

"Yeah. Now it's ruined."

Guilt crept through Liv. Maybe she was meaner than she thought she was. Still, she couldn't bring herself to admit to everyone that she'd been the one to bleach Sabrina's shirt. Not now, when they might almost be kind of friends again.

She finished eating, and as she stood to leave, she glanced at Spencer's table again. He was looking directly at her. He raised his eyebrows, seemingly asking a silent question.

Taking her tray, she headed toward the exit. She dumped the food she hadn't eaten, put the tray away, and walked into the hall.

A hand gripped her arm. "Are you mad at me?"

Liv twisted to face Spencer. "It just looked crowded."

"Like where you sat wasn't. You seemed pretty cozy next to Clay."

"I was planning on sitting by you, but then I saw Natasha was there and I didn't want to intrude. I'm sure you'll have to spend a lot of time together for your project."

Spencer sighed. "It's just a history assignment."

He looked frustrated, which she hated, so she decided to change the subject. "My parents are going out to dinner tonight, so I was thinking we head to my house after school, relax for a while, then put in a little study time before our test. What do you say?"

"I'm down. But do we really have to do the math part?"

"I do. I can't get a bad grade in my best subject."

They walked to class together, and it was almost like everything was back to normal. Almost.

"Are you sure you don't want me to make you something?" Mom asked as Dad tried to lead her out of the house.

Liv turned away from the books she and Spencer had spread out on the coffee table. "Mom, I'm smart enough to feed myself." She made a shooing motion. "Now go. Have a good time."

"Call if you need anything."

"Good-bye, Mom."

Mom sighed and stepped out of view. Dad waved, then followed her into the garage, closing the door behind him.

Spencer dropped his pencil and sat back on the couch. "All day I've been going back and forth if I should tell you something. So I'm just going to spill it."

Liv tucked a leg under her and twisted to face him.

"I looked up your parents on my computer last night. There are a couple of places where you can see if there are complaints against doctors and that kind of thing."

Every muscle in her body tensed, and it suddenly took all her effort to keep the air going in and out of her lungs. "And?"

"They were clean. Tons of glowing reviews, actually. There was something about a trial your Mom was doing on Huntington's disease. I skimmed through it, but it was way over my head. Mostly, it was stuff about the brain. How it works, how the disease affects it—that kind of thing."

What was it Mom had said last night during her fight with Dad? She'd mentioned quitting the trial, but she couldn't remember anything other than that.

Spencer ran a hand through his hair. "Anyway, I wasn't sure if you'd think it was good news or bad news."

"I . . . Of course it's good news." The more information she got, the surer she was she'd jumped to the wrong conclusion. "Maybe I was wrong about my parents. After talking to my dad yesterday, I realized how hard the wreck and my recovery was on them. I think it just freaked them out."

"I'm sure." Spencer put his hand on her knee. "You good, then?"

Liv nodded. "Yeah. Thanks for looking into it."

"No problem. Now, the next question is, what are you going to cook us?"

She raised an eyebrow. "Who said I'm cooking *you* anything?"

"Let's go see what we can find, then. I'm starving."

They walked into the kitchen and she headed to the fridge. She opened the door and stared inside. "My mom made this tomato soup yesterday that was good. The leftovers are in here."

"She made tomato soup instead of opening a can?"

"These days she makes everything from scratch." Liv grabbed the jar out of the fridge.

And then her arm spasmed.

The jar fell to the tile floor and cracked open, splattering red liquid everywhere. For a couple seconds she just stared, feeling like an idiot. "Somebody kill me now."

"It's not a big deal," Spencer said. "Just watch out for the glass."

"It is a big deal. I haven't had an arm spasm in forever, but of course it happens when I'm holding a glass jar."

"Spasm?"

"From the accident. I'm really messed up. Every time I think I'm normal again, I get proven wrong." The spasm. The voices. The crazy dreams and hallucinations. Even blaming Mom and Dad for everything that was wrong.

Liv grabbed a paper towel and tried to soak up the soup. It barely made a dent.

"Where's your dustpan?" Spencer asked.

She pointed to the small closet. He opened the door, got out the dustpan, and scooped up the mess. In no time, the remains of the jar and soup were in the trash.

After wiping the floor with a rag, Liv moved to the sink to wash her hands.

"Doesn't it look like my finger's bleeding?" Spencer said, shoving his hand in front of her face.

She swatted it away. "Stop it. I don't want to see."

"No, look. Blood." He lifted it higher.

Cupping her hands, she filled them with water and tossed it at him. The water hit his face, leaving large drops on his glasses.

"Oh, it's on now." He lunged at her, wrapping his arms around her.

She screeched as he tipped her toward the running water. "No, Spencer! Don't!" The faucet got closer and she hooked her arms around one of his, squeezing in as close as she could to keep from getting wet.

"Not so funny now, is it?"

Water sprayed off the side of the sink, sending drops onto her cheek. "I won't do it again, I swear. Don't get me wet!"

His smile faded and he ran his thumb down her neck. Where her scar was.

She lifted a hand to cover it.

"Is that from the accident?"

"Yeah."

He eased her back down, then leaned forward to turn off the water, bringing their bodies together again. Her heart sped up as she felt the warmth of his body. Her breath caught as his eyes met hers. She put her hands on the sides of his waist, willing him to kiss her.

He stepped back and took off his glasses. Lifting his T-shirt, he rubbed the lenses clean, then put them back on.

Whatever was going on between them was starting to drive her insane. One minute she'd be sure he felt the same. Then nothing. "Spencer?"

"Yeah?"

"You know I like hanging out and doing things on the list, but . . ." Her determination faded, but then she thought about Clay. About Natasha.

I have to know.

"Is there something more going on between us?"

"More?"

She crossed her arms. "Don't act like you don't know what I'm talking about. I'm the socially stilted one, not you."

"It's not that I don't . . . It's just . . ." He blew out his breath. "I can't."

The words hit her like a sledgehammer. A sharp pain shot across her chest and she gripped the counter for support. "Why?"

"Because I . . . And you're . . ." Frustration filled his features, and he shook his head, then dropped his gaze to the floor.

Working to keep the emotion out of her voice, she said, "Then I guess I should tell you that I'm going to the party with Clay tomorrow."

His head whipped up. "Liv, no. Don't go out with him."

"Why not?"

Say it. Say because I want you to go out with me. Because there is *more between us.*

"Because he's a jerk," Spencer said.

Her heart clenched as her last bit of hope disappeared. "He's not a jerk to me."

Spencer threw his hands up. "Fine. Go out with him, then. See if I care."

Anger filled her. "Oh, I'm going to. It's not like I need your permission!"

He stormed out of the kitchen.

From the doorway, she watched him gather his books, sling his backpack over his shoulder, and head for the front door.

He didn't look back. Just walked out and slammed the door behind him.

The silence of the empty house rang in her ears.

Then the sobs broke through.

26

Liv spotted Clay next to his locker, talking to Austin. Because she'd been so upset about what had happened with Spencer, she hadn't called him last night like she'd promised she would. Gathering her courage, she walked over and tapped him on the shoulder. "Can I talk to you?"

Austin gave Clay the nod, then walked away.

"Sorry I didn't call. Your number smudged." She wasn't sure if it had been smudged last night, but it was almost gone this morning, so it was kind of true. "If you haven't made other plans already, I'd like to go out with you tonight."

He smiled. "Yeah?"

His enthusiasm was catching. "Yeah."

"Cool. I'm thinking we'll grab some dinner first, then we'll head out to The Gulch for the party." He put her number and address into his phone, then held out his hand. "Let me see your cell."

He took it, pushed a couple buttons, then gave it back. "Now you can call me whenever." He leveled his blue eyes on her. "And I hope you will."

"My, aren't you Mister Charming this morning?"

His grin widened. "Pick you up at six thirty?"

"It's a date."

"So, I talked to Samuel in class today, and we're going to the party together," Keira said as she and Liv headed for the cafeteria. "It'll be our first official date." She grinned and gave a little squeal. "I'm so glad you told Clay you'd go with him. Tonight's going to be so much fun!" Her face lit up. "Being with Samuel is so easy. We can talk for hours."

Spencer and I can talk for hours. Or just hang out. Things are easy with him.

Used to be easy, anyway.

"This morning he told me I looked beautiful." Sighing, Keira put her hand on her heart. "Isn't that just the sweetest thing ever?"

Spencer's never said much about the way I look. There was that time he told me I looked like a snotty, pretty girl, but maybe I'm not his type. He must like blondes. Wait. Sabrina has brown hair.

Maybe it's because I'm too needy. And clumsy.

Keira's raised eyebrows made her realize her friend was waiting for an answer. "Oh, right. Yeah. Super sweet."

The buzz of simultaneous conversations grew louder as they neared the cafeteria. Keira kept talking as they wove through the lunch line, and Liv halfway listened. As awkward as she felt about how things had ended with Spencer, she still had this urge to go talk to him.

She reached the end of the line and glanced at the table where he normally sat. Natasha and her friends were there, sitting next to him, but he had his headphones in. Looking to the other table, she saw the usual suspects.

She took a few steps toward them and then stopped. *No. Spencer's my friend. Even if we'll never be more than that, I'm not going to just hand him over to annoying Natasha.*

And how interested in her could he be if he's drowning her out with his music?

That thought gave her the courage to turn around.

"Where are you going?" Keira asked.

"I need to talk to Spencer. I'll catch up with you later." Steeling herself for a confrontation, Liv walked to the spot that had been hers until yesterday.

She smiled down at Natasha—she imagined the smile was as fake as the ones Sabrina usually doled out. "Mind scooting down so I can talk to Spencer?"

"Oh, I'm already all set up here." Natasha shot a fake grin right back. "Sorry."

I'm going to throw the hugest wad of gum in your hair.

No, I'm trying to be a nice person. I just didn't realize how challenging it would be.

Spencer looked up from his lunch.

Instead of trying to reason with Natasha, she decided to go to the source. "Can we talk?"

He tugged out his earphones and she held her breath. His expression was so grim, she was afraid he was going to tell her he'd rather not. Or worse—that he'd rather talk to Natasha. "I bet we can find an empty space at an outside table."

Natasha's face dropped, and Liv fought the urge to smirk at the perky blonde.

As she followed Spencer outside, a knot formed in her stomach. Things had been so easy yesterday and now everything felt—well, not easy. They settled at an empty table. The space between them, the quiet, it was all wrong.

"Don't worry," she said. "I'm not going to throw myself at you again."

His shoulders sagged and he sighed. "It's not that. I was on my way to apologize this morning, but you were busy talking to Clay. I assume you told him you'd go out with him."

She nodded.

"I really wish you wouldn't."

"We already went through this." Liv took a deep breath and locked eyes with him. "Everyone wants to find someone to hold hands with, to cuddle up to, someone who likes them for who they are. Clay's made it clear he likes me, so I'm going out with him. I deserve to have that in my life."

"I'm not saying you don't. You do. I . . ." Spencer hung his head, his hair falling over his eyes. "*I* don't."

She put her hand on his arm. "What's that supposed to mean?"

Without looking up, Spencer shook his head. "Nothing. Just forget it." Of course she couldn't forget it, but his closed-off posture showed he wasn't going to say any more, no matter what she did.

The silence grew uncomfortable again. She picked at her food until she couldn't stand it anymore. "I hate this. I just want to go back to the way things were before I messed them all up."

"You didn't mess them up. I swear, it's not you." Spencer finally straightened, but he didn't look her way. "You need a ride home, or is *he* taking you?"

"I can call my mom if it's a big deal."

"I'll take you." He shook his hair off his face and finally looked at her. "I'm done eating. You ready to go in yet?"

"Sure."

On the walk to class, he didn't say a word, and she longed for the carefree vibe they used to have. The rest of the day went about the same—short, stiff conversations. When he drove her home, he turned the music up loud. It didn't feel the same as the times they had listened to the songs so she could experience each one; it felt like he was purposely keeping distance between them.

When Spencer pulled up in front of her house, she grabbed her bag and reached for the door handle. "Have a good weekend."

"Liv, wait."

Dropping her hand, she turned and looked into his big brown eyes.

"Let's go to Prescott. We'll hit the mall, grab dinner—get out of this place for a while."

Staring into his cute face, she wanted to say, *Let's do it.* But he didn't want to take her on a date; he wanted to keep her from going out with Clay. Things were already strained, and the last thing she wanted was to end on a bad note, so she did her best to keep her voice even. "That sounds like fun, but as you know, I've got other plans tonight. We'll have to go to Prescott another day."

Jaw clenched, he shook his head. "I can't believe you won't just take my advice."

"I can't believe you won't just explain what's going on with you." She crossed her arms. "Tell me exactly why, tell me everything right here and now, and I'll consider not going."

Each silent second felt like an eternity. He closed his eyes and pinched the bridge of his nose, and she thought that maybe, just maybe, he was finally going to let her in.

Then he threw his hands up. "Fine. Just go."

"I will!" She flung open the door and climbed out.

"Liv . . ."

Bracing for another retort, she whipped around. "What?!"

"Just . . . be careful."

"Funny, that's the same thing Clay told me when I started spending time with you."

He sighed, then leaned across the console and looked up at her. "You've got my number. If you get in trouble or you want me to come pick you up—anything—call me."

"I'll see you later, Spencer." She closed the door and walked up the sidewalk.

Try as she might, though, she couldn't get the concerned look he'd had on his face out of her mind.

27

Clay opened the door to the restaurant and Liv stepped inside. He hadn't said much on the way over, and she hoped it wasn't because Mom and Dad had scared him. Mom had grilled him about responsible driving, but other than that, it had been short, quick, and relatively painless. Or so she thought.

The hostess led them to a booth, motioned for them to sit, placed a couple of menus on the table, and said someone would be right with them.

After reading through the menu, Liv looked across the table at Clay. "Did my parents freak you out? Because normally you're so chatty and you've hardly said a word."

He lowered his menu and peered over it. "It's been a while since I was on a formal date."

"Formal does sound scary. We should take that part out of it."

His features softened as he smiled at her. "I think that's a great idea."

It felt good not to be the one freaking out for once. Come to think of it, even the voices were quiet tonight.

What do you know? I just might have a shot at being normal yet.

As the meal progressed, conversation got easier. When

they hit a lull, her thoughts drifted to Spencer. "Can I ask you a question?"

Clay leaned forward. "Ask away."

"You and Spencer used to be friends, right?"

He tensed and gave a slow nod. "We were friends for a long time. Until he went off the grid. I don't know what he's told you, but he's the one who stopped talking to us. We all tried. For months."

"What happened? You must have some idea."

Clay ran his finger along the edge of the table, avoiding her gaze.

Why is it so hard for people to be straight with me?

"You're the only one he hangs out with," Clay said when the silence got to the uncomfortable point. "Ask him about it."

"We hang out some, but he doesn't talk much—especially when it comes to the past. I know he was arrested. That's what I heard, anyway. Something about a party."

"He did get arrested. And this kid named Peter ended up in the hospital."

That information gave Liv more questions than answers. "Who's Peter? And how badly was he hurt?"

"He . . ." Clay looked down at his plate. "He ended up in a wheelchair. After it happened, he and his family moved. It was a really sad situation." His mouth pressed into a tight line. "Let's talk about something else."

"Sorry. I didn't mean to . . ." The awkwardness was back and she had no one to blame but herself. Her mind spun over the few facts she'd managed to drag out of Clay.

Spencer couldn't have been arrested because . . . He wouldn't have hurt someone. There's got to be a good explanation.

The waiter came and asked if they wanted dessert.

"I'm full," Liv said.

Clay glanced at the waiter. "Yeah, I think we're done."

Liv stared across the table, wondering how done they were. After her questions, she didn't know if he'd even want to go to the party with her anymore.

Way to blow it with the guy who actually likes you.

Clay lifted the black binder the waiter left on the table, and she reached for her purse.

He waved her off. "I've got it."

Her vision shifted, the hazy image of the Jace guy from her dreams replacing Clay.

"I got it, babe," Jace said. "It is our anniversary, after all."

"The tip, too?" Liv knew how hard it was to be a waitress. And how much it sucked to get stiffed.

"I've got it covered. Also . . ." Jace slid a box across the table to her.

She stared at it a moment, then opened it and lifted out a silver charm bracelet. The heart caught the light; J + L was engraved on the surface. Tears filled her eyes. No one had ever given her something so nice.

Jace leaned in and put his hand on her knee. "I love you, Lin—"

"Liv?" Clay moved, bringing the real world back into focus. She couldn't even pretend she wasn't having full-on hallucinations anymore. That one had sucked her in so deep, she still felt the excitement. The love. The same tears forming in her own eyes.

So much for normal.

Working to clamp down her emotions, she took a deep breath and focused on Clay's blue eyes. "Sorry. What was that?"

"I asked if you were ready to go."

She nodded and placed her napkin on top of the table. As Clay stood and extended his hand, she took it and he pulled her up. But when she got to her feet, he didn't drop it. Hand in hand, they walked out of the restaurant.

Clay used his remote to unlock his gray Impala. He opened the door and looked at her. "I forgot to tell you how pretty you look tonight."

A flutter went through her stomach. "Thank you."

He squeezed her hand, then waved her inside. As he rounded the hood, she took a few deep breaths. *Okay. Everything's cool again. Just don't screw it up now.*

Clay pulled off the road and parked his car next to all the others. "This is the famous Gulch."

The headlights cut a trail through the dark, but she couldn't see much besides dry plants and dirt. "Wow. It's . . ."

"Just a bunch of rocks, brush, and cactuses. But down where the river used to run it looks kind of cool. Mostly we come here because it's far enough from town that no one bothers us."

The ride over had been bumpy, but the conversation had gone pretty well. They'd talked about school, people who'd be at the party, and the few bands she knew. Of course talking about music reminded her of Spencer. Even being out in the desert reminded her of catching lizards with him.

They got out of the car and met in front of the hood. With the sun down, the October night was the perfect temperature. Hundreds of stars lit the inky sky and the full moon cast enough light to see by. The moon always calmed her—something about the way its soft glow broke through, like there was still hope, even surrounded by darkness.

Clay held out his hand. "Be careful for cactuses. When we get closer to the fire pit and The Gulch, it's not as bad. Oh, and snakes. Watch for those, too."

Her gaze shot to the ground. "There are snakes here?"

"Don't worry. We hardly ever see any." He stepped closer, his hand still extended. "Are you going to leave me hanging?"

She grabbed his hand. "Lizards are one thing, but snakes?"

"I won't mention the scorpions, then."

Tightening her grip, she moved right next to him.

"Don't worry, the bad snakes rattle first."

"That's supposed to be comforting?"

He laughed. "Stick with me and you'll be fine."

The fire served as the center of the party. As they neared it, Liv recognized several people from school. Sabrina, Candace, and Taylor were in the middle of the action, laughing and flirting with a group of guys she hadn't seen before.

"Armstrong's here!" Jarvis yelled, slapping Clay on the back. He handed Clay a thick, amber-colored bottle.

She shouldn't have been shocked. She was at a high school party, after all. *What did I think they would do out here in the middle of nowhere? Of course there's alcohol.*

Clay took a giant swig, then handed it back. They stood talking to his friends, and he brought her into the conversation here and there, asking questions and making jokes. And for the first time since she'd moved there, she didn't feel too hot or nervous and fidgety when everyone looked her way.

After a couple minutes, he grabbed her hand and intertwined his fingers through hers. "Come on. I want to show you The Gulch."

Liv waved to the others and then headed into the dark with Clay. It took her eyes a moment to adjust from the bright lights of the fire to the pale light the moon provided.

Whenever a shadow moved, she scooted closer to Clay, hoping they wouldn't see any snakes.

He stopped a few feet before the ground dropped away. "I'm not even sure this is a gulch, but it looks cool."

Even though the light was dim, she could see where the stream had cut a trail. Pale orange striped through the darker red rock. The Gulch wasn't very big—probably about five feet tall and ten feet across. The bold colors stuck out, looking like someone had spent hours painting them into the brown desert. Unlike the land surrounding it, no plants grew on the hard rock walls.

"It's really cool," she said.

Clay downed whatever he had in his cup and wrapped his arm around her waist. Liv twisted toward him, enjoying the way his arms automatically encircled her and pulled her closer. Smiling up at him, she locked her hands behind his back.

He doesn't pull away. Spencer would be pulling away right now, making me feel like an idiot.

She shook her head. *Stop thinking about him.*

"Something wrong?" Clay asked.

"No." She dropped her arms and stepped back. Now she was the one pulling away.

"Want to go hang out with the group for a while?"

"Yeah. I'd like that."

He took her hand in his and they headed back toward the murmur of voices and the glow of the fire. Walking up, Liv saw Keira, who flashed her signature smile—always warm and open. She loved that about Keira.

She made her way over to her one good girlfriend and said hi. Keira introduced Samuel to her—Clay already knew him, apparently. He was cute, and the way he looked at Keira, eyes full of admiration, made it clear he was already smitten.

Good. She needs someone who appreciates how awesome she is.

"I'm going to go get us some drinks," Samuel said, smiling at Keira.

"Sounds like a good idea," Clay said. "I'm sorry, Liv, I should have asked you earlier if you wanted a drink. You want me to grab you a beer?"

She shook her head. "No, thanks."

"How about a soda? I think they've got some Coke."

"Sure."

Clay squeezed her hand, then he and Samuel walked toward the truck with all the coolers in the back.

"So, how's it going?" Keira asked.

Liv stuck her hands in her pockets. "Um. Good."

"Uh-oh. What was the 'um' for?"

Nothing got past Keira. Liv glanced around, then lowered her voice. "Well, at first it was hard to get going, but it got easier, and I'm having fun."

But I can't stop thinking about Spencer.

"No way," Keira said.

I didn't say that out loud, did I?

But Keira wasn't looking at her anymore. Liv followed her line of sight and saw the very guy she'd just been thinking about. *Spencer?*

Natasha appeared out of nowhere and cut him off. Spencer said something to her and nodded at what she said back.

Misery squeezed Liv's heart into a painful knot. *He came here for her.*

Why her? Why not me?

Spencer looked off to the right, then slowly swung left, scanning the crowd. She couldn't stop staring at him. She watched until his gaze landed on her.

From this distance and with the fire it was hard to tell, but she swore his face brightened.

She lifted her hand and waved.

He stepped toward her, leaving Natasha in the middle of her arm-gesturing story. Liv kept her eyes glued to him as he walked toward her. All around him people pointed and stared, but he didn't seem to notice.

When he finally stepped up to her, she shot him a big smile. "Hey. I thought this wasn't your scene."

The light from the fire danced on the lenses of his glasses. He glanced around, blew his breath out, then shook his head. "It's not. Not anymore."

Dying to know why he came, she almost asked. But then she thought better of it.

"So, how's your first party going?" he asked.

She shrugged. "The Gulch is cool."

His face dropped. "Of course he showed you The Gulch. So that probably means . . ."

"What?"

He kicked at the dirt with the toe of his shoe. "Nothing."

"You could drive a girl crazy with all your 'nothings.'"

A grin spread across his face. "What if the girl's already crazy?"

She opened her mouth to respond, but Clay arrived first. "Oh good," he said, narrowing his eyes at Spencer. "You're here." He handed her a big red cup and put his arm around her. Tension filled the space between him and Spencer. She stood there, unsure whether to try to get them talking, or not say anything, or—or just something to stop the weirdness.

"I'll catch you later, Liv." Spencer turned to leave, then abruptly reversed and eyed the cup in her hand. "What are you drinking?"

"Soda." Liv looked to Clay. "Pepsi or Coke?"

"Coke," Clay said.

"And what else?" Spencer jabbed a finger at Clay. "Did you put anything else in there?"

"No."

"Because of her heart, she can't have alcohol. So if you put anything in there, you better come clean."

Now she was back to feeling fidgety and way too hot and definitely not normal. She shot Spencer a look she hoped told him to stop there.

"I know it's supposed to be a secret, but he needs to know how serious this is. You could end up in the hospital. Or worse."

Clay looked at her, the concern in his eyes clear. "I didn't realize you had a heart thing . . . I swear I didn't put anything else in there, though. It's just Coke." He turned to Spencer. "Isn't that *your* trick, Hale? Slip a little alcohol in to help the girl relax?"

The muscles in Spencer's jaw tightened. "You might have her fooled, but I've seen how you get at parties, and I'm not going to let you take advantage of her."

"I just want her to have a good time, and before you showed up she was." Clay dropped the arm he had around her and stepped up to Spencer. "Just leave."

"Leaving's *your* thing, isn't it? When everything goes bad, you run."

Anger flashed in Clay's eyes and he clenched his fists. People had gathered to witness the confrontation, forming a circle around them.

Sensing that a fight was seconds from starting, Liv wedged herself between them. "Stop it." She twisted to Spencer. "Thank you for making sure I'm okay. Right now I'm hanging out with Clay, and everything's fine, so why don't you give us some space?" When he didn't back down, she put a hand on his chest. "Please."

His eyes met hers and his posture relaxed. "Fine. If you need me, I'll be over on the other side of the bonfire."

The crowd parted as Spencer walked away. Gradually, everyone stopped staring and started talking again. Jarvis and Austin came to talk to Clay; Keira and Samuel joined the group a few minutes later. Everything went back to the way it was before—well, close to how it had been before. Instead of just thinking about Spencer, she couldn't stop looking over at him. He kept on the outskirts, not saying much to anyone.

Then Natasha walked up to him, and she fought the urge to go over there and tell the obnoxious girl to stay away.

The more the guys drank, the more adventurous they got. They started challenging each other to do stupid things. Only they thought they were hilarious.

Of all the "firsts" I've checked off, this one has been the least fun.

Every so often Clay would turn and shoot her a smile, and it was nice; it just wasn't what she wanted.

Liv pulled out her phone and looked at the time. "I better get going. I don't want to be late for curfew."

Clay slid his arm off her shoulders and took her hand. "Okay, let's get you home."

He couldn't even walk in a straight line, and she realized they had a problem. "Aren't you too drunk to drive?"

"I'm fine."

The image of a rain-soaked windshield and hazy head-lights coming at her flickered in her mind. The feeling of being completely out of control engulfed her. The screech of metal against metal echoed through her ears. *No, no, no. Do not get in the car with him.*

She yanked her hand from his and took a step back. Hysterical emotions she didn't fully understand overwhelmed her. "You're too drunk. I'm not getting in the car if you're driving."

"Fine. I'll let you drive." He dug his keys out of his pocket and extended them to her.

"I don't know how."

"Don't worry. I'll help you." He swayed and then steadied himself on her.

Liv heard footsteps and turned around to see Spencer coming. "What's going on?" he asked.

"I need to go home, but Clay's too drunk to drive."

"I'll take you," Spencer said.

Clay tightened his arm around her waist. "No way. I'm taking her home."

"You don't want to get hurt, do you?" Spencer's jaw was set, fists clenched by his sides.

Is he threatening Clay?

"And you don't want Liv to get hurt, either. Right? That's why *I'm* going to drive her home." Spencer held out his hand. "Come on, Liv."

She almost took his hand—she really wanted to—but her conscience wouldn't let her leave Clay like this. "What if he tries to drive himself home and something happens?"

Spencer glanced from her to Clay and made a sort of half-sigh, half-groan noise. "Give me your keys, Armstrong."

Clay glowered at him for a moment, then handed him the keys. "Fine." He pulled her toward his car and opened the back door. "You can watch us cuddle in the backseat."

Liv stepped out of Clay's grasp. "I'm going to sit up front

with Spencer. I'm not sure I want this night to end with me being puked on."

Clay fell into the seat, a hurt look on his face.

Spencer shoved the door closed and shot her a sidelong glance. "Funny, I'd think you'd be extremely sure about not wanting to be puked on."

"Very funny."

He held the passenger door open for her, waited for her to get in, and then walked around the front of Clay's car.

"What about your car?" she asked as he slid into the driver's seat.

Spencer shrugged, apparently not all that concerned. "I'll come back for it later."

Liv wanted to hug him—of course, she always wanted to hug him, but tonight, even more than usual. With him behind the wheel, she felt safe again.

"Hey, Hale," Clay said from the backseat as they pulled onto the road, "remember that night we got wasted and woke up with cactus needles all over? There were those two hot chicks there, too. That was a really good party."

Spencer looked over at her, then back at the road. His voice was quiet when he spoke. "Yeah. The reason I know he's a jerk is because I used to be just like him. Bet you're rethinking my friendship now."

"You're not a jerk," she said.

"What did you think about me when we first met?"

"Well, your words said mean, but your actions said nice. So yes, I thought you were rude at first. But then I got to know you, and I don't buy the jerk thing."

"That's because you don't know the whole story."

"So tell me." Liv kept her eyes trained on him. "Just tell me already."

His gaze remained on the road and his mouth set in a straight line.

With every second that passed, it became clearer and clearer that he wasn't going to answer. "You know what? It doesn't matter to me. Because I know who you are now. You're the guy who made sure I was safe tonight, even though I didn't ask you to. That's what matters to me." She reached over and squeezed his hand.

He moved his hand from under hers and she thought he was pulling away, like he always did. Instead, he twisted it so their palms were together, and he laced his fingers with hers.

Heat ran up her arm; her heart raced. Worried the slightest movement or wrong word would cause him to pull away, she held her breath and stayed perfectly still.

Spencer's solemn expression relaxed. Calm replaced the storm.

When Clay groaned, Liv jumped. She'd forgotten he was even in the car with her and Spencer. "Dude, I'm so going to ralph if you don't stop taking those turns so fast."

Great. Now Spencer's going to pull away.

She braced for it, telling herself not to let it hurt her feelings. But Spencer gave her half a smile and squeezed her hand.

Clay's complaints grew louder as they got closer to her house.

"You're going to take care of him, right?" She asked when Spencer turned into her neighborhood.

Spencer let out a long breath. "I'll even let him sober up before dropping him at his house. It'll be just like old times. The old times I was really hoping to stay away from."

Liv wanted to believe things between Spencer and her would be different now. And she really wanted to lean over and kiss his cheek. But she couldn't get up the courage to do it.

You're a strong, independent woman. You don't have to wait around for a guy to make the first move.

But if he snubs you, that'll be twice, you'll look desperate, and—hello—*the guy you started the night with is still in the backseat.*

She glanced over her shoulder at Clay. His eyelids flickered; his face was pale. He rolled forward and threw a hand over his mouth.

Whipping her head away, she was just fast enough not to see it. But she heard it. As Spencer pulled up to her house, she tried to tune out the sounds of Clay redecorating the floor of the backseat with the remnants of his dinner.

Spencer flicked the buttons on the door, rolling down all the windows. "Well, guess you can check going to your first party off the list. Was it all you hoped it would be?"

Liv looked at their hands, still linked, then up to his face. She shot him a smile. "And then some."

28

All weekend, Liv had been anticipating the
moment she'd see Spencer again. His car wasn't in the
parking lot when she arrived at school Monday morning, so
she headed to her locker.

A hand brushed her back, and excitement flooded her.

"Hey, I've been . . ." When she spun around, she discovered it wasn't Spencer, but Clay. "Oh. Hi."

"I'm so sorry about Friday night. I was trying to impress
you and . . ." Clay shook his head. "I made an ass of
myself."

"I was a lot more impressed with the beginning of the
night."

"I hope that . . ." He took a deep breath and then slowly let
it out. "I guess I'm hoping you'll forgive me. That you'll give
me a second chance."

She didn't care enough about him to hold a grudge. "I
forgive you. Everyone makes mistakes." *Some just smell
worse than others.*

"You're the best." Clay surprised her with a hug. "Come
on. I'll walk you to class." He took her books and piled them
on his. "See, I'm working at being a gentleman."

Liv looked around, hoping to spot Spencer. She wanted to
talk to him, to try to figure out where they stood. But there

wasn't enough time now anyway. The bell was going to ring in a few minutes.

Ignoring Clay's extended hand, she stepped down the hall. "Let's get to class, then."

It was a relief when lunch was over. All day she'd been waiting to see Spencer, but he hadn't been in the cafeteria, and she'd ended up reluctantly sitting by Clay when he offered.

Maybe he's not here today, she thought as she headed to class.

But when she got there, Spencer sat at his usual desk in Mr. Barker's classroom, earphones in. He didn't look up when she came into the room. She took the seat behind him and waited for him to turn around.

There's no way he didn't see me.

What did you think he'd do? Proclaim his love for you in the middle of the classroom?

Of course he wouldn't, but she thought she'd be able to see a change if there was one. A stolen glance. An unspoken understanding.

Gag. That's something out of a cheesy chick flick. Guys are never like that in real life.

Unless they actually like you.

Liv stared at the back of his head, getting more frustrated by the second. *Love proclamation or not, it's supposed to be different today. We've come too far to go back to this ignoring crap.*

Sick of waiting for him to say something, she leaned forward and tugged his earphones out.

Spencer turned around and gave her the nod. "What's going on?"

That's what I want to know. "I looked for you at lunch."

"I ate outside."

She searched for something—anything—that would give her a clue as to what was going on in that head of his.

I've been waiting to see him all weekend, and this is it?

He's so frustrating. I don't even know why I like him.

She thought about the list. About how he'd showed up on Friday night. About holding hands with him. About the way she felt around him.

That's why.

When it was obvious he wasn't going to say anything else, she decided to take another stab at conversation. "Are we still getting together at your house after school? You know, to work on our assignment?"

"I guess we need to start sometime."

Well, don't act excited about it or anything. I'd hate to think you actually like spending time with me, you confusing, irritating boy.

He tapped his pencil on her desk, but it was like he was purposely avoiding looking at her. "So what's up?"

Nothing, apparently.

She sighed. "Just trying to figure out an impossible equation."

Liv's attention drifted from the open math book on her lap to Spencer. He'd hardly said a thing on the drive to his house, turning up the music so loud that she hadn't even attempted conversation. Then they'd come into his bedroom, he'd pulled out his math book, and they'd started on their math assignment.

Looking at him didn't provide any of the answers she wanted, but she couldn't stop trying to find them anyway. Spencer had gone to a party and been around people he couldn't stand. He'd swooped in when she needed him. She thought she'd finally broken through to him. Then today, the mask was up again.

"I don't get it," she said.

Spencer pointed his pencil at her paper. "Well if you apply the formula here—"

"Not the math. You. The party. I'm glad you showed up and were there when I needed you . . ." She looked into his face, praying to see a hint of the guy who'd held her hand. "But why? Why'd you do that for me?"

Spencer shrugged. "You're my best friend. Hell, you're my only friend." His eyebrows drew together and his voice came out strained. "When you asked me to make sure Clay got home okay, I thought you were just being nice. I didn't realize . . ." He shook his head. "Never mind." He stood, walked over to his dresser, and started messing with his iPod.

"Realize what?" Liv asked.

The music filling the room changed to Angels & Airwaves's "Breathe."

"Spencer, you're driving me crazy." She scooted to the edge of the bed. "Stop ignoring me and say whatever you were going to say."

He turned away from his dresser. "I saw you with Clay this morning. I'm a little surprised that after Friday night you still want anything to do with him."

"He was just apologizing."

"By putting his hands all over you?" Spencer crossed the room in a couple large strides. "That's the other reason I showed up on Friday. I was jealous."

"Jealous?" She swallowed, her words getting thicker as her heart beat faster.

"Like because you wanted to hang out, or jealous like . . ."

Leaning forward, Spencer put his hands on either side of her. "Like I wanted to tear his arms off when he had them around you."

Liv tilted her head up. Mere inches separated their lips. Her breath caught as he moved closer.

His lips brushed hers.

"Liv, your mom is—" Lori stood in the open doorway, eyes wide.

"Busted," Spencer whispered under his breath, straightening up.

"Liv, your mom is here to pick you up." Lori folded her arms and shot Spencer a stern look. "I think it's best if you two stick to the living room from now on."

Heat crept into her cheeks as she gathered her books and shoved them into her backpack. It was embarrassing, but it was also incredibly disappointing. Couldn't Lori have waited just a few more minutes?

Liv slung her backpack over one shoulder and glanced at Spencer. "See you tomorrow."

He reached out and squeezed her hand. "Definitely."

As Liv walked out of the room, Lori pulled her into a tight hug. Only seconds ago, Lori had seemed mad; now, she was hugging her so tightly she was starting to wonder if she'd ever let go.

Parents were so weird sometimes.

Liv said good-bye to Katie on the way out and then climbed into Mom's car.

"Did you get done everything you needed to?" Mom asked.

Math-wise, sure. Kissing-wise, definitely not. "I guess it's a good start."

"Well, I finished running errands early and figured I'd save Spencer a trip. We learned the best recipe today. It's really simple, too. You use . . ."

Mom went on and on about her new recipe, and Liv tried to listen. But her thoughts drifted to Spencer. How he'd said he was jealous, and how soft his lips had felt when they touched hers.

29

Liv slid into class as the bell rang. Last night she could hardly sleep, anticipating seeing Spencer again. Unfortunately, Dad had to go to work early, and Mom was running behind schedule, making her almost late for school, so she had to wait longer.

Each class ticked by at a snail's pace, and when lunch finally came, she was so antsy she could hardly stand it. Keira tried to talk to her as they walked to the cafeteria, but she couldn't focus on anything but the fact that she was about to see Spencer for the first time since their almost-kiss.

She breathed a sigh of relief when she saw him in his usual spot.

Then Natasha and her friends sat down next to him.

Why won't that girl leave him alone already?

Since Natasha had sat across from Spencer, in what should be her spot, Liv walked over to the table and sat right next to him.

Natasha frowned, a crease forming between her eyebrows. With a huff, she turned to Spencer. "So as I was saying before we were interrupted, if we go with the Tea Party thing—"

"Tea party?" Liv nudged Spencer. "You're having a tea party and you forgot to tell me?"

Spencer put his hand on her knee and grinned at her. "I'm not going to invite you if you mock it."

"We're talking about the Boston Tea Party," Natasha said, her tone exasperated.

"Then I'm out," Liv said. "Calling something a party doesn't automatically make it fun. I learned that the hard way."

Spencer squeezed her knee and butterflies shot through her stomach. "I don't know. I'm starting to think something good came from the last one I went to."

Natasha was speechless after that. Or maybe she kept talking, but Liv simply didn't notice.

On their way out of the cafeteria, Spencer grabbed Liv's hand, intertwining his fingers with hers.

"Exactly how many girls are hung up on you?" she asked as they started down the hall.

He shot her a sidelong glance. "No girls are hung up on me."

"I can name three right now."

He twisted to face her and slid his arms around her waist. "I only care about one of them."

"Who said I was one of them?"

A wicked grin parted his lips. "Who said I was talking about you?"

She smacked him on the arm and he hugged her tighter.

Someone cleared her throat. Out of the corner of her eye, Liv saw Mrs. Tully. "You two don't want to be late for class."

I swear. The universe is totally against us.

Waiting for Spencer to come out of those red double doors had never been so hard. She hadn't even bothered with digging her book from her bag. She sat on the bench, drumming her fingers, growing more impatient by the minute.

What seemed like an eternity later, he finally stepped out of the school. By the time he got to the bench, she was already standing. Then she felt stupid. And nervous.

I don't know what I'm doing. What if our heads bump together, or what if I suck at kissing, or what if he's changed his mind and—

Spencer held out a folded piece of paper.

"You wrote me a note?" she asked.

"It's the list. It's getting long, and we need to start marking things off." He tapped her hand with the paper. "Take it. See which one you want to do."

"I'm not feeling the list thing today."

"I added more stuff, though. We'll do whatever you want."

Sighing, she took the paper out of his hands. *What I want is for you to kiss me already.*

Throw out a flirty line. Let him do the rest.

Think confidence. Take the initiative.

She looked up at him. She wasn't that confident. So she unfolded the list and skimmed down it.

1. ~~McDonald's~~
2. ~~Catch a lizard~~
3. Sports: baseball, basketball, volleyball
4. Movies: Lord of the Rings trilogy. Matrix trilogy. The three Spiderman movies.
5. Music: ~~30 Seconds to Mars~~, Radiohead, 311, ~~Green Day~~, Shinedown, White Stripes, Weezer, ~~Cage the Elephant~~, ~~Angels & Airwaves~~
6. Swim
7. Bike

8. Drive
9. Teach Liv to give a compliment once in a while.
10. Bowling
11. Miniature golf
12. ~~Start a fire~~

She stared at the last item.

13. Kiss Spencer

She looked up from the list. Spencer stepped forward, wrapped his arms around her, and pressed his mouth to hers.

Her lips automatically moved against his, parting as he pulled her closer and kissed her deeper. She wasn't sure if it was her first kiss, but it was the first kiss she remembered, and it was definitely worth the wait.

30

With the kissing accomplished, Liv and Spencer decided to check another thing off the list. The plan was to go to Spencer's house and take out the second *Lord of the Rings* movie.

"By the way," she said as they drove down Main Street, "the other night I was listening to the radio and heard a song I really liked. Imagine my surprise when the deejay said it was by 311."

"I told you they were good," he said. "Which song was it?"

"'Love Song.'"

He stopped for a red light. "That's, like, their worst song." He hooked up his iPod so it would come through his car stereo. "Here's their self-titled album. It's one of their best."

The only good part about the music was watching Spencer bob his head to the beat as he drove. He turned down his street. "See, it's good."

She wrinkled her nose. "I hate it."

"That's it. You just lost two—no, three cool points."

"Not my cool points—" She clasped her hands and turned to him. "Please, anything but that."

Spencer pulled into his driveway. "Don't worry. Kissing racks up the cool points, so you've got a few to spare."

"Well, in that case . . ." Liv leaned toward him.

He met her in the middle. He brought his hand to her cheek as he kissed her, and lightly rubbed his thumb along her jaw.

Happy was an understatement.

They got out of the car and headed toward the front door. Spencer inserted the key, then gave the door a funny look. He grabbed Liv's hand and walked inside. "Katie, you forgot to lock the door. You've got to always . . ." His posture tensed.

Liv peeked around him to see what was going on.

"Hello, son." Spencer's dad sat on the couch. Katie was next to him. "I figured you'd have to come home sometime."

"What are you doing here?" Spencer asked, an icy edge to his voice.

Liv stood there, feeling out of place.

Katie's eyes widened. "You and Liv are holding hands! Does that mean that you're going out?"

Ignoring Katie's question, Spencer tightened his grip on Liv's hand. "Let's go."

Mr. Hale stood. "I just need to talk to you for a minute, son. It's important, and since you won't return my calls, I decided to stop by." He gestured to the couch. "Please sit down."

Spencer hesitated, then slowly led her to the couch. She sat in the middle, between Spencer and Katie; Mr. Hale grabbed a chair from the kitchen table and placed it across from them.

Mr. Hale glanced at her. "We were never formally introduced. I'm Carl."

"This is Liv," Spencer said. "Now, get on with whatever's so important."

The anger in Spencer's voice, the way he looked at his dad, reminded her of how he'd been back when she first met him.

It scared her, especially since she'd finally broken through to him.

And the hurt it caused Mr. Hale was evident by the sorrow in his eyes. He pressed his lips together. "Dana and I are getting married. And we want you two to be in the wedding. Katie, you'll be a junior bridesmaid, and Spencer . . . what do you say? Will you be my best man?"

"You cheated on Mom, left us for Dana, and you want me to be part of your wedding? No, thanks." Spencer stood, pulling her with him. He made a beeline for the front door, charged out of the house, and slammed the door shut behind them.

Earlier, everything had been perfect; now, she didn't know what to do.

Spencer kept his grip on her hand. "Walk with me?"

"Sure."

After a couple minutes of silence, Spencer glanced at her. "Sorry about that. I didn't mean for you to get dragged into it."

"You know you can talk to me about anything."

"I know," he said. But the silence that followed told her he wasn't going to.

A car drove by, and Spencer moved her from his left to his right.

"What's with the switch-up?" Liv asked.

"I want to be between you and the street. That way if rocks fly up or whatever . . ."

"You'll take the hit for me?" She leaned into him. "My hero."

Tightening the arm he had around her waist, he kissed her forehead.

They'd just turned onto Main Street when her stomach

growled. She put a hand over it to try to quiet it, but the sound only got louder.

"Are you hungry?"

Because she'd been distracted at lunch by the fact that Spencer's hand was on her knee, she hadn't eaten much. "Yeah." She glanced down the street. The red roof of a Chinese restaurant caught her eye.

Her gaze locked onto the building, a mixture of anxiety and excitement zinging through her veins. *Yes, there. Go into that one.*

She pointed. "We need to go there."

Liv stared at her chopsticks.

Spencer scooted forward and the plastic-y material of the red booth he was sitting on creaked. "I can never work those things. That's why I stick with a fork."

That wasn't it, though. Something tickled her memory. After a moment of staring at the chopsticks, waiting for it to come to her, she set them down on the cherry wood table.

As they sat eating, she'd occasionally get a whiff of something that would send the familiar pricking across her scalp, like there was something she needed to know about the restaurant.

What? What is it about this place that I need to know?

She ran her fingers across the table and eyed the chopsticks again. She glanced at the gold statue in the corner, something so familiar about the cross-legged figure, yet not quite right.

Try to remember . . .

Her vision went hazy, but before any images caught hold, a sharp pain spiked behind her eyes. She blinked and shook her head. Her heart was beating too fast and the noise of the restaurant echoed in her ears.

The waitress came by and refilled Spencer's drink.

Liv took a couple more bites of her food, then scooted her plate to the side. One of her chopsticks rolled to the edge of the table, half on, half off.

She stared at it for a moment. Then, without knowing exactly why, she smacked the end. The stick flipped up. Midair, she caught it in her hand.

Spencer's mouth dropped. "Okay, that was impressive. Especially considering how horrible your coordination is." He grabbed his chopsticks, set one on the end of the table, and flipped it. Into the empty booth behind him.

Liv laughed. "Smooth."

The couple seated to their left gave them disapproving looks.

Spencer leaned his forearms on the table. "You got lucky the first time. There's no way you can do that again."

She set her other chopstick on the table, smacked the end, flipping it into the air . . . and caught it.

Of course Spencer had to try again. When he attempted to catch it, he sent the stick flying toward her.

"Ah!" She dodged and it hit to the left of her. "If my light-ning-quick reflexes hadn't kicked in, I'd be missing an eye right now."

"Sorry. But for the record"—a smile spread across his face—"I think you could make an eye patch look good."

She laughed again.

The looks from the people at the other table had moved from disapproval to contempt.

"You're just jealous you can't do this." She retrieved the chopstick next to her, flipped it, and caught it.

He gaped at her. "How are you doing that?"

Liv shrugged. "I really don't know. Sometimes things just come to me." She grinned at him. "It is nice to find something I'm better at than you."

"I'm sure you don't remember, but there's this rule about not showing up your boyfriend. It hurts his ego."

Her heart picked up speed as she looked into his brown eyes. "You're my boyfriend?"

"If you want me to be."

A lightness entered her chest, happiness washed over her, and she knew she had a goofy grin on her face, but she didn't even care. For the first time since she'd woken up from her coma, her life felt right. Complete, even. "I think I could handle that."

31

Spencer rushed over to Liv as she started up the steps to the school. "If it isn't the champion chopsticker." He grabbed her hand and laced his fingers with hers.

She grinned, her skin tingling from the contact. "That's right. I'm the best chopsticker around. Scratch that sport off the list."

"So it's a sport now?"

"Hey, if there's a chance at losing an eye, it's a sport."

"That would mean the Three Stooges are a sport."

She lowered her eyebrows. "Yeah, I don't know what that is."

"You never . . .?" He shook his head. "We'll have to add that to the list."

Hand-in-hand, they entered the school. Sabrina and her group stood in their normal spot, just inside the front door. Sabrina muttered something—an expletive if she had to guess—and the entire group turned and stared.

"I'd hate to leave them with any unanswered questions," Spencer said.

Liv opened her mouth to ask what he meant. He cut her off with a kiss that made her momentarily forget they weren't alone.

Then his arm slid around her waist and they started down the hall.

She leaned her head against his shoulder. "I have a feeling today is going to be very interesting."

Keira shoved her books in her locker. "I've never felt this way about a guy before," she said with a sigh. "Every time I'm with Samuel, I think it'll never get better. But then I see him again and it does. I'm in serious like with that boy."

Thanks to the kiss in the hall that basically announced to everyone she and Spencer were together, Liv knew exactly how Keira felt. Dizzy. Warm. So excited that she practically skipped everywhere she went. It made concentrating in classes almost impossible.

"You've got it, too," Keira said. "It's written all over your face. Not to mention I saw that kiss this morning. When are you going to hook a sister up with the details?"

"Well, I liked him for a while, but he kept pulling away. But over the last few days . . ." Thinking of how great everything was now sent a thrill through her stomach. "We finally crossed into more, and I'm really happy."

Sabrina walked up, her expression far from friendly. "Come on, Keira. I need to talk to you."

Keira shot Liv an apologetic look and turned to go.

Sabrina took a few steps, then turned back and looked her in the eye. "I know him better than you do. I was there for him when his dad left. I was the one who stuck by his side, even when he started treating me like crap. And in the end, I got ignored, cheated on, and dumped without any explanation. Don't think he won't do the same to you."

Not knowing what to say to that, Liv simply stared. *She's just jealous. She'd say anything to mess up things between Spencer and me.*

"I'm not making it up." Sabrina nudged Keira. "Tell her. You're the only one she'll believe."

Keira's face dropped. "He was really drunk at that party, Sabrina. I'm sure he didn't—"

"That's supposed to make it okay?" Sabrina shrieked.

"I'm not saying . . ." Keira bit her lip. "It's true. He cheated on her at the end-of-the-year party with this skanky girl from Sedona." She mouthed, *I'm sorry.*

"I'm not some mean girl out to get you," Sabrina said. "Admittedly, I wasn't thrilled when you moved here and everyone was always talking about you, though I guess that's not your fault. But I don't think you're as nice as you pretend to be, either. I can see through your naive confused girl act."

Liv almost said it wasn't an act, but her brain was still tripping over the information about Spencer.

"So I'm not going to tell you not to date Spencer—go ahead, I'm over him." Her eyes locked onto Liv's. "I'm just telling you that you might want to be careful."

Liv's mind spun as she headed to lunch. She kept telling herself it didn't matter, but Sabrina's words had gotten to her. Rounding the corner, she almost bumped into Clay.

"Clay, hey."

"I hear you and Hale are a thing now," he said.

"Yeah, it just kind of happened. I did have fun with you, and you're a nice guy, it's just that—"

"Whatever." He shook his head and walked away.

This day is getting worse by the minute.

By the time she sat across from Spencer, she felt tired and irritated. She said a feeble hi and dug into her food.

"You're quiet," Spencer said.

"I wish today was over already."

"Well, I've got some good news. I don't have to stay after school, so you won't have to wait around for me."

"So you're done with your . . . whatever?"

"I don't have it today, anyway. So, what do you want to do?"

Keeping things from her wasn't new, but because of Sabrina's comments, it bothered her more today.

He always pushes me for details, but any time I push him, he shuts down.

It's supposed to be different now.

Or maybe he'll never let me in.

"Earth to Liv?"

"What?" She remembered the question. "Oh. I don't care. We can do whatever."

"So swimming?"

"Except that."

"Why?"

"You first."

Eyebrows knit together, he studied her. "Me first, what?"

"You never tell me why anything."

Spencer reached across the table and took her hand. "What's going on?"

"What's going on with you?" she asked right back.

"This conversation would be a lot easier if I knew what you were talking about."

"I'm talking about everything. You hold everything in."

"I don't hold everything in."

Liv raised her eyebrows. "Oh yeah? What about your dad? He shows up and tells you he's getting married, and you storm out of the house. The rest of the night, you didn't say a word about him, but I know it's got to be on your mind. He's getting remarried. That's big news."

Spencer pulled his hand away. "There's nothing to discuss. I'm not going to the wedding. End of story."

"Not end of story. There's got to be a reason why."

"Because going would be like telling him it's okay that he left us to start a new family. What he did to my mom . . ." The muscles along his jaw tightened. "He's a hypocrite. All growing up, he preached about honesty and responsibilities, then he just bailed."

"I could tell he cares about you, though. Couldn't you see how hard he was trying? How sad he was when you didn't want to listen?"

"After what he's done, he deserves to be sad."

"At least he's trying to keep you in his life," Liv said.

"Marrying Dana isn't trying. Besides, he'll just get sick of her and cheat again, so there's no point in going to their wedding and acting like it'll work." Spencer narrowed his eyes at her. "This is really what you're being so weird about? That my dad and I aren't getting along?"

"I care about you. It's not weird to want to talk about these things."

"What do you want to know? That my dad decided he was in love with someone else, then left to be with her and didn't bother talking to Katie or me for six months?" He threw up his hands. "What else do you want to know?"

"How about what you do after school, or why you're not friends with anyone anymore. Or why people tell me I should be careful around you."

"This is exactly why I tried to keep my distance." He shook his head. "I've got to take care of some things before class," he said, standing up. Then he walked away, leaving her sitting there alone, wishing she would've kept her stupid mouth shut.

Keira caught up to her after math class. The math class she and Spencer had spent ignoring each other.

"What I said about Spencer kissing that girl, that was true, but Sabrina was trying to make him jealous with this other guy first. She always leaves that part out of the story." Keira leaned closer. "The party was at this huge house—some kid's parents were gone or whatever—and people from Sedona and Jerome came, too. Spencer and Sabrina were both drunk, and she thought he was ignoring her, so she started flirting with this other guy. Instead of getting his attention the way she thought it would, he went up to this girl from Sedona and kissed her. So Sabrina walked over and told him, and I quote, 'You're being just like your jackass father.'"

The harshness of those words made her jaw drop. "No way. That's low, even for Sabrina."

"Yeah, so they got into this huge fight. I was the designated driver that night, and Sabrina demanded that I take her home. It ended up being a good thing because the cops came soon after."

"And that's when that kid got hurt and Spencer got arrested?"

"That's the story. Most kids were either gone or too drunk to remember exactly how it all ended."

"Sounds like quite a party," Liv said.

"It was crazy." Keira shook her head. "Things got out of control that night. Anyway, I wanted to tell you the full story, because I didn't want what Sabrina said to mess up things with you and Spencer."

As well-placed as Keira's intentions were, it didn't keep them from being too late.

Everything Liv did took greater effort than usual. Walking down the hall; putting her books in her locker; keeping herself from bursting into tears.

I can't believe I let Sabrina get to me.

So much for not being a follower.

Steadying herself on her locker door, she tried to figure out what she needed to take home. She'd have to wait for Mom's cooking class to let out so she could call and get a ride.

Unless I go tell Spencer I'm sorry and he forgives me. And that's what she wanted to do, but at the same time, the fact that he kept so many secrets from her still bugged her.

Do I want to be the girl who lets everything go, who never gets any answers?

How about being the girl who actually has *a boyfriend?*

Tears were threatening again and she blinked them back. Just when she'd thought she was going to get to be a happy, normal girl with a perfect boyfriend, everything got all screwed up again.

Taking a deep breath, she pushed back her emotions, slammed her locker door, and turned around.

A couple yards down the hall, people rushing around him, stood Spencer, his gaze on her.

Time to decide what kind of girl I'm going to be. Can I let go of his past, not even knowing what it is? And how important is the past anyway?

She thought about the realistic dreams and the hazy memories she kept having: Elizabeth; fighting with friends; the drunk cheerleader; the gum. Had she done any of those things?

I don't even know about my own past, and here I am, demanding he tell me all about his.

Right now, all she knew was that the distance between her and Spencer caused her physical pain. Her chest hurt so badly she could hardly breathe.

His eyes didn't leave hers as he walked toward her.

With every step, her heart squeezed tighter and tighter until it felt like it had stopped beating altogether.

And then he was standing in front of her. "Not doing this would be easier if you weren't my only friend."

Oh my gosh. He's breaking up with me.

A giant lump formed in her throat.

"Or if you weren't so fun to be around." He ran his hand down her arm. "Or if you weren't so damn cute."

Liv took a deep breath, trying and failing to keep her voice steady. "You think I'm cute?"

"Damn cute." A fleeting smile crossed his lips, then his expression returned to serious. "You're the one person whose opinion I care about. When I'm with you, the past disappears, and I'm a better person."

She closed the gap between them and wrapped her arms around his waist.

His arms encircled her and his lips brushed her temple as he spoke. "I knew I was a goner after we went lizard hunting."

She looked up at him. "Then why'd you fight it so long?"

He turned his head away. "I don't deserve to be happy. I've done some awful things, Liv."

"When I came here, I didn't know who I was. I had a hard time just being in public." She put her hand on the side of his face. "Meeting you is the best thing that ever happened to me. Nothing you—or anyone else for that matter—say will change what I think about you."

He grabbed her hand and pulled her toward the exit. "I guess there's only one way to prove your theory."

32

When Spencer said he wanted to prove her theory, the last place she thought they'd end up was the grocery store.

"So, what are we here for?" she asked as she and Spencer walked inside.

"Before we sit down and face reality, I'm reminding you of the perks of dating a bag boy."

Liv shot him a smile. "Why do good girls always go for bag boys?"

He shook his head, a smile beginning to break free. "Funny." He paused in front of the meat section. "Hamburgers are a little trickier than hot dogs, but we could cook them if you'd rather have one."

She turned her attention to the meat display in front of her. Looking at the blood pooling in the packages of beef made her dizzy.

Blood poured down, soaking her shirt, leaving large drops on her jeans.

You're going to die.

Diverting her eyes to the floor, she backed away from the meat. She turned and gripped the edge of one of the nearby freezers and took a couple of deep breaths.

Spencer put his hand on her back. "Are you okay?"

"It's the blood." She closed her eyes. "There was . . ." A wave of nausea rolled through her stomach. From the memory, from the awful feeling of the life slowly draining from her, or from that thought—*You're going to die*—she wasn't sure.

"Maybe I should take you home," he said.

She forced herself up. She was finally going to learn more about him, and what happened at that infamous party. No way she was giving that up. "I'm fine. Let's just stick with hot dogs."

They loaded up on hot dogs, candy, and root beer—using Spencer's discount—then got back into his car and headed to Dead Horse Ranch.

Spencer pulled up to the same spot they'd come before. They gathered wood for a fire and stacked it in the pit. "Now we'll see if you were paying attention," he said, handing her the lighter.

Liv lit the kindling and gently blew on it. At first nothing. Then the flame spread. "How many cool points is that worth?"

"So many that you finally get your wish of being in charge of them."

Sitting on the blanket, they ate their food and watched the fire. The moon looked bigger and closer than usual. Like if they drove across the desert she could reach out and touch it.

Spencer took her hand in his. "I guess there's no such thing as a secret in a small town. That's how my dad got caught. Someone saw him out at a bar with Dana and told my mom."

"That must've been awful for Lori."

"She didn't want to believe it—things get blown out of proportion in a small town, too. But when my mom confronted him, he told her that he'd fallen in love with Dana, and that he wanted to be with her." Sadness crept across Spencer's features. "I think it would've been easier if I hadn't been so close to him. We played ball, went bowling, watched sports, all that normal father-and-son stuff. One day he's the dad I admired, the next everything fell apart and he was just gone."

Spencer ran a hand through his hair. "He always told me that the one thing he'd never tolerate was a liar. If he caught me telling a lie, I got whooped. When my baseball went through Mrs. O'Brian's window, he marched me over, had me apologize, and made me do her yard work all summer." His mouth set in a tight line. "Then he ended up being the biggest liar of all. My mom was devastated."

"At least she had you," she said.

He hung his head. "She didn't, though. I was pissed at my dad, at life, at everything. I started fighting with her, getting in trouble at school and drinking all the time. Then the end-of-the-year party came . . ." His eyes lifted to hers. "I'm sure you've heard parts of the story."

"No one seems to know what really happened. But it doesn't matter."

"As wasted as I was, I remember exactly what happened. And believe me, it mattered to one person."

Her voice came out just above a whisper. "The kid who got hurt?"

"You know how it happened?"

She shook her head. "Just that he's in a wheelchair."

"It's my fault."

"Spencer, whatever happened—"

"It's my fault, Liv. It's my fault he's in that wheelchair." The agony in his voice made her want to cry. She tightened her grip on his hand.

"Peter moved here freshman year. He was a huge nerd, had

no sports skills, and was overweight. I'd never really talked to him before that night. He was just a guy who wanted to be *in*, and when he came to the party, we all took advantage of that. So yeah, I was drunk—we were all drunk. Sabrina and I were dating, we got into a fight, and I made out with some other chick." His shoulders slumped. "Definitely not my finest hour. But that wasn't even the worst thing I did ..."

The muscles in his neck and jaw tightened, and she could tell how hard he was fighting to hold it together. "Toward the end of the night, Peter comes up to me, Clay, Austin, and Jarvis. The guy's wasted, spouting off all this junk about how he's got a black belt in karate. So we started challenging him to do stuff. He danced, he did kicks, and he tried to break a board."

The flames reflected off Spencer's lenses, and for a moment the only sound was the crackling of the fire. Liv didn't move, didn't breathe, as a tortured expression overtook his face. "I dared him to jump off the roof onto the trampoline."

She brought her hands to her mouth, knowing that the rest of the story was going to be bad.

"I didn't think he'd even be able to climb that high. He'd barely gotten up on the roof when someone yelled that the cops were there. People scattered in all directions. And Peter ..." Spencer swallowed and then choked out the next words. "Jumped. And landed on the concrete patio.

"I don't know how many others saw, but no one slowed down. I ran over and told him to get up, that we had to go. Then I saw the blood. His eyes were wide, and when he looked up, I saw the fear." All the color drained from Spencer's face; sorrow filled his voice. "He told me he couldn't feel his legs. And the way he looked at me—like I'd know what to do, like I'd be able to help him somehow."

Spencer used his thumb to wipe the tear rolling down Liv's cheek. She hadn't even realized she'd started crying. She wanted to say something to him that would make it all okay, but the ache in her throat made it impossible to talk, and even if she could speak, she had no idea what to say.

"The cops came and arrested me for underage drinking. They wouldn't even let me stay with Peter." He shook his head. "A fall like that, a stupid stunt, and now he'll never walk again. I'm the one who told him to jump. Like with your accident. One wrong move, one instant. And you can never take it back."

Spencer's eyes glazed over. "I ruined his life. I'm the guy who ruined someone's life for a joke. That's why I don't deserve to be happy. I don't deserve to be with someone like you."

The torment he obviously felt broke her heart. More than anything, she wanted to make it better—to be able to take his pain away. Pushing up on her knees, she wrapped her arms around him.

He tensed.

Then he put his arms around her and rested his head on her shoulder. The right words didn't come, so she simply held on, wishing she'd never have to let go.

"Are you okay?" Mom asked her when she walked into the living room to tell her that she was home.

Liv was emotionally and physically drained, but she thought she'd done a good job of masking it. "How'd you—?"

"Mothers can sense these things." Mom patted the cushion next to her. "Have a seat." Liv sat, and Mom tucked her hair behind her ear. "So, what's going on?"

Explaining wasn't going to be easy. She didn't want to get into the whole story—especially because it wasn't her story to tell. "I guess I just realized how everything we do affects not only our lives, but people around us, too. It sucks that one weak moment could change the entire course of someone's life."

The creases in Mom's forehead deepened. "Language, Olivia. *Sucks* is not a word I want to hear from you. As for the sentiment behind the language, what happened to bring this all up?"

Again, she thought about Spencer and the night that had changed his and Peter's lives forever. "I got to thinking about how decisions we make, one little moment, could change everything. Like with my accident. I wrecked, and now I have no memories. You and Dad had to help me recover and we moved. All that basically happened because of something I did."

"There was the storm, and who knows how many other factors involved. I don't want you to feel bad because of the accident." Mom leveled her gaze on her, eyebrows raised. "You hear me?"

Liv nodded. "I do. I guess I'm just wondering how we get over our past mistakes." *And how do I help Spencer get over his? How do I make him realize what a good person he is?*

Mom pressed her lips together, seemingly deep in thought, then let out a long exhale. "Life is full of hard choices, and making mistakes is part of that. There are decisions I've made that have caused grief not only for myself, but also for people I care about, and people I don't even know. And I might feel guilt over them for the rest of my life . . . but I'd probably do them again because of what's happened in my life because of it.

"You talk about one moment changing everything. You coming into our lives, that definitely changed everything, and I'll be forever grateful you lived through that accident." Mom draped her arm around Liv's shoulders and pulled her in next to her. "You're one of my proudest accomplishments, Olivia. I'd be lost without you."

Resting her head against Mom's shoulder, she caught a whiff of her vanilla perfume. The familiar smell, being able to talk to her like this, made her realize how much they'd both grown since moving to Cottonwood. Little by little Mom was learning to let go, and she was getting the hang of life, figuring out who she really was.

Once in a while, she still longed to remember, longed to find the missing pieces in the puzzle. But then she remembered the heart-wrenching look on Spencer's face, the deep regret in his eyes.

She thought about how she knew her parents were hiding something. Words Dad had said on their walk the other night popped into her mind: *You know your mother and I would do anything for you, right?*

Cold spread through her entire body. All this time, she thought Mom and Dad were hiding because *they'd* done something in Minnesota. The thought suddenly occurred to her that they might be hiding something *she* had done. And it was clear they were terrified someone might find out about it.

Maybe Spencer was right when he said I was better off not remembering all the crappy things I've done.

33

As they went through their morning at school,
Liv would occasionally catch Spencer looking at her, this
indecipherable expression on his face. Then he'd give her a
smile, grab her hand, kiss her cheek, or some other gesture
that made her heart go all fluttery.

After lunch, he pulled her into a remote area in the hall
and wrapped his arms around her waist. "I was so worried
that after last night . . ." He placed his forehead against hers.
"I don't know how I got so lucky."

"You don't give yourself enough credit. You're one of the
most awesome people I've ever met."

"Yeah, but you don't remember most of the people you've
met, so that's not saying much."

She gave him a playful shove. "Come on, you know what
I'm saying."

He caught her arm, yanked her back to him, and kissed
her. She parted her lips as he deepened the kiss, slipping his
tongue in to meet hers.

A group neared, their conversation growing louder, and
Spencer pulled back. More and more people entered the
hallway, ruining their chance to be alone.

With a sigh, he grabbed her hand and led her down the
hall. As they rounded the corner, they came face-to-face with

Clay. His features hardened; Spencer's grip tightened.

This is ridiculous. "Hey, Clay, how's it going?"

Clay mumbled a "fine," then kept walking, and she twisted to face Spencer. "So, when are you and Clay going to get over your thing?"

"Our thing?"

"I know you used to be friends, and I know that you stopped talking to everyone after the party, but I guess I'm not getting exactly why."

"That night, I realized all the people who were supposed to be my friends just left. They didn't even care that Peter was hurt." His expression hardened. "That's not the kind of friends I want to have."

Liv glanced around. They didn't have much time before class started. "When I went out with Clay—"

"I don't want to hear about that. I know he showed you The Gulch, which is his signature . . ." He shook his head. "I'd rather pretend it didn't happen."

"Nothing did happen. I mean, we never kissed or anything, if that's what you were thinking."

That news took some of the tension out of his features.

"Before we went to The Gulch, I wanted to find out more about the notorious party. Really, I wanted to know more about you. So I asked him what happened. He didn't say much, only that someone was hurt, but I could tell he felt horrible about it." She squeezed Spencer's hand. "You two probably have more in common than you think."

He stood there for a moment, shifting his weight from side to side. "I don't know what to say to that. No matter what, I'm a hypocrite. For not forgiving him, and for not forgiving my dad. I'd like to say I can let it all go, but I'm not as good as you are."

"It's not about me." The halls had cleared. There wasn't enough time to get into this. She tipped onto her toes and kissed his cheek. "I just want you to be happy."

"What if not dealing with any of that, and just being with you, is what makes me happy?"

"Okay."

Spencer's eyebrows shot up. "Just like that?"

"Just like that."

"If only it were that easy." He tugged on her hand, pulling her toward Mr. Barker's classroom. They walked in and took their seats, and Mr. Barker started his lecture. About ten minutes in, he let them work on their group assignment.

Spencer scooted his desk next to hers. "All I can think about now is my dad. It's not that I don't want to forgive him, but it's hard to forget all the hurt he's caused our family."

Liv propped her elbow on her desk, her cheek on her fist. "Look, it's easy for me to tell you to forget about the past, because I don't really have one. I think the changes you've made in your life are admirable." She smiled at him. "And you know I'm crazy about you."

He shook his head. "I don't think I'll ever be good enough for you."

"It's because of you, because of things like the list, that I've decided it doesn't matter if I ever get my memories back. I'd be a different person if I never met you."

"I *was* a different person before I met you."

Her stomach did a little flip, and she wished she wasn't sitting in math class, surrounded by other students.

"How's it coming?" Mr. Barker asked from behind them.

Liv glanced down at her blank paper, trying to come up with a response.

"We got stopped on a couple problems," Spencer said. "But we're going to get it all figured out."

It wasn't until she and Spencer had driven to the middle of nowhere that she started to rethink her decision. "Are you sure this is a good idea?" she asked as she rounded the hood of Spencer's car.

He held the driver's side door open. "The worst you can do is take out some cactuses, and I'm sure no one would care if a few went missing."

She settled into the driver's seat but didn't touch the steering wheel until Spencer got back in and buckled his seat belt. On the ride out, he'd gone over the basics. It sounded simple enough, but sitting behind the wheel was different than hearing about it. Her stomach knotted and her pulse quickened.

"Push in the clutch . . ." Spencer waited for her to do it. "Okay, put it into first gear."

Liv maneuvered the gearshift. "There?"

"Yep. Now slowly ease off the clutch and give it some gas."

The first three times, the car stalled out. On the fourth try, she was able to keep the engine running. After a half mile or so of barely moving, she decided to try second gear. Only the gearshift wasn't cooperating. It made a horrible grinding noise as she tried to force it into place. "It's not going."

Spencer put his hand over hers and helped her glide it into place.

She let out the clutch and drove farther down the deserted back road. "This is pretty fun."

Drops of rain hit the windshield. At first it was just a few, then more and more splattered against the glass. In a dream-like trance, she watched the water roll down.

Rain pelted her windshield. Everything was so blurry. Liv wiped the tears from her cheeks, then scooted forward, straining to see through the rain. Her wipers never got that one stripe in her line of sight. She turned the knob so they would go faster, but instead of the wipers speeding up, everything went dark.

Headlights cut through the black. They were coming at her. Coming fast.

She slammed on the brakes, hard as she could.

The car shuddered to a stop. Her breaths came out in ragged gasps.

"Whoa," Spencer said. "What happened?"

Nothing but desert was in front of her. The rain wasn't even heavy enough to need the wipers. But that car coming for her . . .

It seemed so real.

Before she could stop them, tears filled her eyes.

Spencer put his hand on her shoulder. "It's not a big deal. Getting the clutch down is tricky."

"It's not that. The rain . . . and the car was coming . . ." Sitting in the seat felt suffocating, and she had to get out. She undid her seat belt, threw open the door, and stepped away from the car.

Drops of rain landed on her head and arms. She tipped her head to the sky and closed her eyes. Over and over, she saw the headlights coming for her.

She felt a hand on her back. She opened her eyes and looked at Spencer.

"What happened?" he asked.

"Driving and the rain, it triggered something. I think it

was a memory. Of right before my car accident." She shook her head. "Just when I decide to stop worrying about my lost memories, one slams into me."

"Well, maybe that's a good sign. Maybe you'll get more and more back."

That thought no longer comforted her; in fact, it terrified her. Because something felt very, very wrong. Because if that memory had been real—if she'd crashed into another car and not a tree—it meant Mom and Dad *had* lied to her.

And if they had lied . . .

34

Every nerve in her body was on alert. She was
dizzy and nauseous; a sharp pain shot across her head.

*We moved halfway across the nation; they were all about
a fresh start; they're always weird when I ask about the past.*
Everything she'd overheard Mom and Dad say, the voices
and visions. She'd suspected it all along, but now there was
no denying that something awful had happened. An awful so
huge that they'd fled from their old life.

"You look like you're going to pass out." Spencer's arm
came around her waist.

Her knees felt like they were going to give way.

Spencer's grip tightened. "There's too much cactus to sit
you down here. Let's get back to the car."

*What could be so horrible that my parents would do any-
thing to keep it from me?*

Spencer eased her onto the hood of his car and sat next to
her. "You're starting to scare me. I'm not really sure what to
do right now."

"Sorry." She leaned her head on his shoulder and he put
his arm around her. "I'm okay. I just need a minute. I'm . . ."
Well, she wasn't exactly sure what she was. "Overwhelmed."

"Is it like in the movies, where you suddenly remember
everything?"

"No, nothing like that. I don't know if that would be good or bad."

For a moment, they sat in silence. Spencer pointed across the horizon. "You see the rainbow?"

Red, yellow, blue, and violet striped through the gray sky. "I guess we can cross two things off the list. Seeing my first rainbow and driving."

"Yeah, I wouldn't say you know how to drive just yet."

"Thanks for that," she said, elbowing him.

"Sorry, I couldn't resist." Using the arm around her shoulders, he pulled her closer and kissed her forehead. "Come on. We'll go for ice cream. Ice cream makes everything better."

She wished ice cream could erase the memory of the car coming at her. She knew it wouldn't, but when Spencer slid off the hood and extended his hand, she took it.

Getting ice cream *had* made her feel better for a little while. What was even more effective was sitting in Spencer's car, kissing him until her lips tingled and she was short of breath.

But as soon as she started up the sidewalk to her house, everything felt wrong again. From the outside, it looked like the perfect house with the perfect family living there. She remembered when she was always on the inside looking out. Now that she was on the outside, she could see everything about to crack.

What's going to be left when it does?

The sense of wrongness increased the second she walked inside. This was supposed to be her safe place; right now, it felt like she was standing on a ledge and might slip at any moment.

Mom stepped out of the kitchen. "I was about to call you. Dinner's almost ready."

The progress they'd made yesterday, the heart-to-heart—all of it felt false now. She couldn't look at Mom, didn't want to be around her. "I'm not hungry. Spencer and I had ice cream."

"I don't like you ruining your appetite with junk."

Well, I don't like that you and Dad lie to me.

She couldn't say that out loud, though. What if she'd gotten the image from a movie or something and just didn't realize it?

That sounds like something Mom would say to explain it all away.

But she knows the brain better than I do. Who am I to question a brilliant neurologist?

At this point, she was actually hoping it was a false memory. There had to be a way to be sure. Only she no longer trusted the two people who could tell her the truth.

She looked at Mom, who had a worried look on her face as she gave her the once-over. *What are you not telling me?*

"Olivia, did you hear what I said?"

Clenching her jaw to fight the fiery anger building up in her, Liv put her hand on her stomach. "You know, you're right. I shouldn't have had that ice cream. I'm going to go to my room and lie down for a little bit."

Before the accusations flew from her mouth or Mom could say anything else, she rushed upstairs. Her mind spun for a way to find out more on her own. She paused outside the office door, glanced over her shoulder, then ducked inside.

Liv pulled open drawers, riffling through papers, trying to find anything that might lead her to the truth. Home documents, receipts—a bunch of files that didn't give her any answers. She shoved them back and saw a flat black box.

It thumped against the side of the drawer as she lifted it out by the handle.

On top of the box was silver, a lock on the left and a keypad on the right, with a large knob in the middle. She twisted the knob. Nothing. She pulled, tugged, and tried to use a letter opener. But the lock remained set.

After banging her fist against it a couple times—that didn't work, either—she stared at it, trying to figure out how she could get inside. She jerked up her head when she heard a knock, not on the office door, but down the hall.

"Livie?" Dad knocked again. It would only take him a couple of seconds to find out she wasn't in her room.

Heart racing, she shoved the box back in the drawer. She heard Dad's approaching footsteps and tried to slam the drawer, but the box was sticking up, the corner catching.

"Livie, are you in there?" The doorknob twisted.

Liv forced down the box and kicked the drawer closed as the door swung open. She shot out of her seat, sure guilt was written all over her face. For a moment, she and Dad regarded each other, a strange silence between them.

"I was using the computer." She pointed at it, like he wouldn't know what she was talking about, then added, "For school."

Dad shoved his hands in his pockets and nodded. "Mom wanted me to try to get you to come down for dinner."

"Like I told *Mom*, I'm not hungry." Her heart squeezed as she looked at Dad. He'd always been her rock, the guy she knew she could count on. But now . . . she didn't know anything anymore. "Besides, I've got lots of homework I need to get done."

She started out the door, but he stepped into her path. "Everything okay?"

Tears crawled up her throat. No, it wasn't. "I just had a long day. Good night, Dad."

"Good night." He squeezed her shoulder. "Love you."

Liv kept her lips clamped, unable to say it back. Not now. She wasn't sure if she'd yell or cry. She pushed past him, went into her room, and lay back on the bed.

The illusion that had been passing for her life was fading now, faster and faster with her suspicions confirmed about her parents lying to her.

Now all she had to do was uncover the truth.

And hope there was something left of her when she was done.

Liv asked the couple seated in the booth if they needed anything else. When they said they didn't, she tucked a stray strand of hair behind her ear, placed the bill on the table, and smiled. "Have a good night, then."

She walked past the frosted glass divider with the etched catfish, lily pads, and cherry blossoms, and stopped in front of the golden, chubby Buddha statue. The silver charms on her bracelet clanked against the statue as she rubbed his belly. In theory, rubbing Buddha's belly was good luck; in reality, she hadn't noticed much change in her life, but she kept doing it anyway. She needed all the luck she could get.

She dropped her hand and headed to the red booth in the corner, where Huan was waiting for her.

She sat down and glanced at her watch.

Five more minutes and I'm out of here.

"So, what were we on?" Liv asked.

Huan brushed his straight black hair out of his eyes. "You need eight in a row to win."

She set the end of the chopstick on the table. She smacked the end of it and caught it in the air. "You're going down."

She repeated the flip-and-catch six more times. She set up for the eighth attempt. The attempt that would make her tonight's champion.

Huan's gaze drifted to the door. "Your boyfriend's here. He doesn't look very happy."

Liv looked to the door and saw Jace. She held up a finger, then turned her attention back to the chopstick. Focusing on it, she smacked the end. It flipped in the air but went too low. She tried to catch it anyway, but she wasn't fast enough. It bounced off the table to the floor. "Dang it!"

"Nice try," Huan said. "We'll have a rematch tomorrow."

"You're on." She picked up the chopstick and tossed it on the table, then hurried to the back. She punched out, told Mrs. Táo good night, and walked up front to where Jace was waiting.

His brows were furrowed, his jaw set. "Why are you always flirting with him?"

"Not this again. Like I've told you a million times, Huan and I just pass the time together. You making a big deal about it is starting to get old."

"Walking in and seeing you two together is starting to get old."

Knowing this was an argument that could go on for hours, she asked, "Can we get going already? We're late enough as it is."

She pulled her hood up, hoping it'd keep her dry from the rain coming down outside.

Jace grabbed her hand and headed out of Táo's Restaurant, taking large strides she could hardly keep up with. A bolt of lightning tore through the sky, followed by a loud clap of thunder.

When they reached the parking lot, Jace turned to her. "My truck's low on gas."

Liv dug her keys out of her pocket. "We can take my car, then."

He grabbed two cases of beer out of his truck and transferred them to the back of her white 1988 Pontiac Grand Am. He took the keys from her, and they got into the car.

She twisted toward him, leaning her back on the car door. "So how was practice?"

"Rainy."

Looks like he's in a mood again. At least once we get to the party, Courtney will be there.

The rain got heavier, coming down in thick sheets, and by the time Jace pulled up to Martin's, water ran down the edge of the roads, and there were puddles everywhere.

Jace handed her a case of beer and carried the other one inside. The party was already in full swing. Music blared; empty beer bottles were everywhere. She spotted Courtney in the corner.

"You made it!" *Courtney stood up, stumbled over, and threw her arms around her.* "I'm so wasted."

Liv turned her head away from her friend's alcohol-saturated breath. "I noticed."

"I probably should slow down." *Courtney thrust the cup toward her.* "Here, it's cran and vodka. You can have the rest."

After downing the contents of Courtney's cup, Liv grabbed a beer and settled on the couch. Tonight's dinner rush had exhausted her. Working at Táo's was part of her plan to get out of this town and away from Mom. It was also the only way she could afford to buy clothes she wouldn't be embarrassed of wearing in public.

As she sat, drinking her beer, people wandered in and out of the room. By the time she finished it, her head felt pleasantly fuzzy. She hadn't seen Jace in a while, and decided she should go try to make up with him. Half the time she liked that he got jealous, and half the time she hated it. But she loved him, and he was always there for her, especially when she needed to vent about Mom.

He wasn't in the next room, or the kitchen.

"Have you seen Jace?" she asked Martin.

"I think he's in the basement playing pool."

She walked downstairs, turned the corner, and stared at Jace and Courtney. Kissing.

Courtney saw her first. She pulled away, eyes wide.

Liv spun away, charged up the stairs, and headed out of the house. The rain soaked through her sweatshirt in a matter of seconds. She got all the way to her car before realizing Jace still had her keys.

"Wait!" Jace yelled, coming out of the house. He ran across the yard to her. "It's not what you think."

"I saw you kissing her. It's exactly what I think."

"It didn't mean anything, though. I was telling her I was mad at you, that I was sick of seeing you with Huan, and she came on to me."

"It didn't look like you were pushing her away."

"It was just a drunken mistake. I don't care about her; I care about you."

Tears ran down her cheeks, mixing in with the rain. "You and Courtney were the only people I thought I could count on, and you both betrayed me." She undid the clasp on her bracelet. "Take your stupid love bracelet," she said, throwing it at him, "and never talk to me again."

"Don't be like that. You know I love you."

He reached for her and she stepped back. "Just give me my keys."

"You've had too much to drink."

"Between catching you and Courtney and the pouring rain, I'm all sobered up." She held out her hand. "Now, give them to me."

Grumbling, he dug the keys out of his pocket. "Fine. Go, then!"

"I will!" Liv snatched them out of his hand and got into her car. Heading home wasn't an option. Mom would be drunk and some random guy would be there. She started the engine. She tugged on her seat belt but it kept catching, so she gave up on it. She accelerated out of the driveway and headed toward the outskirts of town, with no set destination in mind.

Her eyes burned as more tears filled them. How am I ever going to get out of here now? All my plans were tied up with Courtney and Jace.

She took a right onto a back dirt road. The rain had turned it into a muddy mess. Her tires slipped and she could hardly see. Everything was so blurry. She wiped the tears from her cheeks, then scooted forward, straining to see through the rain. Her wipers never got that one stripe in her line of sight. She turned the knob so they would go faster, but instead of the wipers speeding up, everything went dark.

Headlights cut through the black. They were coming at her. Coming fast.

She slammed on the brakes. Instead of slowing, she sped up. Dropping her head, she threw her arms in front of her.

When Liv woke up, her hair was matted to her forehead and neck. Her breath came out in ragged bursts. She inhaled deeply, trying to calm her racing heart. That had been the most vivid, realistic dream yet.

The ones where she was blond always left her feeling awful. At first because she wasn't a good person; now because of how hard her life was.

Her life or my life?

Feeling like her head was about to explode, she pressed her fingers to her temples.

How am I supposed to know what's real and what's just a dream?

She remembered the dream where the girl's mom had slapped her. Just the memory made her cheek burn.

But the woman who'd slapped her hadn't looked anything like Mom, and Mom would never slap her. So that meant it couldn't have been a memory.

Looking different, dreaming about people who didn't exist—it was all so confusing. She wanted to believe Mom was right about her brain making the images up to keep functioning. It didn't explain how deeply she missed Elizabeth, or knowing the cheer she was supposed to do in her dream, or a dozen other questions she had. But no other explanations made any sense, either.

She had never wanted to know and not know something so badly.

35

Liv used her spoon to push her cereal around the bowl. It had been in the milk so long, it was now mush. Every time she'd lifted her spoon to take a bite, though, she ended up putting it back down without eating. She pictured that box in the office over and over, wondering if it held all the answers. Wondering if she'd open it and find nothing and be back at the beginning again.

Dad came into the kitchen, newspaper tucked under his arm.

"Good morning." Mom kissed Dad on the cheek, then came over with a pitcher, glasses, and Liv's pillbox. Mom set the pills in front of Liv, then picked up the pitcher and started pouring it. The juice came out in thick chunks.

Liv wrinkled her nose as Mom pushed a glass her way. "What is that?"

"Good for you," Mom said.

"That means gross."

"It's a fruit and vegetable smoothie, and since you had ice cream for dinner last night, I expect you to drink it." Mom placed a glass in front of Dad and one in front of herself, then sat in her usual chair.

Dad opened his paper and handed the crossword section to Mom, who immediately started working on it, and Liv took a drink of her juice—which wasn't great, but not as bad as she thought it would be. Sun streamed through the window as they sat, eating their breakfast like a happy, all-American family.

Lies. Lies. Lies.

Still, she sat, playing her part. Biding her time. Feeling like she was slowly going insane.

Mom frowned, then leaned down and felt Liv's forehead, something she hadn't done in weeks. "Are you feeling okay? You look flushed."

Liv stared into Mom eyes, like she might be able to pull out the truth if she looked hard enough. Being home today might make it easier to dig for clues, but it'd also mean being around Mom and not Spencer. "I'm fine."

It was just a dream. Just a dream.

She kept hoping that repeating it over and over would make it true.

But it didn't.

She pushed away from the table and rushed upstairs. Once she was inside her bedroom, she called Spencer. "Do you know how to pick a lock?"

The line was so quiet, she checked to see if the call disconnected. Her phone said it hadn't. "Spencer?"

"Why do you need to pick a lock?"

"I might not if you know a way to figure out the combination. But I need your help. Can you come over? Like, now?"

"I'll be right there."

As soon as Spencer showed up, Liv told Mom they needed to print off something for their math assignment and dragged him upstairs. She closed the office door and locked it.

Spencer put his hands on her shoulders. "What's going on?"

Silence stretched between them as she tried to figure out how much she wanted to tell him. Spencer was the one good thing in her life. They'd only been officially going out for four days, and it'd already been filled with plenty of ups and downs. But she had to know what Mom and Dad were hiding, and she needed help.

"You can tell me anything," he said.

"It's just, sometimes lies look so much like the truth. And when you can't tell between the two, how do you know which one will make you happy? Maybe the lie will make you happier. And if you're happier with the lie, would you really want to know the truth?"

His eyebrows lowered as he studied her. "I'm not sure what you're talking about, but I know telling you the truth made me feel better and more miserable at the same time."

She took a deep breath and blew it out. "I think my parents lied to me about the car wreck. I don't think I hit a tree; I think I hit another car."

"But why would they keep that from you?"

Liv looked into those brown eyes of his. "That's what I'm afraid to find out."

For a moment, neither of them said anything. Then Spencer exhaled. "What makes you think you hit another car?"

"Well, when I was driving yesterday and I had that flashback thing or whatever it was, I saw headlights coming at me. I swear it was a memory, but according to my parents I wrecked into a tree. Then there's the fact they act weird any time I bring up the accident."

"And if someone else was involved, but your parents don't want you to know, that must mean . . ."

An icy knot formed in her chest. "It means the other person probably didn't make it." Saying it aloud made her feel even worse. "You think that's it?"

"I don't know. If they lied . . ." He squeezed her hand. "I'm sure your parents are only trying to protect you. If I could forget that night with Peter . . ." The regret that crossed his face said the rest.

Spencer's tormented expression was enough to make her think twice about how much she wanted to know about her accident. As with Spencer, what was done was done. Opening up the past would just hurt everyone, and obviously she had enough issues to overcome as it was.

It was a nice idea, ignoring everything she'd uncovered. But then she thought of the box at the bottom of the drawer, of how she could no longer look Mom or Dad in the eye without feeling so much bitterness she thought it would choke her. Of how everything inside her was screaming that she needed to find the truth or she'd never fully be able to move on with her life.

"I have to know what really happened." She pulled open the drawer and tugged out the box. Spencer pulled a screwdriver out of his pocket. "This was my plan, but I don't think . . ." He jabbed it into the lock, but it didn't turn. He tried to wedge the screwdriver under the lid. Nothing. He took a paper clip out of the top drawer of the desk, straightened it, and inserted it into the lock. After a minute or so, he grumbled and tossed it aside. "I know you think I'm some kind of criminal, but I don't normally do things like this."

"I don't think you're a criminal. I just didn't know who else to call."

"Well, don't I feel special." He slid the screwdriver back in his pocket. "Have you tried to guess the combination?"

"Since there're ten thousand possibilities, no."

"Right, but people use numbers they can remember. Like birthdays."

The clock on the wall above their heads ticked loudly, like it was taunting them with the fact that they were running out of time. The buttons beeped out as she entered Dad's birthday. Then Mom's. Then her own. "Nothing."

"Maybe an anniversary," Spencer said.

"I don't know—" Liv remembered the photo album. She took it off the bookshelf and flipped it to the page with Mom and Dad's wedding photos. There was a wedding announcement taped next to the pictures.

Holding her breath, she hovered her finger over the numbers. *Nine. Two.* It didn't make any noise, so she looked to Spencer. "I don't know the year, and I need two more digits."

He leaned over her. "You've got to add a zero in front of the month and day." He pressed zero, nine, zero, two.

The top clicked, similar to the sound of a door unlocking.

Spencer hooked his fingers around her hip as she reached for the box with shaky hands. She opened the lid and stared inside.

Spencer's grip tightened. "Holy shit."

36

All Liv could do for a moment was stare. Inside were stacks of hundred-dollar bills. The stacks had a thick paper band around them that said $10,000. *One, two, three, four. Forty grand.*

In addition to the money, there was paperwork with foreign bank accounts and three passports. The picture in her passport showed her face still puffy, with dark circles under her eyes.

"Why would they have all this?" she asked.

"Maybe they're planning a trip?" From Spencer's tone, she could tell he didn't actually believe it.

She took out the map inside. Someone had highlighted routes from Cottonwood to three different places in Mexico. "And this?"

"Maybe a trip to Mexico?"

Liv tilted her head and looked at him. Then she returned her attention to the box. "This is in case something bad happens." Thoughts swirled around her head in a jumbled mess. Her dream; the theory that if someone else was in the wreck, they must not have made it. A sick feeling settled in her gut. "I think I was drunk the night of the wreck. Every time I remember it, it's fuzzy. Not like my other memories, but like I wasn't in control. Like *I* was what was fuzzy."

Her heart dropped. "What if I killed someone?"

"You didn't." Spencer put his hands on her waist.

She hugged him, wanting it to be true. But even if he was right about that, all her instincts were screaming that something horrible had gone down that night. "My parents have an Escape to Mexico Plan. That doesn't exactly scream *innocent*."

"There must be some explanation. Your parents are so not the criminal type."

No, they weren't. Which meant something huge had motivated them to prepare like they had.

How far had her parents gone to cover up whatever happened? How far were they willing to go to make sure the truth stayed buried?

"Olivia?" Mom called. It sounded like she was nearing the top of the stairs.

"Almost finished!" The map wouldn't fold right, the crinkling sounding way too loud. Heart slamming against her chest, Liv finally got it folded flat, locked the box, and shoved it back in the drawer. She grabbed the photo album off the desk, planning on putting it back, but a voice whispered, *Take it.*

With no time to question why, she shoved it in her bag. The zipper took some convincing, but she finally got it closed. She looked at Spencer, holding his gaze for a beat, then they left the office.

Mom was at the top of the stairs. "You two are going to be late to school if you don't hurry."

"We're going right now." Liv grabbed Spencer's hand and held it tight, glad he'd been with her when she'd found that box. Now they just had to figure out what it all meant.

School dragged, and by lunch, she felt like she'd been there for at least eight hours. She got her food and almost bumped into Sabrina.

"Liv," Sabrina said, offering a tight smile. It wasn't exactly friendly but it wasn't exactly mean, either. The nice thing was how little she cared. It was such a light, freeing feeling to not base her life on someone else's opinion of her.

Liv nodded. "Sabrina."

She started to move past her, but Sabrina said, "Wait. Look, maybe you really are as nice as everyone thinks. Keira told me I've been a total bitch to you, and maybe she's a little bit right."

Liv raised her eyebrows, biting back a *Maybe?* and also thinking, *Go, Keira!*

"We both made mistakes." Sabrina glanced at Spencer, and a hint of sadness broke through her stony expression, so quickly it was gone before it fully caught hold. But it was enough for her to know Sabrina was talking more about her and Spencer's relationship than hers with Liv. Apparently there were actual feelings buried underneath that pretty exterior.

Sabrina gripped her tray tighter and looked over at Keira—who was standing a couple paces away, pretending not to watch what was going down—then back at Liv. "So I'm sorry or whatever."

"And I'm sorry or whatever that the back of your shirt got bleached in science lab," Liv said. "It was an accident, I swear, and I'll pay for a new shirt if you want me to."

Sabrina's nostrils flared, and she was sure the mean girl would come right back. But then the anger seeped out and Sabrina gave a half shrug. "Guess that makes us about even."

"Guess so."

And even though she no longer cared what Sabrina thought, it felt like in that moment, a truce formed between them. A real one this time. She smiled at Keira, who had a triumphant grin on her face, then walked across the room.

Spencer watched her as she settled across from him, then covered her hand with his. "How you holding up?"

She shrugged. "I can't stop thinking about it. I'm so mad at my mom and dad right now, and yet . . . I miss them. If that makes sense."

"I get it. In all the madness this morning, I didn't get a chance to tell you that I called my dad last night."

"Oh? So how'd it go?"

He tipped his head one way, then the other. "Better than usual. We'll never have the same kind of relationship we used to, but we're going to try to have one again. It's pretty much all your fault, too."

She smiled at him. "That's great, Spencer. I'm so proud."

"That's not all I did last night, either. It took more hours of practice than I care to admit, but I think . . ." He pulled out a pencil and balanced it on the table. He smacked the end. It flipped in the air and he caught it. "Impressed?"

Liv remembered her dream, how she and that Huan guy had been playing the same game. Then she thought back to being in the Chinese restaurant with Spencer, and how she'd automatically known how to flip and catch those chopsticks. Which meant at least some elements of her dreams involving the blond girl were true.

She groaned and dropped her head in her hands.

"Not the reaction I was hoping for," Spencer said.

"I'm sorry. It's very impressive, really. It just made me realize my theory has too many holes."

"Which theory?"

She bit her lip. "You wouldn't believe me, even if I could find a way to explain it. And that's a big if."

"So first you give me a pity compliment, then you insult my intelligence." He put a hand on his chest. "Ouch, baby, ouch."

Liv couldn't help smiling. She nodded at Spencer's pencil. "You want to have a competition? We'll see how many flips and catches in a row we can do."

He tilted his head and raised an eyebrow. "You think I can be distracted that easily?"

"I was hoping." When his expression showed he wasn't letting it go, she added, "The other thing will have to wait until after school."

He handed over the pencil. "Okay, let's see what you got."

After she beat Spencer—his four in a row to her six—they got up to go.

Clay was leaving the cafeteria at the same time and they did that stutter, you-go, no-you thing. Spencer pulled Liv into the hall. Then his muscles tensed, he stopped, and he turned to face Clay.

"Hey, man, I'm . . . I'm sorry things went down the way they did."

Clay's eyebrows shot up, the surprise on his face clear. He looked from Spencer to her, then back at Spencer. He lifted a hand and rubbed it along his jaw. "I'm sorry I left. I should've had your back." For a moment, they stood there, then he gave one sharp nod. "See you guys around."

She watched him walk away, then turned to Spencer. "That's it? You guys are good now?"

"Well, we're dudes. We're not going to have some hug-fest." He drew her to him. "Now you and me, on the other hand . . ."

She sank into the hug, dropping her head on his chest and holding him tight. This day was going freakishly well as far as school and friends went. It probably would've seemed like more of a win if the huge weight of that morning wasn't still hanging over her head.

♪♫

While waiting for Spencer, Liv sat on her usual bench and looked through the photo album. With her just-a-dream theory in shambles, she needed a new one. One that involved Mom and Dad having passports, money, and a map to Mexico all ready to go.

No answers came as she studied the photos. *This is useless.*

She was so engrossed in trying to figure it all out, that when Spencer walked up and said, "Hey," she jumped.

"Sorry. I didn't mean to scare you." He sat next to her.

"I've looked through my parents' photo album, but I'm not finding what I'm looking for."

"What are you looking for?"

"I don't know."

"Well, that explains why you can't find it."

She shot him a look she hoped conveyed she didn't find him funny.

He took her hand in his. "Can't you just talk to your parents? Tell them what you remembered and ask them for the truth."

"I've tried. They'll just take advantage of the fact that I can't remember anything and lie. Ever since I woke up from that coma, it's been one lie after another." She twisted to face him. "Sometimes I'm not . . . I'm not me. Except I am . . ." She shook her head. "I'm not explaining it very well." Her chest squeezed and she had to blink to keep the tears from coming. "It's like I've got all these pieces, but none of them fit together. The more I try to make them, the more broken I feel."

Spencer cupped her cheek, looking at her as though she might shatter right before his eyes. Part of her felt like it wasn't entirely impossible. "Liv . . ." Instead of saying anything more, he lowered his lips to hers. The kiss took on an urgent edge, from her or from him, she wasn't quite sure. "Let's get out of here."

She still needed to know the truth about her past—she couldn't go back now. But she could see the desperation in his eyes, a mix of fear and need. The same fear and need that echoed within her. So before doing something that had the potential to ruin everything, she could spend a few hours with her boyfriend, pretending her life wasn't so screwed up. She let him pull her to her feet and took a moment to soak in the feel of his hand against hers, the way he smelled like warm sunshine, and the way his hair curled around his ears and the top of his glasses.

The way that being with him had made her feel whole in a way nothing else had.

Spencer pulled up to a beige rancher with a red door and rock-and-gravel landscaping. "Good. No lights are on."

"Why?" Liv asked. "Are we breaking in?"

"Yeah, I figured that's something else we ought to check off the list." He looked at her, fighting to keep his expression serious, then a smile broke free. "This is my dad's place. He told me I could use his pool whenever."

When Spencer had mentioned going swimming, she told him she didn't want to be around a bunch of people. Then he'd said he knew a place they'd be alone. He claimed that swimming was the best thing for blocking out the rest of the world—said it in a way she could tell he'd used it many times before. She'd run out of excuses, anyway, so she'd finally, albeit reluctantly, agreed.

They got out of the car and walked up to the front door. Spencer knocked, and when there was no answer, he reached into the planter and grabbed a key. He led her through the house and outside to the pool.

He took off his glasses and set them on a table, then pulled off his T-shirt and tossed it on one of the nearby lounge chairs.

And suddenly the little bit of courage she'd managed to build up on the drive over disappeared. Her throat went dry, her heart hammered against her rib cage, and her rapid pulse throbbed through her head. "I don't think I can do this."

He stepped closer, put his hand on the side of her neck, and ran his thumb along her jaw. "We'll start in the shallow end, and even the deepest part doesn't go over five feet. I'll be right beside you the whole time."

"It's not that . . . Well, it is. But it's not *just* that." The point had been to forget about her problems for a little while, but she thought about the scar on her chest, and the kid with the Frisbee telling her how disgusting it looked, and she couldn't bear it if Spencer looked at her the same way.

His eyebrows drew together. "What is it, then?"

A couple months back, she wouldn't have even considered it. But now the scar had faded to light pink, and she wanted to feel strong; she wanted to shake off her insecurities. Unfortunately, it was easier to want than to actually do.

Just get it over with. Taking a deep breath, she peeled off the shirt covering her navy bikini top. Then, feeling immediately self-conscious, she put a hand over her scar.

Spencer grabbed her hand and lifted it off. "That's what you're worried about?"

"It looks gross."

He leaned down and kissed the raised line on her chest, then moved his lips up to the scar on her neck. "Obviously I haven't done a very good job of expressing how beautiful I think you are."

A lump formed in her throat and she blinked back tears.

His fingers traced the top of her scar. "It makes me think how lucky you are to be alive."

Liv wrapped her arms around his waist, kissed him, then rested her head on his bare chest. She could hear his heart beating out a steady rhythm, and she did feel lucky to be alive. The stress she'd felt moments ago melted away. She stepped back and smiled up at him. "Now that the hard part's over, I guess it's time to try swimming."

Liv wrapped her hair in a towel and squeezed out as much moisture as she could. Swimming with Spencer had been just the pick-me-up she needed. Opening herself like that had made her feel stronger, like she could face anything now.

Looking into the mirror on the bathroom wall, she could see the change, too. The girl reflected back at her was finally familiar. In need of a good hair-combing, but familiar. She brushed her hair out, gathered all her belongings, and went to stuff them in her bag. The photo album was still in there, taking up most of the room. She didn't want it to get wet, so she pulled it out and stuck it on the edge of the sink.

Spencer knocked. "You ready yet?"

"Yeah. I'm just gathering all my stuff." Liv unlocked the door and swung it open. Spencer's hair was damp and his glasses were back on. A grin spread across his face as he stepped into the bathroom.

He's so freaking cute. And he's smart, and he makes me feel amazing, and I love being with him. And I just love him.

Slinging her bag over her shoulder, she stepped in for a kiss. But her bag bumped into the album and it fell to the floor. "Oops. Looks like I need to work on my smooth moves," she joked.

"Well, you've always been a little clumsy."

She smacked his chest with the back of her hand. "You better watch it, or I won't ever finish the move I was working on." She crouched down to pick up the album. The photo of Mom pregnant caught her attention. Down at the bottom right corner were red numbers. The date the photo was taken.

Her blood ran cold as she stared at it.

She did the math again, sure there had to be a mistake. But it wasn't like it was hard math to do.

"Earth to Liv," Spencer said. "You okay down there?"

Her eyes remained fixed on that date. "Ten. My mom can't be pregnant with me in this picture, because that would make me ten years old. Which means . . ."

Terror gripped her heart. *Elizabeth. That would be about the right age for her. And when Mom had looked at the picture, she'd gotten choked up.*

What if Elizabeth was with me when the car wrecked?

The scenario unfolded in her mind. Driving drunk with her sister. Who wasn't here anymore. She lifted her hands to her mouth, praying for it to not be true, but the more she thought about it, the more it made sense.

She picked up the book and tapped the picture. "This proves that my parents are lying to me. You remember how I told you I thought I remembered a sister named Elizabeth?

This picture means she might be real. And if she is, I've got to know. There has to be an article about my crash, or a police report, or something. Some way of figuring out what happened."

He shook his head. "I don't know if it's a good i—"

"I need to know what happened, Spencer." She locked eyes with him, and her voice shook with emotion. "Please help me."

He studied her for a moment. Finally, he extended his hand to her. "Come on, then."

37

Spencer led Liv into a small room with a packed bookshelf, big gray filing cabinet, and paper-covered computer desk tucked in the corner. He moved the mouse, and the computer screen lit up. Another couple clicks and the Internet browser opened. "Okay, we're online."

He grabbed the chair in the corner and set it to the left of the computer desk. "Have a seat." Then he entered information into a search engine. "I'm not exactly sure what to look for, so this might take a while."

She scooted closer to him. "Thanks. For helping me with this."

He turned to her, and the tenderness in his eyes made her heart squeeze. "I probably shouldn't tell you this, but you could talk me into pretty much anything."

She brushed his hair off his face, gave him a quick kiss, then rested her head on his shoulder.

The search was taking forever, and she was about ready to call it off for the day. Needing to stretch her legs, she headed to the kitchen for water. When she stepped back into the office, two glasses in hand, Spencer leaned closer to the screen. "No way . . ."

Liv set the glasses on a side table. "What?"

He clicked the mouse, exited the screen he was on, and turned away from the computer. "It's nothing." He stood, keeping his body between her and the screen. "It's getting late, and my dad and Dana will probably be home soon. We'll have to try some other time."

"I can tell you're lying." She crossed her arms and narrowed her eyes. "What is it? Tell me."

"Liv . . ." He sighed. "It's big. Huge. It might ruin everything." He squeezed her shoulder, imploring her with his eyes. "Can't you just trust me on this?"

"I trust you. But I need to know." She stepped past him.

His arms came around her, and he gripped her wrist as her hand closed on the mouse. "Just wait. Sleep on it."

She jerked her arm out of his grasp and pulled up the history. It was a jumbled mess, so she set it to sort by order visited and scrolled to the bottom. She clicked on the last link.

Spencer moved in front of the computer, blocking her view. "Let me look at it tonight, make sure it's got all the facts, then I'll show it to you tomorrow, I promise."

Teeth clenched, she said, "Move."

"Just—"

"I need to know what the hell's going on. Now, move." Keeping her eyes on his, she said, "Please."

He threw up his arms and got out of the way.

Liv stared at the picture.

Her picture.

Missing, it said across the top. Her knees felt like they were about to give way. She flopped into the computer chair. This couldn't be right. This wasn't the secret she'd been thinking. "Maybe this girl just looks like me," she whispered. But as she read more about Vivienne Clark, she learned that she had a sister named Elizabeth. A sister who was ten years old.

At the bottom, there was an added plea from the family, mentioning the fact that Vivienne—or Viv, as the family referred to her in the article—had a heart condition and needed medication.

"It's weird, too," Spencer said, leaning over her and scrolling down. "This girl went missing on the same day."

Lindsay Rogers was blond. Liv couldn't even try to focus on the words next to her picture. She looked exactly like the cheerleader from her dreams.

"According to her boyfriend, he tried to stop her from leaving a party because she was drunk, but she wouldn't listen to him. Her mom said that she never showed up at home, and no one has seen her since."

Liv scanned through the information Spencer had summed up. Then she got to the part about Lindsay working at Táo's Chinese Restaurant and her shaking hand sent the cursor bouncing wildly across the screen.

She clicked back to the picture of Vivienne Clark.

The picture of what she saw when she looked in a mirror.

Spencer put his hand on her shoulder. "You know, you're right. That just looks like you. I'm sure there's a good explanation."

"It doesn't make any sense," she choked out, her mind spinning as everything she thought she knew unraveled. "One ... but both? How could it? What ...?" Her breath came out in quick, shallow gasps. "Not the blond cheerleader."

What the boyfriend had said about the party, the way the girls looked, it was all too much. Too confusing. The words onscreen blurred together as her mind reached to find a logical explanation that wasn't there.

"You think you knew the blond girl?"

"I think . . . I . . ." The room spun, images bleeding in and out of focus. All the dreams and visions from two very different girls. The conflicting voices in her head.

Liv saw the headlights coming at her; she saw the blood soaking her shirt, leaving large drops on her jeans, and thinking she was going to die. Searing pain shot through her head, making it feel like it was splitting in two.

Splitting in two.

In the back of her mind, she heard Dad saying he and Mom had come across the wreck. He'd talked about all the blood, then said he and Mom had done the best they could with their skills.

I didn't wake up in a hospital. She'd woken in a bedroom, hooked up to medical equipment with Mom looking over her.

What did they do to me? She thought of the pink line on her chest, then lifted her fingers to where staples used to be. *Who am I?*

What *am I?*

"You think . . . what?" Spencer asked.

"I can't even say it out loud. Because you'll never believe me. Because I don't even know if *I* believe me."

38

Liv ran up the stairs, threw open her closet, and started shoving clothes into a suitcase.

Mom poked her head in. "Olivia, darling, what are you doing?"

Ignoring the question, she threw her pajamas onto the growing pile of clothes and grabbed her toothbrush from the bathroom, adding it to the rest of her supplies.

"Young lady, you tell me what's going on this instant."

"You don't get to know! *I* didn't get to know, and now you can see how you like it!" The suitcase fastened with a *click*. She heaved it off the bed and headed for the door.

Mom grabbed her arm as she tried to step into the hall.

"I know, Mom," Liv said, jerking free. "I saw pictures of two missing girls. One looks exactly like me, and the other— well, the other has been showing up in my dreams. I'm still working out all the details, but I know it means you're a liar."

Mom's eyes widened; her mouth dropped open. "It's . . . I . . . I can explain."

"I can't believe anything you say." She rushed past Mom, down the stairs, and charged out the front door, slamming it behind her. Her chest felt like it was on fire as she flung open the back door of Spencer's car and threw her suitcase on the seat.

Mom stepped out on the porch, tears streaming down her face. "Olivia, please wait. I can explain."

Liv got into the car and pulled the door closed.

Spencer's attention was on the doorway. "Are you sure we shouldn't—?"

"Just go." The tears she'd been trying to hold back broke free. "Please. Just go." She buried her head in her hands as Spencer turned the car around and drove away.

The noise of the sliding glass door sounded loud in the quiet.

Liv took the can of root beer Spencer extended to her. Now that the sun had gone down, there was a chill in the air. It was about the only time she remembered feeling cold since they'd moved here. Or maybe the cold was more about what she'd found out earlier today.

Spencer sat next to her on the patio swing. "My mom just got off the phone with yours. She and your dad were going to come over—"

Liv whipped her head toward him.

"But my mom convinced them to give you some space. You can stay here with us tonight."

She breathed a sigh of relief. No way could she face them now. *I don't know if I can even look at them ever again.*

She shivered and Spencer put his arm around her. "I'd ask if you're okay, but I know that's a stupid question."

With his arm around her, she did feel better. And warmer. If only she could shut off her thoughts for a while. "Tell me something to get my mind off of it all."

Spencer took a swig of his soda, then stared at the top of his can for a moment. "Mr. Harmsen and I finished building the plane today."

"You built a plane?"

"One of those model planes."

"With Mr. Harmsen? Isn't he the school counselor?"

"Yeah."

"Why'd you build a plane with him?"

Spencer gave her a sidelong glance. "The long or the short version?"

She leaned her head on his shoulder. "The longer the better."

"Well, after my dad left and I started getting into trouble, my mom decided I should talk to someone. Of course, I didn't want to, but Mom made it clear it wasn't really an optional thing. So I sat through a few sessions with Mr. Harmsen. He had this huge model airplane, and when I asked him about it, he talked about the hours he'd spent putting it together, painting it and getting it to look just right. Then he asked what I thought."

Spencer shifted, looking uncomfortable. "Remember, this was back when I was a jerk. And I felt so damn angry all the time. About everything. Anyway, I walked over to his plane, threw it on the ground, and stomped on it. I told him I thought his sessions were as big a waste of time as building that plane was. Then I walked out.

"I felt awful just after—even in my jerk phase, I knew I'd crossed a line. So when school started up this semester, we worked out a deal. Three days a week we'd work on building a new plane, no talk of anything else, but two of the days, we'd talk about the serious stuff. After what happened at the end of the year, we talk about Peter a lot." Winding his fingers through her hair, Spencer shook his head. "I still can't believe you want to be with me. Or did that story change your mind?"

"I wish you'd stop being so hard on yourself. In fact, if you think about it, you and I probably never would've started talking if you hadn't stayed after school to meet with him."

"If that's supposed to make me feel better, it worked." He kissed her cheek. "I know you don't think I'll believe you, or that I won't understand, but I've found that sometimes talking things out really does help."

Looking up at the starry night, she wondered how much to tell him. "You know how I told you that I have these dreams that feel more like memories?"

"Uh-huh."

"Well, sometimes when I dream, I look different. I'm blond. And a cheerleader. Like the other missing girl." She glanced at him to gauge his reaction. He wasn't looking at her like she was crazy; he looked more amused than anything. "What's with the face?"

"I'm just picturing you in a cheerleader uniform."

Liv bumped him with her shoulder. "This is serious stuff."

Using the arm he had around her, Spencer pulled her closer. "I am serious. You'd look cute in a cheerleading uniform."

She shook her head, but she couldn't help smiling.

"Okay, no more jokes. I just couldn't stand how sad you looked." His fingers stroked the back of her neck. "So, what do you think it all means?"

She took a deep breath and blew it out. "Isn't that the million-dollar question."

Liv kissed Spencer good night, changed into her pajamas, and crept into Katie's room. She lay down on the air mattress Lori had set up for her and stared at the plastic, glow-in-the-dark stars on Katie's ceiling.

Katie rolled over in her bed, the dim glow of her alarm clock lighting her face. "It's too bad we didn't have a chance to do the normal sleepover stuff. Next time, we'll need to get a girly movie."

"You're on." As Liv looked at Katie, she was reminded once again of Elizabeth. "Did I ever tell you about a girl your age I knew named Elizabeth?"

Katie shook her head. "Tell me about her."

"I distracted her parents so she could hide her peas."

"I like peas, but zucchini, ugh, that stuff is disgusting. I shudder. It's like my throat shuts down to try to keep it away."

Liv smiled. *No wonder I think of Elizabeth whenever I'm around Katie. They really are so much alike.*

Katie's face dropped and she looked like she was about to cry. "Spencer's so much better when you're here, then Mom's better, and you're so nice to me, and I like you so much, and . . ." She trained those big eyes on her, and when she spoke, her voice squeaked. "Please don't move away."

Liv's chest constricted. "I like you, too, and obviously I'm crazy about your brother." The thought of leaving made her want to cry. She swallowed past the lump in her throat and tried to give Katie a reassuring smile. "I'm not planning on going anywhere."

But today she'd found out that what you plan and what happens aren't even close to the same thing.

"I don't want to lie," Elizabeth said.

Liv turned toward her sister, who was sitting on her Hello Kitty comforter, a scowl on her face. Talk about not giving an inch.

All her life, she'd followed the rules and stood up for what she believed in. For one night she wanted to be the girl who broke free and did whatever she felt like without thinking about the consequences. She wanted to be the girl who went to a party to meet a guy.

"Just tell them I had to pick up a book from the library." Liv had already checked one out so she could sell her cover story if she had to. "I'll be back in an hour and a half, two tops."

"I can't believe you're friends with Jackie again, even after how crappy she treated you. Mom and Dad were right. That girl's bad news."

"Don't even start. Friendships in high school are complicated. You're way too young to understand."

"But not too young to have to lie for you." Elizabeth crossed her arms.

"Hey, I lie for you all the time. You want me to tell Mom that you're not really eating your peas?"

"That's not the same thing. This isn't disgusting vegetables; this is you sneaking out of the house when you're supposed to be taking care of me. I know I said I don't need a babysitter, but I don't want to be all alone in the house. Besides, you promised we'd watch a movie."

Liv tugged on her black Converse shoes and bent over to tie the laces.

The party was a big one, and even though Mom and Dad had said she couldn't go, she'd decided to swing by, just for an hour. Mostly because that's where Andrew would be. Jackie had apologized to her a couple of days ago. It wasn't like it was spontaneous—Jackie was now fighting with her other group of friends. But still, Jackie hated to apologize and she'd done it anyway. She even confessed she was jealous because Andrew was into Liv. At first she didn't know whether to believe that, but Andrew had actually talked to her earlier today, and he'd told her she should come find him at the party. He wasn't like other boys. Yes, he was cute, but he was smart, too.

When Liv stood, Elizabeth was still frowning, giving her that puppy-dog, don't-leave-me face.

"Stop being a baby." Liv misted on some perfume. "I'll be back before your movie's even over."

Elizabeth walked to the dresser and took something off it. The jeweled red bow of her Hello Kitty keychain caught the light as she held it out to her. "It's my lucky keychain. I want you to take it tonight."

"If this is supposed to make me feel guilty—"

Elizabeth grabbed the key ring out of Liv's hand and clipped the keychain on. "Good luck with Andrew. Don't trust Jackie too much."

Liv hugged her sister. "You're the best. I'll lock up, and I'll be back soon. Everything will be fine, you'll see."

She hurried out of the house, fired up her car, and buzzed down the road, glancing at the map on her phone for guidance. With every turn, the smaller and more abandoned the roads got until she ended up in the middle of nowhere. She lifted the phone again, trying to figure out where she'd taken the wrong turn.

Then she decided she was being punished for leaving Elizabeth. I get it, okay. I'm going back home.

Liv turned the car around, anxious to get back to Elizabeth and tell her how sorry she was for leaving her. They'd paint their nails and she'd even let Elizabeth play in her makeup. To hell with Jackie. And Andrew and his adorable dimples.

She turned up her Flyleaf CD and moved closer to the steering wheel, straining to see through the rain. What's . . .?

A dark object was in the road.

Is that a . . . ?

The headlights weren't on, and she could just make out the dark outline of the car. It was coming fast. Coming straight for her. She slammed on her brakes, but with the mud, she kept sliding.

The airbag went off.

Metal scraped against metal.

The side of the car slammed against something.

From the corner of her eye, she saw a glimmer of red as light bounced off the swinging Hello Kitty keychain.

Elizabeth.

Faint and distant, mixed in with the sound of rain pounding metal, her CD played on.

Blood poured down, soaking her shirt, leaving large drops on her jeans. Lifting her head was impossible. Everything hurt.

You're going to die.

Liv brought her shaking hands to her face. When she pulled them away, she expected them to be covered in blood, but they were clean. She sat up, trying to catch her breath.

Moonlight spilled in through the window, illuminating Katie's sleeping form, reminding her that she wasn't in her own bed. That everything was wrong.

The car that hit her was the blond cheerleader's— Lindsay's. Liv's chest burned. She pulled her shirt away from her skin and peered down at her scar. Her heart beat faster, like it was confirming her thoughts. Proving how strong and healthy it was now.

It was her heart.

No wonder she's been haunting me. Tears blurred her vision. She stared out the window at the moon, but it no longer looked like hope. It looked faceless and lost, smoth-ered in all the dark clouds.

Just like her.

Smothered. Choking. Fading.

Slipping.

Falling.

Drowning.

As quietly as she could, she slipped off the covers and tiptoed out of the room. She padded to the kitchen, got a glass from the cupboard, and filled it with milk.

Lori walked into the kitchen and flipped on the light. "Oh! I thought I heard someone."

"I'm sorry," Liv said, swiping tears off her cheeks. "I just . . . I woke up and needed a drink."

"That's fine. You're welcome to anything. In fact, why don't you have a seat and I'll see if I can find some cookies."

Liv pulled out a chair and sat at the kitchen table while Lori rummaged through the cupboard. Lori took a couple chocolate chip cookies out of a plastic package and offered them to her. "Thanks," she said, grabbing one.

For a moment, they sat and ate their cookies in silence.

"Your mom called. More than once, actually."

Liv's chest tightened. Even after everything she'd found out today—even though it didn't make sense—she still wanted to be wrapped in Mom's arms, with Mom telling her it would all be okay.

"She's really worried about you," Lori said. "Both of your parents are."

Liv searched for a response, but tears lodged in her throat, and she didn't know what to say, anyway.

"They love you. Come what may, through the good and the bad, parents love their children."

"I love them, too." As mad as she was, and as confused as she was, she did love them.

But the missing girls. The heart that shouldn't be mine.

Pain radiated from her stolen heart. Again, she felt lost, completely adrift in this new world where she was no longer sure who or what she was. Where she felt responsible for a girl's death. She sniffed, fighting to keep control of her emotions. "What if love isn't enough to fix things, though? What if there's something that ruins it all?"

Lori grabbed another cookie. "Well, without all the facts, I'm not sure how ruined it is or isn't. But I don't think all's lost. When you love people, you don't give up on them. No matter what."

39

Liv leaned across the car and kissed Spencer's cheek. "Thanks for everything."

"Call if you need me," Spencer said. "I can get someone to cover my shift. I'll do whatever you need me to."

"It'll be okay. I'll give you a call later, though." She took a deep breath, grabbed her suitcase out of the back, and carried it up the sidewalk.

She paused in front of the door, her courage faltering. Last night she'd hardly slept, thinking about having someone else's heart, wondering how she'd ended up in Mom and Dad's care.

Mom and Dad. A sharp pain shot through her chest. Henry and Victoria Stein weren't even her real parents. *So why did they take care of me?*

All the questions swirled through her head again, pushing her to confront them so she could put the final pieces together. Another deep breath. In and out. In and out.

The instant she walked in, Mom was at the door. She threw her arms around her, hugging her so tightly she could hardly breathe. "I was so worried."

Dad appeared by her side seconds later, his eyes red and bloodshot. In fact, both of them looked disheveled, like they hadn't slept any more than she had.

"Time to tell me everything," she said, looking from Mom to Dad. "I want to know what really happened the night of the wreck, and this time, I don't want you to lie to me."

Dad took the suitcase from her and set it aside. He swept his arm toward the living room. "I think you're going to want to sit down for this."

Mom and Dad told her about all the procedures they'd gone through to try to have a child, and how after years with no success, Mom finally got pregnant, only to lose the baby halfway through the pregnancy. After that devastating miscarriage, the doctors told her that she'd most likely never carry a baby full-term.

Having a child was one of their greatest desires, so they decided to adopt. It was a long process, but they eventually met a young pregnant woman who had decided to give her baby up for adoption. They met with her and she told them the amazing news—she'd picked them to be the baby girl's parents. The paperwork was filled out, the nursery was painted, clothes bought, everything ready to go.

"So the night of your accident, we'd gotten the call that Abby was having our baby." Mom looked at her, tears glistening in her eyes. "We sat in the waiting area for several hours. The nurse came out and got us, we went into the room . . . I was filled with such joy, knowing my dreams were about to come true. Knowing I was about to hold my baby for the first time.

"I looked at Abby, who was holding our perfect baby girl. Chubby cheeks, ten tiny fingers, ten little toes. Then I saw the way Abby was looking at the baby in her arms. The love and awe filling her features was so apparent, and

I just knew . . ." Mom pressed her lips together and tears ran down her cheeks. "She looked up at us and said, 'I'm sorry, but I can't.' And just like that, our dream was shattered again."

Dad put his arm over Mom's shoulders. "So we did the only thing we knew to do. We drove home. There was a horrible storm and the rain was pouring. Everything was slick and muddy and it took forever to drive from the hospital. We were almost home when we saw the two wrecked cars."

Liv scooted to the edge of her seat.

Mom picked up the story, and her recollection of that night was so vivid, Liv could see it.

Headlights illuminating two cars off the side of the road, hoods accordioned together, engines still steaming.

She could hear the faint music, smell the damp earth mixed with the sweet liquid pouring from underneath the cars. She could see Dad putting his fingers on the neck of the blond girl sprawled across the hood—Lindsay. The rain carrying the girl's blood in red streams down the side of the white car.

She heard the grinding noise the wipers made as they worked across the buckled glass of the other car's windshield.

And there she was in the other car—her body, anyway. Injured head resting on the deflated airbag, blood-covered clothes, Elizabeth's Hello Kitty keychain hanging from the ignition.

"Dad had already started working on stopping the other girl's hemorrhages," Mom said. "I got into the car with you. The depressed skull fracture alone . . . I've seen a lot of brain injuries in my life, and yours . . ." Mom's chin quivered. "I took off my scarf and wrapped your wounds the best I could. Knowing neither of you would make it to the hospital in time, we took you to my nearby lab where I'd been working on a cure for Huntington's disease."

Mom lifted her red-rimmed eyes. "The brain injuries to the other girl were very bad. Compound depressed skull fracture with internal cranial cavity exposed to the outside environment." She shook her head. "It's not an injury she'd ever recover from. Even if she lived, she'd be in a vegetative state for life."

She lifted her clasped hands to her lips. "But you, you only had one damaged area on the right side of your brain, the only healthy part the other girl had left. So I used my skills to graft it in."

The hairs on the back of Liv's neck rose, and she slowly brought a hand to her head. "You're saying . . .? My brain is . . . it's made up of two different brains?"

"I did what I had to do to save you. The surgery I performed was highly experimental, but I had to try. If I hadn't done it your brain never would have functioned properly. It's why you'll never completely get your memories back." Mom leaned forward. "It was risky, but I couldn't let you go through life without a shot at normalcy, and I couldn't let you die. Not when there was a chance to save you."

The opposing thoughts, the weird dreams—it all made sense now. While completely not making sense at all. This was crazy.

Liv moved a hand over her chest. "What about the heart surgery?" Her stomach rolled, and for a moment, she thought she was going to puke. "What? You figured you'd used the girl's brain, you might as well take all her other good organs, too?"

"Your ribs punctured your chest," Dad said. "From what I saw, you already had a weak heart, and it was severely damaged in the wreck . . ." His face paled. "The only other option was letting you die, so I performed a heart transplant. Using the other girl's . . ." He closed his eyes and dropped his head, unable to say the rest.

But he didn't have to. All the air left her lungs and suddenly the room felt too big and too small at the same time. It was what she'd guessed, but having it confirmed made it that much worse.

Just when I started to feel like I know who I am, I find out that I'm two people, and suddenly, everything I thought I knew seems wrong. I don't know who I am, because I'm not anyone. I'm parts. Pieces.

A science experiment.

A monster.

Tears ran down her cheeks. She didn't try to stop them or bother with wiping them away. At this point, she wasn't even sure she could move. And if she did, which part of her would be moving? Vivienne? Lindsay?

There was no Liv. Olivia. Livie. It didn't matter what anyone called her. The name didn't change what she was.

"I was the one who pushed your father to do the transplant," Mom said, her voice sounding tiny and far away. "But we had a choice to make, if you could even call it that. We could let your life slip away, or we could give you a new one. Even if you and the other girl *had* gotten to the hospital in time, neither of you would've made a full recovery.

"When I realized that what we'd done . . ." Mom's voice shook and she seemed to be struggling for words. "Well, with all the foreign tissue, you were no longer who you started out as that night. You became two people's daughters all at once, but no one's at the same time. So knowing you'd need someone who could take care of you, the kind of care required after those extreme surgeries, I decided the best thing to do was to raise you as our daughter. I thought of you as our miracle." She gave her a weary smile. "And you are truly a miracle."

"I'm sure this is overwhelming," Dad said, "but we both love you very much. We've dealt with guilt over our decision, because of the other families involved, and because of all we had to do to cover it up, but we've never regretted saving you. In fact, I thank my lucky stars every day that you're in my life."

"See, we don't really know what we're doing. This whole parenting thing is new to us, and I know we've made mistakes, but like your father said, we love you very much. More than I even knew was possible. That's why I can't bring myself to regret what we did. Because the idea of you not being in this world . . ." Mom wiped the tears from her cheeks, then scooted forward, anxiety filling her features. "So now you know everything. How are you? Are you okay?"

Liv was still dealing with that rug-being-pulled-out-from-under-her sensation, no longer sure of anything anymore. "I don't know what to think. But I'm most definitely not okay."

Finding out that you used to be two people is more than confusing. It's more than life-changing. It's so much more than anything, that there aren't words to describe it.

Liv lay back in her bed, mourning the loss of parents she never knew. She felt bad for Lindsay, who never got that math scholarship or the love she really needed from her mother; that after her rough life, she'd lost everything she did love in one night, and was so desperate and hurt over it that she got into her car drunk and drove to her death.

She wept for Elizabeth, waiting all night for her sister to come home, when she never would. She cried for Vivienne, who struggled with whether she wanted to give up her convictions to fit in, because no matter how much she tried to act like she didn't care, she wanted to fit in somewhere, too. And when it came down to it, she loved her sister—would've done anything for her—and was trying to do the right thing by turning around to go back home.

Her mind returned to the wreck, her thoughts spinning over Mom and Dad's unbelievable story. She pictured them coming across the two cars, doing all they could, and knowing they could only save one person. By using organs from the other.

A shudder ran through her as she thought about the blood and the brains and the heart. She was a freak of nature—no, not nature; she was a freak of science. An experiment.

Mom had called her something else, though. She'd called her a miracle.

Liv stood and looked in the mirror. She thought about how unfamiliar her reflection used to be. In time, she'd come to recognize herself; she'd gotten more secure with who she was, even without her memories. Really, both girls had pushed her to learn and grow in different ways, even though they'd also driven her crazy. She wasn't the perky cheerleader, yet she wasn't the nonconformist outsider, either.

Vivienne Clark and Lindsay Rogers had died the night of the accident. And here she was in their place. Their memories were fuzzy. Hers were real.

At that moment, something inside her changed. Her body felt lighter, her mind clearer. Then there was only the quiet of her room, and her own thoughts. The strange, unbelievable truth was what she'd needed to set the voices inside her head free.

I'm just me now.

She glanced at the clock. *Finally. I thought five o'clock would never come.*

Waiting for Spencer to get off work had been torturous. She grabbed her phone and dialed his number. *Pick up, pick up, pick up.*

"Hey, I was just about to call you," Spencer said.

"I was hoping we could talk. In person."

As they drove to Dead Horse Ranch, Spencer held her hand, talked about music, and everything almost felt normal again.

He kept glancing at her, obviously waiting for her to tell him what had happened, but as she'd said when he picked her up, it wasn't a riding-in-the-car discussion. Part of her wanted to blurt it out and get it over with, but she was also scared to tell him everything.

He parked and they got out of the car, took the blanket from his trunk, and spread it on the ground. As they sat looking over the river, she noticed everything: the sound of the water rushing against the rocks; how the leaves on the trees were starting to turn yellow; the rabbit hopping away from them.

"Okay, I've held it in as long as I can," Spencer said, twisting to face her. "What happened?"

Explaining the whole story to him took a while, but out it came, one word at a time, until he had the whole truth. When she finished, he just stared.

Panic welled up in her. "Was it too much? I always feel like I tell you too much."

He shook his head. "Not too much. It's just . . . Whoa."

"Yeah. Definitely whoa."

He took a few breaths, his chest rising and falling with each one. His eyes locked onto hers. "What are you going to do?"

A giant lump formed in her throat. "I don't know. As much as I'd love to see Elizabeth again, I only remember flashes and nothing else. And from what I know about Lindsay, she and her mom didn't exactly get along. In fact, her life was a pretty big mess." Liv looked out over the water. "My parents did what they had to do to save my life. They'd be in huge trouble if anyone found out—they'd lose their medical licenses, maybe even end up in jail. The fact of the matter is, I don't think I belong anywhere else. Maybe we're not a conventional family, but we're a family. I know they love me, and I love them."

She blinked back her tears and swallowed. "What do you think?"

"Well, I think you belong here, but that's just me being selfish." He put his hand on the side of her face and ran his thumb along the top of her cheek. "If your parents hadn't come along, you wouldn't be here, and . . . I don't even want to think about that." Heat ran through her as he gazed into her eyes, saying so much with a simple look. "I was miserable before I met you. So the thought of you . . . that would mean . . ." He took a deep breath. "I love you, Liv."

The words filled her with joy, but it seemed incomprehensible, especially after what she'd just told him. "How can you love me? You don't even know who I really am. *I* don't even know who I really am."

He lowered his head and brushed his lips against hers. "I love whoever you are." He kissed her, lightly at first. Then he slipped his hand behind her neck, pulling her closer and kissing her with growing urgency. Like it might be the last time they ever kissed.

When their lips separated, it took her a moment to catch her breath. "I never would've made it through all this without you." She leaned into him, felt the security of her body pressed against his, and inhaled his recently showered, soapy scent. "I love you, too, by the way."

He took her hand in his, intertwining their fingers.

Leaning against him, feeling the warmth radiate off him, listening to his breath go in and out, she knew she was exactly where she belonged.

Epilogue

Liv no longer worried about keeping her hair over the scar on her neck or hiding the faded scar on her chest. Over time her arm spasm had completely disappeared. She knew how to ride a bike; she knew how to drive. Sports were still shaky, but she managed. The only thing Spencer refused to take off the list was "Teach Liv to give a compliment." Not because she never complimented him—she did all the time—but because he thought it was funny to hold it over her head.

Last month, she and Spencer had graduated from high school. Next fall, they'd be attending ASU together—she and Keira were going to be roommates. The drive from Phoenix to Cottonwood wasn't too bad, so they'd all make frequent visits back home.

Everything in her life was as it was supposed to be. With one exception.

She pulled up to the curb and double-checked she was at the right address. *1725. This is it.*

Liv looked at Spencer. "I don't feel so brave now that we're finally here."

"You've thought about this for almost two years," he said. "It's time."

"But what if I'm doing more harm than good?"

"There's no way that knowing you could do harm." He put his hand on her thigh and squeezed. "We came all this way. You can do this."

She took off her sunglasses and smoothed down her hair. "Okay. I can do this." She blew out a shaky breath. "Wish me luck."

Spencer leaned across the car and kissed her lips, lingering for a couple of seconds. "Good luck. I'll be right here if you need me."

Rapid pulse pounding through her head, she opened the door and climbed out. Her legs ached from the hours in the car, and it was nice to stretch them. Rochester didn't have the dry, desert air she was used to. The landscape was greener, the air full of moisture. Taking a deep breath, she started up the sidewalk. The lawn was neatly trimmed; flowers lined the sidewalk; two huge trees shaded the front yard; and the white, two-story house had dark-blue shutters. It was the quintessential American home.

No memories hit her as she took it all in. She thought she'd recognize something, but it all looked foreign.

Then she saw a brunette girl through the large window. She was the reason she'd come all this way. Liv stared at the more mature version of Elizabeth.

For two years, she had lived her life as Olivia Francesca Stein. She'd left the two girls she used to be behind her. While the voices had disappeared the night she'd learned the truth about who she was, there was still the occasional tug; the dream that made her think of her sister. So once she turned eighteen, she'd made up her mind to come see her. Parts of the story she'd tell the Clarks would be true—the amnesia, and being raised by loving parents. How exactly her parents had come to be her parents and the details about how she was actually two people, she'd keep from them.

After all the months she'd spent thinking about this moment, wondering if it was the right thing to do, here she was, standing in the doorway to her old life. The life Vivienne Clark would've lived if she hadn't been in a head-on collision.

Elizabeth turned toward the window. Her eyes widened. She dropped whatever had been in her hands and leaned closer to the glass. She yelled something over her shoulder— Liv couldn't make out the words, but it sounded more like excitement than fear.

It was just the push she needed to take the final steps. She walked up to the front door, raised her fist, and knocked.

Keep reading for a bonus scene from

All the
Broken Pieces,

as told in Spencer's point of view . . .

First Day of School

Spencer

—

Bitter feelings welled up in Spencer the second he pulled into the school parking lot. People he'd known forever but now had no desire to ever see again disappeared inside the red double doors of the school. All summer he'd dreaded the moment he'd have to come back and face the guys and girls who used to be his friends. No doubt there'd be rumors and speculation, but he would have to do everything he could to just ignore it.

He turned up his music and leaned back in the seat of his car, wanting to delay the inevitable for as long as he could. Over the summer, some of his classmates had tried talking to him—usually while he was bagging groceries or stocking shelves at Safeway—and it was always uncomfortable. A few tried to pretend like nothing had happened, like they'd never abandoned him and the guy who'd needed help.

Of course, it's my fault he needed help in the first place.

Spencer shook his head. No thinking about that night. Not right now, when he needed all his energy to deal with the cowards who'd kept on living their regularly shallow lives, no thought to the person who no longer had that option. He yanked out his earphones, shoved them in his bag, and left the car. The day was already hot, the sun shining, temperature steadily rising. Hot enough to make his glasses slide down his nose so that the black frames were in his line of sight.

He pushed them back in place and entered the school. First thing he saw was his ex-girlfriend, Sabrina, with her friends surrounding her the way they always did. Her dark hair was straight and shiny and her skirt was short, showing off her legs and most definitely pushing the dress code. He knew from waiting on her couch while her dad made uncomfortable small talk that she spent hours putting herself together so she looked that good.

Her gaze met his, and Spencer quickly darted in the opposite direction before she could corner him for a heart-to-heart. It had taken two weeks of ignoring her calls for her to get the hint and stop calling. After what she'd done, he'd never understand why she thought they'd be able to smooth things over and pick up their relationship like nothing happened.

It's better to avoid them all. Spencer found his new locker, shoved his supplies inside, and rushed toward the first floor. He got all the way down the stairs before realizing Mrs. Tulley's classroom had moved. He sighed, knowing this meant more chances of people wanting to stop and do the fake *so good to see you again/how was your summer* thing.

Familiar faces passed him on all sides but he charged forward, jaw set so they could see he wanted to be left alone.

Nothing ever changed in this town.

Everything was the same.

Every*one* was the same. Except for him. He'd never be the same again—he was going to make sure of that.

He glanced up as he neared the stairs. A girl who was most definitely not the same was coming down the steps. Dark hair, dressed in jeans and a gray T-shirt with a jeweled heart on front that caught the light. She had big eyes, a cute little nose, full lips, and looked totally lost.

Spencer's throat went dry, and even though he knew he was

staring, he couldn't seem to look away. No doubt she'd fit in with Sabrina and her group.

That thought helped him remember why it didn't matter how pretty or sweet she looked. *She'll be just like the rest of them within a week, if she's not already. Better to stay away than get sucked into that mess again.*

The binder in her arm fell down the stairs and popped open, and papers scattered everywhere. For a moment, she just frowned at it, her shoulders slumped. Other people walked across the mess, not even bothering to step over the papers. The girl finally sprang into motion, rushing down the steps and scooping up the papers, her cheeks turning pink. Spencer's brain told him to keep going, but his feet slowed as he neared, and then he was picking up the mess along with her.

He sat back, shook the hair out of his eyes, and got his first look at her up close. Her large hazel eyes stood out against her pale skin. He had kind of been hoping she'd be cross-eyed or have crazy teeth—something so he wouldn't think about how much he'd like to see her smile. She was naturally pretty without the help of a lot of makeup.

All these questions whirred through his head: *Where'd you move from? Why'd you move here? Need someone to show you around?*

He thrust the papers toward her. He hadn't bothered talking to anyone besides Mom or his sister, Katie—who really did most of the talking for all of them—in a long time. Meanwhile, the girl was just staring at him, blinking, and his heart was doing this strange squeeze thing he didn't like at all. She needed to stop looking at him like that. Now. Before he forgot that this year he wasn't getting sucked into all the social bullshit.

He waved the papers in front of her to wake her out of whatever trance she was in. "Do you want them or not?"

Her eyes widened and she took the papers from him. "Thanks. Everything just kinda spilled. I don't know if I would've been able to get it all without your help."

"Yeah, well, the people here aren't the most helpful bunch." He ran his gaze over her again. With those looks, guys would be tripping over themselves to ask her out. "I'm sure you'll be fine, though."

She tilted her head in this cute, sorta confused way, a crease forming between her eyebrows. Her lips even went a bit pouty. "What do you mean by that?"

Acting clueless. Like she didn't realize she was pretty and hadn't had years of guys doing whatever she wanted when she blinked those big eyes. "Yep, you'll fit in just fine."

He stood, readjusted his bag, and headed upstairs, trying to force her face out of his mind.

The first person Spencer saw as he exited the food line in the cafeteria was the new girl. So far she hadn't been in any of his classes. People were talking about her, though, so he knew her name was Liv Stein. She was just standing in the middle of the room, holding her tray of food, looking unsure where to go next.

Might as well point her in the right direction so she can make friends. He shouldn't care, but she looked so sad standing there all alone. "Popular table's over there." He jerked his head toward the spot where he'd sat all last year. Sabrina was already there with her group of girls that did whatever she said, along with Clay and the rest of the guys.

Liv glanced toward the table, then looked back at him. Danger. Those eyes could get him in trouble if he didn't watch out. "Where do you sit?"

"Not there." Before he did something stupid and asked her to join him, he walked past her, sat at a table in the corner, and put in his earphones. He turned the music nice and loud so he could drown out everyone else. Half a day, and he was already itching to bolt. He had to stay late to talk to the school counselor, too. At least the guy was nice, even if Spencer didn't want to sit around and talk about how the first day back at school went.

Liv settled in next to Keira. *Good pick. Keira's one of the nicer ones.*

Liv pulled her hair forward and kept her eyes on her food. Keira pointed to everyone, no doubt introducing Liv to the group. The guys were staring and smiling at her. After living around the same people for most of their lives, new people were always a novelty. Extra bonus points if that someone looked like Liv.

What are you doing? You're just as bad as they are. Worse, even. She's probably better off with them, even though they won't think twice about stabbing her in the back if it'll get them out of trouble.

Spencer forced his attention to whatever meat the gray square was supposed to be, letting the lyrics of his music wash over him.

Before he left the table, he glanced the new girl's way. *Looks like she's fitting in great there.* He told himself he didn't care, but he had the strangest urge to go pull her away.

He dumped his tray and walked out the door. After a while, she'd be just another girl here. A pretty girl, sure, but just a girl. The newness would wear off, and then he could stop thinking she might be different. How she might be someone he could actually talk to.

Acknowledgments

Huge thanks and hugs to all the people who helped this book get to where it is now! For Julia Allen, Brandy Vallance, Robert Spiller, and Susan McConnell. You guys have taught me so much about writing, and more than that, have become dear friends. Thanks to Anne Eliot, a talented author and one of my closest friends—the night we met was fate. You've talked me off the ledge so, so many times and provided laughs when I really needed them. To Kika MacFarlane, for being the first teen to fall in love with Spencer, to think my book was worth getting grounded over, and for telling me I couldn't give up on this story. To Jenna Shattuck and the other yaromance.com girls for being my teen readers and being so cool.

Thanks to my fabulous editor, Stacy Cantor Abrams, and her also-fabulous assistant editor, Alycia Tornetta. This story wouldn't be where it was today if not for you two. To everyone at Entangled for all the support. All the authors, editors, and Danielle Barclay and Elana Johnson for help with publicity—you have all been so amazing. (Also, thanks to Stacey O'Neale for getting me started with the PR stuff.) Thanks to Lisa Burstein and Rachel Harris who answer my freak-out e-mails, encourage me, and make me laugh.

To my mom, dad, brothers, and sisters, for putting up with all the writing talk. Love you guys! Shout-out to my BIL, Jeremy, for proofing query letters and answering endless grammar questions. To Amanda, Malinda, Ariane, and Christy for reading my early books and telling me they were good, even though the writing needed a lot of work. Thanks to my kids who are just the best and understand when Mommy's working. And last but not least, huge, super-sloppy-kiss thanks to my husband, Michael, who puts up with writer mood swings and has read novel after novel to provide feedback and tell me when my guys aren't talking like guys. Thanks for not telling me I was crazy when I came up with the plot for this book, even though you later told me you thought it (along with saying I made it work and it was the best book I'd ever written). Thanks for believing in me. Without your support, I would've given up long ago.

Pretty Amy

a novel by Lisa Burstein

Sometimes date is a four-letter word...

Amy is fine living in the shadows of beautiful Lila and uber-cool Cassie, because at least she's somewhat beautiful and uber-cool by association. But when their dates stand them up for prom, and the girls take matters into their own hands—earning them a night in jail outfitted in satin, stilettos, and Spanx—Amy discovers even a prom spent in handcuffs might be better than the humiliating "rehabilitation techniques" now filling up her summer. Even worse, with Lila and Cassie parentally banned, Amy feels like she has nothing—like she is nothing.

Navigating unlikely alliances with her new coworker, two very different boys, and possibly even her parents, Amy struggles to decide if it's worth being a best friend when it makes you a public enemy. Bringing readers along on an often hilarious and heartwarming journey, Amy finds that maybe getting a life only happens once you think your life is over.

Coming to a bookstore near you

05.15.2012

GRAVITY
Melissa West

In the future, only one rule will matter:
Don't. Ever. Peek.

Seventeen-year-old Ari Alexander just broke that rule and saw the last person she expected hovering above her bed—arrogant Jackson Locke, the most popular boy in her school. She expects instant execution or some kind of freak alien punishment, but instead, Jackson issues a challenge: help him, or everyone on Earth will die.

Ari knows she should report him, but everything about Jackson makes her question what she's been taught about his kind. And against her instincts, she's falling for him.

But Ari isn't just any girl, and Jackson wants more than her attention. She's a military legacy who's been trained by her father and exposed to war strategies and societal information no one can know—especially an alien spy, like Jackson. Giving Jackson the information he needs will betray her father and her country, but keeping silent will start a war.

Gravity
drops
10.09.2012